Harlequin  Romances

WELCOME
TO THE WONDERFUL WORLD
OF *Harlequin Romances*

Interesting, informative and entertaining,
each Harlequin Romance portrays an appealing
and original love story. With a varied array
of settings, we may lure you on an African safari,
to a quaint Welsh village or an exotic riviera
location — anywhere and everywhere that adventurous
men and women fall in love.

As publishers of Harlequin Romances, we're
extremely proud of our books. Since 1949,
Harlequin Enterprises has built its publishing
reputation on the solid base of quality and
originality. Our stories are the most popular
paperback romances sold in North America; every
month, eight new titles are released and sold at
nearly every book-selling store in Canada and the
United States.

A free catalogue listing all available Harlequin Romances
can be yours by writing to the:

HARLEQUIN READER SERVICE,
(In the U.S.) M.P.O. Box 707, Niagara Falls, N.Y. 14302
(In Canada) Stratford, Ontario, Canada N5A 6W4

or use order coupon at back of books.

We sincerely hope you enjoy reading
this Harlequin Romance.

Yours truly,

THE PUBLISHERS
Harlequin Romances

CHILD OF TAHITI

by

REBECCA CAINE

Harlequin Books

TORONTO • LONDON • NEW YORK • AMSTERDAM • SYDNEY • WINNIPEG

Original hardcover edition published in 1976
by Mills & Boon Limited

ISBN 0-373-02045-7

Harlequin edition published February 1977

Printed in U.S.A.

CHAPTER ONE

THE plane was coming over from the south-east, low under the brilliant morning sun, and the increasing roar of its jets made a harsh, alien intrusion on the lovely pagan peace of the island. A vividly plumed bird rose from the undergrowth with a shrill cry, immediately to be echoed by its fellows, and suddenly the island seemed alive with raucous sound.

The boy and the girl stood still, unheeding. His hands were on her slender shoulders and his head tilted down to her, a sunlit duo silhouetted against the long silver sweep of the deserted beach. And then the girl's lips moved, their cry muted against the encroaching roar. She gave a sudden thrust with small hands and broke free.

'No, Pierre!'

'But, *chérie* . . .' His whimsical smile still teased and his hands tried again to capture the eluding shoulders. 'I only wanted . . . you will be sorry when I have gone!'

'I won't! Leave go—I won't be sorry.' The slight figure in the scanty white bikini was immature in its fierce defensiveness. 'Why should I care if I never see you again?'

'Never is an awfully long time.' Dark eyes laughed down into distraught blue ones that betrayed the give-away sparkle of unshed tears. 'I thought you liked me a little bit more than that, *ma petite*.'

'Like you! You conceited idiot! Why should I like you more than that? What's so special about *you*, Pierre Lamont?'

The attempted carelessness of the questions vied oddly with the tone in which they were uttered, and Pierre's handsome features assumed mock reproach.

'But I thought you were my special little friend, who would never quarrel with me. And here we are; quarrelling!' He made an expressive gesture. 'I wonder . . . is it that you are not quite so *petite* as I believed? That perhaps you are a tiny bit jealous because I——'

'Jealous! Me? Because——' Her voice rose thinly and the scream of the jets blotted out the rest of the choked denial as she tore herself out of his grasp and fled along the beach.

5

'But, Tina! *Chérie*—come back!' He took a pace forward, then let his hands fall to his sides.

He stared after the small, fleeing figure, and the great plane zoomed overhead. It cast a huge dark shadow on the water, like the ghost of a great bird, and for a moment Tina checked her headlong flight to stare up at the silver capsule.

She shaded her eyes against the sun and blinked away her tears, then some ancient pagan instinct she scarcely knew she possessed made her flinch and run blindly along the coral strand lest the great dark shadow should darken herself as it crossed her path.

But it had gone. The shadow diminished, the deafening roar began to dim to a whine, and it was far over the sea, dropping still lower in the sky as it homed down towards the runway of Tahiti's airport.

Tina looked at the misted green peaks of her home island, humped out there in the jewel-blue sea, and slowed her steps. There was no sound of pursuit, no beguiling Gallic lilt to win her back and make her betray more than she ever meant to betray to a living soul, and at last she stopped to draw great gasping breaths. A line of boundary stones marked the beach a short way ahead, and beyond them the sickle of white sand curved more steeply about the limpid green oval of the lagoon. She glanced back, saw no sign of Pierre, and went on with slow dragging steps, past the marker stones, her toes trailing through the warm creamy ripples at the water's edge.

Presently she came to a wide grove of palms and paused for a moment before she turned and struck up the high shelving beach. She threw herself down under the shade of the tall silent sentinels and lay prone, her hot face pressed hard against the soft darkness made by her forearms. What did it matter? Why was she bothered? She didn't care if Pierre went back to France and ... She was a fool to mourn for all those crazy little dreams, for all those tender little fantasies born of a certain light she'd imagined in a man's eyes ... all the small appealing signs she'd misread out of the naïvety of inexperience—like an alphabet backwards. What a fool she had been! Idiot heart. Believing he was attracted to her. All those weeks she'd looked forward to, lived for, her visit to Kaloha.

Her lips quivered, trying to keep back her anguish, and

she beat the sandy earth with hot, clenched little fists. Was this what love did to one? If it was, she wanted none of it. Let Pierre go back to Europe. Let him ... A convulsive shudder ran through her body and the storm of emotion refused to be contained any longer.

The palm fronds shifted fitfully above, making a cool green shifting shade in which the colours of flirting wings streaked in darting flashes of brilliance. Far out beyond the reef, beyond the cool lagoon, the surf boomed out its eternal thunder and tossed its wild white curtains of spume high into the blue. But Tina heard none of it, nor saw it, as she lay spent after the storm of passionate tears. Even her warning instincts were numbed, blind and deaf to the approach of footsteps through the grove, to the long shadow that sprang ahead of them and fell across her body.

The man's voice was deep, its first exclamation of surprise sharp, its second one more demanding.

He bent over her, a flickering dawn of alarm in the peremptory hand he put on her shoulder, and she stirred with shock, starting up as the head and broad shoulders loomed down mistily above her tear-drenched eyes.

A trace of disbelief entered his expression, then vanished. 'For a moment I thought ... What's the matter?' he demanded.

She stared blankly at him, tasting the salt bitterness of her own tears, then the brief moment of shock abated and she trembled. She turned away wordlessly, brushing at her eyes with a sand-coated arm.

The newcomer frowned. 'What's the matter?' he repeated. 'Are you hurt, or something?'

'No—go away!' she choked, hating him without reason, hating the whole world, anyone or anything that witnessed her foolish grief. 'Go away,' she repeated.

His brows went up consideringly. 'But I don't choose to go away.' He paused, the frown re-forming, but more in puzzlement this time. 'This is my beach you're weeping all over, you know. Who are you, anyway?'

Again his hand closed over her shoulder as she remained deaf to his questions. Then the somewhat arrogant presence of him got through to her and she whirled round.

'Just leave me alone! You can charge me for weeping all over your beastly beach, but just——' The shape of him blurred and wavered and swam in her vision, then something snapped in her and a wild, unreasoning anger drove out all other feeling.

'*Go away!*' She began to cry it over and over again, then when he failed to move she beat against his chest with small hammering fists. She was on the point of hysteria now, beyond all reasoning except the need to make him go away and leave her to deal in her own way with the tempest of raw emotion that racked her heart.

He exclaimed sharply, then caught at her small flailing fists, but she did not heed the shocked words with which he attempted to calm her. She struggled, the instinct for freedom coming uppermost, and tried to tear her hands free. But the fingers imprisoning her wrists were like vices, and suddenly there was pain. She had forgotten the rasping discomfort needle-sharp grains of sand could cause to tender skin under intense pressure, and as her fierce wrenching movements brought no relief a hatred surged up against this new enemy who had materialised from nowhere to inflict fresh hurt with his superior male strength.

She cried out, then lashed out with her feet. The next moment she was free and gasping from the sharp slap he dealt her across her face.

'*Oh!*' Her hand flew to her cheek, nursing it, and she stared at him with incredulous eyes. 'You—you——!'

'Little wildcat!' he exclaimed grimly. 'Are you crazy?'

'You hit me!' She took a step back, sober now with shock. 'How dare you?'

'It's the only answer to hysterical females.'

'I'm not hysterical! It's all your fault. I never asked you to interfere.' Her hands went out to ward him off, and he checked before the frail gesture of defence. 'You're the one who flipped. How dare you say those things to me?' she choked, backing away towards the beach.

His sudden cry of warning came too late as she started to run. Too late she saw the heap of tangled sea-wrack and driftwood left by the tide. She ran blindly into it and stumbled, making a desperate attempt to regain her balance, then the heap of wrack shifted under her foot and she fell with a curiously twisting slow motion on to her side.

The stranger watched. When Tina did not move immediately he took a few steps forward.

'Are you all right?' he asked at last.

There was no reply and he went nearer to the slender form crumpled on the sand and wrack. 'Are you okay?' he repeated.

A petulant movement stirred her shoulders. 'I—I don't know,' she mumbled.

'Well, hadn't you better find out—before I leave you to your tantrums?'

The scorn in his voice stung as much as the marks of his fingers on her flushed cheek. Trembling with anger and humiliation, she started to scramble up, only to gasp with pain and sink back on the sand.

'You've done some damage, it seems.' He surveyed her dispassionately. 'Is it very bad?'

'I don't know and I don't care.' She rubbed at her ankle, willing the throbbing pain to go away so that she could escape this impossible man before anything else happened to her. 'Just go away, will you?'

'I'm very tempted to.' His tone was dry. 'But my conscience says otherwise.'

'Give in to temptation. Be like Oscar Wilde,' she gritted, and flung a twisted piece of flotsam aside.

He gave an impatient gesture. 'Can you stand up?'

She shook her head and stared stubbornly along the shore. Nothing registered. The hotel and the beach gardens were out of sight. She could see only sea and sand and sunlight, and the blue-grey peaks that crowned the island, a combination that, along with the inevitable palms, made up many of the islands, yet from this angle made strangeness of one she thought she had come to know very well during the past few days. But then she had never come along the beach this way; they—she and Pierre and Fay and Paul—always went exploring the other way, towards the one tiny port that Kaloha boasted. Although hadn't she suggested the other day that they come this way for a change? And Pierre had said there was nothing, it led to the plantation end; frightfully dull, he laughed, trying to mimic a plummy English accent and only succeeding in reducing them all into mirth; it had sounded funny, one exaggerated accent overlaid with a French one.

She shivered, the pain starting all over again at the

thought of Pierre. It brought a sense of isolation and an irrational belief that if only she could stare unblinkingly into this strangeness she could pretend it had never happened, begin to forget ...

'How far have you to go?'

The deep, infuriating voice again. She nursed her ankle. 'Nowhere.'

'Oh, for——!' He ran his fingers through his hair, controlling his impatience with an obvious effort. 'What a baby you are. Try talking sense for a change, will you? Who do you belong to?'

'Nobody.'

The muffled little response was scarcely perceptible and he checked an exclamation. 'You *are* feeling sorry for yourself. Nowhere to go. Nobody to go to. I'm afraid I can't quite believe *that*, young lady.'

'You don't have to. You don't have to believe anything.' Suddenly tears welled up again and in an agony of self-pity she buried her face in her hands. 'I wish I didn't have to go back there. I wish I was dead!' she choked.

There was a space of silence. For a long while the stranger stared down at her and his eyes grew troubled. He said quietly: 'I don't know what it's all about, but you don't really wish that, you know.'

'I do,' she whispered stubbornly. 'How do you know how I feel, anyway?'

'I don't,' he said flatly, watching her move again to touch an ankle that was beginning to swell. 'But I can see that you need a helping hand, even though you've done your best to convince me that you don't deserve it.' He took a deep breath and held out his hand. 'Are you going to accept it?'

Tina looked up unwillingly with eyes that were reddened with weeping, then avoided his steady gaze as she slowly put out her own hand. Without speaking he helped her to her feet and supported her slight weight while she tested the injured ankle. She set her lips, but they twisted as she tried to step forward.

'Where do you live?' His grasp tightened as she winced.

'I don't live here—I'm only staying here with Fay—she's just got married and they've taken the hotel along at——'

'I've seen it. But it's nearly a mile from here,' he cut in.

10

'I don't think you'll make it, frankly.'

'I'll have to,' she said hopelessly. 'I didn't think I'd come so far along the beach.'

'But you did, under stress, it seems.' He hesitated. 'Will you promise not to throw another fit of hysterics if I suggest some first aid?'

His voice sounded farther away than he was, and now that she was standing up she felt an alarming weakness making her unsteady. Her fingers were curling themselves, entirely of their own accord, very tightly round his forearm, and some instinct told her that if that rocklike support was withdrawn something odd might happen to her.

Tina had never fainted once during the course of her young life, nor had she ever experienced the frightening effects that emotional stress can cause, especially on a body that has waited overlong for food.

She must have made some sign, for the stranger said abruptly: 'You're just about out on your feet, aren't you? Come on, it isn't very far—hang on.'

The sandy path through the grove seemed to go on and on under her halting steps, and the world took on a strange quality of unreality. The trees closed in a lacy canopy overhead, shedding gold dapples among the tangle of vines and wild tropical growth that made green walls alongside the pathway. She leaned blindly on the broad muscular strength of the stranger and ceased to wonder where, why, or who ... it was taking all her powers of concentration to prevent her left ankle from buckling under her at every step, and when he stopped she had no idea if they'd come ten yards or ten miles.

The path had ended at a flight of rough steps cut into the earth and curving up a steep incline. She bit her lip and made to ascend, then a pressure on her shoulder checked the attempt. The next moment powerful arms cut under her waist and knees and she was swung up hard against the stranger's chest.

'Heavens! Are you made of feathers and snowflakes?' he exclaimed softly.

The vibrations of his voice made their own physical communication deep in the warm throat her cheek was against. That warmth and his strength induced a fresh awareness of despair and weariness, to which her body suddenly cried out

11

its plea to submit to that weariness and accept the sense of security a strange fate had so unexpectedly offered. In a moment of fantasy she imagined it was her father who held her thus and whispered those fanciful words. Soft, humorous, the artist in him choosing such a quaint turn of expression to tease ... exactly the kind of thing her adored father would say in one of his more grandiloquent moods. But his moods would change with the speed of quicksilver. When they reached the top of the steps her father would quite likely stagger, clump across the veranda and dump her down on the divan, then groan, 'Feathers of lead! Snowflake cement!' as he pretended to gasp with utter exhaustion.

But this man did not gasp. He carried her carefully and effortlessly up the veranda steps and across hollow-sounding boards. There was a screen door centre, facing the steps, and a rattan lounger with white cushions along to the left, immediately under one of the windows of this long, low bungalow. The stranger set her down, easing her gently on to the lounger, and murmured, 'I won't be a moment,' before he shouldered through the screen. As he disappeared within she heard him call, 'Kim!' and his steps fade.

She did not move, except to turn her head and look about her with a dawning of curiosity. She could see the whole eastern sweep of the lagoon from where she lay. It was as smooth as a pool of luminous crystal, shaded with green and amethyst, lapped by the curling white tongue of coral beach and fringed by the great girding of reef. No living creature disturbed the scene, even the palms were unmoving, etched in a breezeless lull that created the illusion of an artist's impression stretching away into infinity. How her father would love it; that particular blending of hues and grouping of nature's scenic effects. The ever-changing face of the ocean and the expressions of the islands never failed to make him reach for his brushes. But what would he say if he could see her now? Spirited into the domain of a stranger, a strange and mysterious male who was as arrogant and compelling as any hero of legend ... Perhaps he would say she was dreaming it all. Perhaps if she blinked it would all disappear, magically taking with it all this morning's misery and humiliation ...

She started quite violently when she heard the man's

voice and his shadow fell across her. She blinked up like a nervous little cat, catching back an exclamation. At home the screen doors squeaked like banshees every time anyone opened them, but this one had given so silently she had had no warning of the stranger's return. But the coldness of a glass thrust into her hand restored a semblance of normality and slowly she raised it to her lips.

He saw her grimace, and a trace of a smile relieved the soberness of his mouth. 'Yes, there's a dash of brandy in it. Kim's making coffee. It won't be long.'

'Oh ... don't make coffee especially for me,' she said.

He brushed aside the protest. 'It's no bother. I usually have coffee about this time.' He was drawing a chair near and sitting down as he spoke. 'Let's have a look at that ankle.'

Without waiting for her assent he raised the affected foot and rested it on his knee, probing the ankle with strong fingers and raising his brows when she winced. 'That hurt?'

'A bit. Have I broken anything in it, do you think?'

'Heavens, no! I think you've just ricked it badly.' He looked up as a Chinese boy came to the doorway, bringing a blue plastic bowl and a yellow towel. 'Here we are—thank you, Kim.'

There were pieces of ice floating in the water, and without wasting any time the stranger began to bathe her ankle. It struck so cold she shivered, and he smiled crookedly as with quick methodical movements he packed ice chips into the folds of a handkerchief and bound it firmly round her ankle.

'It'll melt all too soon,' he told her, putting the folded towel on the cushion and placing her foot over it. 'Now finish that drink.'

'Thank you—you shouldn't have gone to all that bother.' Her voice was steadier now and something, probably the brandy, had made her feel less agitated. She held out the glass to him. 'I don't think I need any more if I'm going to have coffee. I—I'm all right now.'

'I'd never have guessed it.' His tone was dry as he took the glass. 'No, stay where you are until you've pulled yourself together,' he enjoined forcefully as she stirred.

'But the ice is melting,' Tina protested. 'It's soaking through the towel—it'll go all over the cushion.'

'It doesn't matter. Just keep that foot still for a while.'

She followed the line of his glance and for the first time she became conscious of herself under his gaze. Most of her —the scanty white bikini covered very little of her—was still sand-streaked, and her long thin limbs bore adhering traces of the heap of seaweed into which she'd fallen. There was a long green frond sticking to her tummy, and the bikini no longer had the sparkling white freshness of when she donned it an hour or so ago before she ran down the beach with Pierre, to plunge hand-in-hand with him into the sea.

Pierre! He didn't even care what happened to her. It was all his fault! Her mouth tightened and she brushed angrily at the fine coral sand. She'd hurt herself, and lashed out like a wildcat at a total stranger. Who'd promptly slapped her face! Suddenly the waves of self-pity washed over her again and she quivered. If only she'd never been born!

'Chilly?' asked her rescuer.

'No.' Stubbornly she stared down at the white cushions, knowing he was watching her, then raised her gaze to the line of *toa* trees which made a windbreak at the side of the garden. At last, almost unwillingly, her eyes slid to the face of the man who watched her so steadily.

The grey eyes were calm, almost dispassionate now in their survey, and suddenly a confliction of impulses beseiged her. She realised he was trying to be kind to her in his brusque way, even though he'd hit her, and she wanted to tell him why she'd gone nearly berserk down there on the beach. Then he'd be sorry he'd hit her like that. Then she wanted to cry again. Only this time she wanted him to understand and comfort her ... She uttered a sigh, her lips parting to begin the trembling words forming in her imagination. Then she saw the maturity in his strong features, and a different kind of understanding in his eyes, and a surge of hot colour flowed into her cheeks.

She was drawing back, beginning the little gesture of deceit and the murmur about the hot sun that would excuse the embarrassing scarlet, then the boy, Kim, made a welcome diversion as he arrived, bringing a battered old silver tray with a coffee pot and china on it. He set it down on a low table near the veranda rail and hovered.

'That's fine—thanks, Kim,' said the man, getting to his

14

feet. He waved the boy away and turned to busy himself at the tray.

He had his back to her, and she watched him, prompted by the first stirrings of curiosity. His hair was thick and dark but conservatively cut. His shoulders were broad and muscular, as though they were well used to physical exertion, and she had already experienced the effortless strength of his arms. Yet his hands betrayed no clumsiness with coffee pot or cups, and though firm and strong in perfect proportion to the rest of his big six-foot frame they had a well-kept look about them and clean nails that didn't quite go with manual toil. Nor did his clothes give any definite clues. He sported neither the fashionably gaudy wear in which the tourists blossomed forth from their hotels in Papeete, nor the immaculate tropic kit of the businessmen, and he certainly didn't affect the deliberately tattered gear of the drop-outs. His pants and shirt were of well and oft-laundered linen, its original bush khaki tone faded to a pale greeny beige, but they were tailored and handstitched to that casual perfection only superb tailoring could attain. So he wasn't business; he wasn't official; he didn't look like a planter, he certainly wasn't a poor white, and he was no banana tourist. So to what category *did* he belong?

Tina, who after her years on the islands thought she could recognise most of them by now, frowned with puzzlement. There was one thing of which she *was* certain; he was English. And that made him more puzzling still. For Englishmen weren't all that thick on the ground of the islands ... She must ask Fay the moment she got back ...

He turned with the cup of coffee in his hand and caught her staring. A faint flicker of his dark brows acknowledged this, but he did not speak as he passed her the cup of coffee. There were biscuits on a chrome dish with a scalloped edge, and he put these where she could reach them without getting up.

'Thank you.' She took a biscuit, aware of a slight restraint, and he nodded, leaning back as though he were uninterested. He sipped his own coffee, until she gave a small exclamation. He glanced at her inquiringly.

'I've eaten nearly all the biscuits,' she said guiltily. 'I wasn't thinking. I'm sorry.'

'What for? You must have been hungry.'

15

'I am—I mean I was,' she amended hastily. 'You see, I've just remembered that I didn't have any breakfast. We came out first, for a swim, and then ...' Her voice tailed off and the shadows returned to cloud her face. With an effort she summoned youthful courage and made a wry grimace. 'Heavens, you must think me a proper little pig, wading into them like that!'

'They were brought for you—finish them,' he shrugged.

'May I?'

'Of course. And a second cup of coffee might not come amiss.' He did the refill, then sauntered across the veranda to lean casually on the rail and look out across the blue Pacific. Presently he swung round and surveyed her with grave eyes.

He nodded slowly. 'Yes, I think you're recovering.'

'Oh ...' She sat up, instantly taking this as a cue that she should be thinking of departing, and her cup tipped over, splashing its dregs over her wrist and one of the white cushions. Cursing her awkwardness, she righted the cup and rubbed hastily at the brown smears on the white material.

'Don't bother—it doesn't matter,' he said quickly.

'Oh, but it does!' She chewed at her lip. He seemed to have perceived so much about her in a very short time, and under the maturity of that level gaze she felt painfully conscious of her youth, like a nervous child facing a strange adult's authority. It imbued her with a sudden urge to escape from him and made her hands tremble as she leaned forward to put the cup and saucer on the tray. She almost dropped them when he moved suddenly to take them from her hand. Then with his free hand he touched her ruffled hair and said on a note of wry amusement:

'He probably isn't worth it, you know.'

'H-he ...' Her mouth parted. 'Who?'

'Whoever you're running away from.' The tanned hand fell away in front of her eyes and reached down for the sneaker he had taken from the damaged foot. 'Though I know I'm wasting my breath saying it.'

She looked down. 'I'm not running away from anything, if that's what you mean. Least of all a man.'

The tears were dangerously near again, just as she had congratulated herself on regaining control. She clasped her hands tightly, willing herself not to give way again.

16

The slightly cynical detachment left his expression. He watched the small twisting hands, the giveaway whiteness of tension over the thin bones, and a sigh escaped him. He slipped the sneaker over her toes and stood up.

'I'm sorry, I didn't mean to upset you. But it seems a logical conclusion. When a girl reaches a state of such emotional distress that she vows she doesn't want to go on living there has to be some reason for it. I hate to admit it, but invariably one of my own sex has had something to do with it.'

She sat with bowed head, and he leaned back against the rail, his hands stretched out along it at either side.

'How old are you?' he asked abruptly.

'How old do I look?' she retorted defiantly.

'About fourteen and a half.'

His face was in shadow, with the sun behind him, and she could not see his expression, but the brilliant light was full on her small taut features, revealing her outrage.

'I shall be sixteen in April!'

His mouth curved ironically. 'And this is May! I'm not so far out, after all. And you're fifteen—and a month. Oh, please don't cry again!' He moved forward, shaking his head. 'I was merely trying to offer a word of comfort from a man's angle. It *is* the young Frenchman, isn't it?'

'How did you know?'

'I saw you the other day, when I was out in the boat. Frankly, now I know you're just a kid, I think you need spanking. You thought no one could see you, I suppose?'

Tina could see the grimness round his mouth now, and without thinking she cried: 'How dare you spy on us! It was only the very first time Pierre ever——'

'The first time *anyone* had kissed you. I know,' he broke in. 'That was fairly obvious.'

Tina twisted away so that he could not see her anguished expression. To think that he had witnessed that first, tentative seeking kiss, that began as a teasing gesture and then became the tender, deepening embrace that had almost stopped her heart and made her begin to believe ecstatically that Pierre felt the same joyous love as herself. Then Pierre had given a sigh, and somehow the kiss had changed, and then something had made her pull away from him, as though she were afraid that the second kiss could spoil the

17

magic of that first wondrous moment of Pierre's lips touching her own, as though the first kiss could never happen again exactly the same way. And this man had ...

'You were wise enough to run away,' he said dryly, 'I'll grant you that. Don't you know he's at least eight years too old for you? On second thoughts, *he* deserves the hiding.'

'He doesn't!' Rage fought with tears. 'How dare you? He *isn't* too old. You sound just like my father.'

'Your father's probably a very wise man. Does he know that his daughter's fooling about with a French boy when she ought to be in school?'

She stood up unsteadily, drawing control around her with childish dignity. 'My father knows where I am, and he trusts me. Now ... I enjoyed your coffee, but I can't say the same for your words of comfort.'

'The truth isn't always comforting,' he said more gently, 'and Englishmen aren't noted for their Gallic charm of phrase. But there's one thing at least I can say, and do.' He held out one hand. 'See if that ankle will carry you this far.'

She obeyed before she thought to question the command, taking the strong muscular hand extended to her as she winced and was forced to throw her weight on to one leg.

He did not relax his grip, and for a moment he studied her ungainly stance, the way the handkerchief-bound foot was tucked childishly behind the undamaged ankle. Suddenly he said:

'I'm sorry I slapped you, down there on the beach.'

A little startled by the unexpected apology she searched his face warily and saw nothing to suggest anything other than sincerity. She swallowed hard and decided to accept the olive branch. 'It—it's all right,' she said awkwardly. 'I guess I flipped first.'

He nodded and released her hand. Then his mouth curved in a lazy smile and he turned away. 'Don't be surprised—even I can manage this kind of peace-offering.'

He reached up to the cascade of blossom on the overhanging tree and selected a big bloom, inspecting it carefully for lurking insects before he turned back to her. He tucked it gently into her hair, and the tantalising little grin touched his mouth again as he looked into her wide startled eyes.

'You'll have to wait a while before you can wear the

18

flower of love. But when you do, I hope the man who puts it there will never make you weep for him.'

Something in his voice and the unexpected gesture brought the tautness back into her throat, but a different kind of tautness this time. She put her hand up to the heavy magnolia and exclaimed: 'I don't like the scent of tiare anyway—it's too sickly—Aunt Wynne says it always gives her a headache. This is far nicer. More subtle.'

He inclined his head slightly when the small spate of confidence ended rather breathlessly. 'But I didn't mean that literally. The wearing of the flower is merely a symbol. When love flowers for you, real love, you'll know the difference—that is, if you even remember a young Frenchman who once made you weep for him.'

Tina looked away. 'He's going back tomorrow,' she said in a low voice. 'He's going to be married, to a girl he's known all his life—a sort of arranged marriage. Like they still have in some of the old families. You know ...?'

He nodded. 'I know.'

'I—I thought he liked me, and he—he'd write to me, and,' she paused and swallowed hard, 'and one day he'd come back for good, to help Paul run the hotel—he said he'd fallen in love with the Islands. But he ...'

She stopped, unable to go on, and her mouth quivered as she remembered Pierre's kiss, his lilting voice as he said softly: *So this is the last time I shall be able to flirt with my* petite *island Luana—next time I see you I shall be a married man,* chérie!'

Her head jerked up proudly. She would *not* allow Pierre to make her weep again! She said firmly, 'But I don't care if he doesn't come back. Anyway, I have to look after my father. He needs me.'

'You're very fond of your father?'

'He's the most wonderful person in the world.' She leaned on the veranda rail and her eyes lost some of their hurt. 'He's terribly clever as well—he's John Raimond, the artist. He's famous, you know.'

The stranger turned his head. 'I'd like to say that I know his work, but that wouldn't be strictly true. I'm no art expert. But I've heard of him. I thought he lived in Tahiti.'

'We do, but I came to stay with Fay and Paul for——'

'I remember. You said you were staying with friends.'

19

She nodded eagerly. 'Yes, you see Fay and Paul were married three months ago—Fay lived next door to us until then—and now they've taken over the little guest house in Akaia and they're going to try to extend it into an hotel now that the tourists are starting to come here, so they'll be settling permanently on Kaloha. Paul is Pierre's elder brother—he's quite gorgeous really, but I'm going to miss Fay terribly. She's like the sister I never had.'

'No brother, either?'

'No.' Tina looked down at the tangle of green ferns and the cluster of white-petalled tiare blossom whose heady scent drifted up from the heavily wooded slope. The garden seemed almost to tumble down into the sea, she thought inconsequentially, then glimpsed the steep rough steps up which the stranger had carried her. Oh, God! She *had* made an idiot of herself. Then she sensed his regard and his idly spoken question still hanging on the air, and she thought it was not as idle an interest as it seemed. He was genuinely concerned about her. Suddenly the feeling brought a warmth and a confidence she did not question. She said slowly: 'There's only Daddy and I now, since ... I nearly had a brother, but my mother died when he was born. There were complications, and they couldn't save her, or the baby.'

There was a pause, then, 'How old were you at the time?'

'Seven.' Tina's face shuttered on the memory. 'Sometimes it seems ages ago. Sometimes it seems just like last week.' She turned away abruptly. 'I'd better get back. They'll think I'm lost.'

He also moved, towards the door. 'I'll take you back, if you can ride pillion?'

'Oh, yes, but ...', she looked at him doubtfully. 'It'll be a bother for you. I'll be okay.'

'It's no bother. Ten minutes along the track.'

He moved indoors, leaving her little option but to follow or make her way back down the steps and along the beach. After a moment's hesitation she went into the cool shadowy interior. But there wasn't time to indulge in any curious looks about her, and she gained only a blurred impression of a simply furnished living room and a tiled hallway with doors at each side before she was out into the blinding sunlight again and limping unsteadily across a flat expanse of lawn to where the tall stranger waited beside a wicket gate. An old Mobibike stood outside, on a dusty narrow track that curled away into the plantation that reached right up to the front of the house. As he opened the gate she suddenly recognised the scent that lingered on the atmosphere.

'It's vanilla, isn't it?'

He said, 'Yes,' but seemed disinclined to enlarge any further on the subject, and again she experienced that flicker of curiosity. She could see now that this was the start of the vanilla plantation—Fay had told her that half the island was given over to its cultivation, but she hadn't given it a second thought—and it was obvious that this man had something to do with it. Yet somehow he did not fill the planter image.

'You'd better have this.'

She became aware that he was standing there impatiently, and the tone of his voice told her that it was the second time he had spoken. He was also holding out a blue garment.

'Just for the ride,' he said, as though addressing a two-year-old.

Tina flushed scarlet. 'I'm sorry, I didn't ...' She stared at the blue cotton shirt, then at his impatient expression, and then remembered her somewhat scanty attire.

'Yes,' he said dryly, 'you're not exactly dressed for pillion riding through a plantation.'

She flushed again. Of course he was right. The track looked dry and dusty, the wheels would kick it up, and there were the insects, and the delightfully cool breeze of speed would rapidly become less comfortable.

The garment almost enveloped her, the short cuffed sleeves slopping below her elbows, the big open collar making her slender neck look like a thin stem rising from it. She avoided looking at him as he helped her on the pillion, then mounted himself.

She sat very stiffly, gripping the little bars, oddly disturbed by the sudden proximity of that broad back curved slightly in front of her.

'Hold on to me if you're not steady,' he called over his shoulder, 'though we're not likely to break any speed limits!'

She shook her head, not realising that the silent response

21

was unseen, and the engine throbbed into life. A moment later they were into the shade of the grove, amid the rows of slender supporting trees entwined by the planifolia vines, and the air was dark, warm and moist with the heavy sweetness of the pods. She noticed windbreaks of banana trees every so often, and then a sudden swerve round a sharp bend almost unseated her and she was forced to grab the broad waist in front.

'What did I tell you?' He seemed unconcerned by the sudden clutch of small arms round his middle, and she sensed his grin.

She stayed silent, holding her body tense against any more similar occurrences, until the vanillery began to thin and the island views opened out again. A few more minutes and another curve brought the more familiar terrain near the hotel into sight, and then she remembered something. She said abruptly: 'This sounds awful, but would you mind not coming in?'

He slowed down. 'I never had any intention of making this a social visit.'

There was a slight edge to his tone, and she said quickly, 'I'm sorry, I didn't mean it like that. But they'll fuss. I don't know if Pierre ... I just want to sneak in and get cleaned up first, before ...'

If he wondered at the reason left unspoken he gave no sign. Under the shade of a yellow-leaved *bourao* he stopped the machine. 'I'll drop you here, then.'

He waited until she scrambled off, and enigmity had returned to his expression.

She hesitated, aware of, yet not defining a feeling of something awaiting completion before she took her leave. 'Thanks for bringing me back,' she said at last, then went on awkwardly, 'I've just realised ... I don't know your name, Mr ...?'

His smile flickered briefly. 'Do names matter that much? Away you go before someone spots you. And remember what I said.'

'You said quite a lot of things, Mr Mystery.' Her wide, direct gaze rested on his face. 'I'll try, though.'

'Just remember one. In a couple of years you'll have fallen in love so many times you'll have forgotten what Pierre even looks like.'

Her lips compressed. 'Never!'

'Like to bet on it?'

'I don't need to. I——' She stopped indignantly. 'You're laughing at me again. Oh, you——!' Her mouth pursed in a grimace of rage as he raised one hand in a laconic salute and swung into a big U-turn across the track. In moments he was out of sight and only the settling slicks of dust from his machine remained.

'Of all the——!' Tina hung on to the gate with one hand while she tore the big white handkerchief off her ankle and squashed it into a tight ball in her palm. Forgetting the voluminous—on her!—garment she still wore, she tried to compose her expression as she limped with heavily assumed nonchalance towards the house and prayed no one would emerge until she'd reached her room. For once luck was on her side, and no over-observant adult crossed her path to remark on her absence and the somewhat odd picture she must be presenting. In the safety of her room she grabbed her wrap and winced at the still considerable discomfort of her damaged ankle. It was all Pierre's fault. And as for Mr Mystery, whatever his name was, with his advice and his smirk ...

Men! She was through with the lot of them from now on!

CHAPTER TWO

What a party!

Tina flopped into a chair and fanned her hot cheeks. It was long after midnight, the last guest—Joey, of course!—had just gone and the wide airy room wore the battered look left by recent noisy revelries. Now there was only Aunt Wynne, restoring a fallen cushion to its rightful place, her daughter Fay, who was rescuing an overturned glass from a small pool of shandy behind a chair, and the tall, slightly stooped figure of John Raimond, standing by the patio door and filling the last pipe of the day. He turned, as though sensing Tina's regard, and looked at his daughter with affectionate eyes.

'Had enough?'

Tina shook her head, exchanging a conspiratorial grin with Fay. 'I wish it was just starting all over again.'

'Heaven forbid!' John turned a despairing glance to Aunt Wynne. 'What it is to be young. How does it feel to be eighteen, anyway?'

'Wonderful!'

'Any different from being seventeen?'

'Of course! Worlds different!' Tina breathed a deep sigh of happiness. 'It's been the most wonderful party, and most wonderful day, ever.'

'Has it, darling?' John Raimond's eyes lost their bantering look. 'I'm glad.'

Tina looked at the three people who had always made the security of her world, and a tremulous emotion suddenly came to mist her eyes and bring a lump to her throat. It was true; they had given her a supreme day to celebrate her coming of age, and it seemed like a seal on the love they had given her for as long as she could remember, especially so since that still remembered day of tragedy eleven years ago ...

The title 'Aunt Wynne' was a courtesy one. The kindly plump woman now beginning to gather up party litter was their nearest neighbour, and for the past decade she had endeavoured to make up for the loss of Tina's mother, while Fay, three years older than Tina, had become the sister she had never had. Yes, Tina mused, she had been truly blessed and should count herself lucky to be surrounded with so much affection.

She sprang up sharply, divining Aunt Wynne's intention of moving kitchenwards to start on the chaos that had swept in there like a tide. 'No, you've done enough today. Leave that. I—I'll never be able to thank you, all of you, for today, and everything.'

'Well, we're not sure if you deserve it.' Her father looked a little amused at the emotional speech. 'But we'll give you the benefit of the doubt.'

His dry tone banished the moment of pathos and restored the former lighthearted atmosphere. Quickly Tina began to gather up dirty glasses, turning a reproachful glance on him as she did so and fully aware of the twin imps of mischief lurking in his eyes.

'See what a flint-hearted father I have—begrudging me a little bit of birthday pleasure,' she said mournfully. 'He'll have me back in my rags tomorrow, hawking leis to the

24

tourists and touting for custom.'

John Raimond maintained his mock-solemn expression. 'And see what a congenital liar I've fathered, folks.'

'Am I not my father's daughter?' She scowled at him, then, unable to keep her mirth in check, reached up to kiss his cheek. 'Now hadn't you better go and pack? You know you've to catch the early plane and you'll only get in a flap if you leave everything until morning. I'm just going to do the glasses and set the places for breakfast in case we sleep in,' she chattered on over her shoulder. 'But we mustn't sleep in, or you'll miss the plane, and Paul's coming over first thing. Oh, I wish he'd been here today.'

'So do I.' Fay followed the younger girl into the long kitchen that led off the rear of the Raimonds' bungalow and picked up a glass-cloth. 'It's ages since we had a day off together. But he hates us both to be away overnight, especially when we're so busy.'

Tina nodded, knowing that the hotel over on Kaloha was fully booked that week by a party of American tourists. But apart from the now successful hotel business on which the young couple had worked so hard for nearly three years there were the two-year-old twin sons whom Paul idolised. They were the principal reason for Paul's absence from the birthday celebration. It would have meant leaving them and the hotel for the best part of a day; also, little Jacques, senior to his twin by exactly seventeen and a half minutes, had suffered a tummy upset and slight fever a few days previously, and Fay had decided, much to Tina's disappointment, that he and André had better stay at home, away from the excitement and the temptation to consume too many party goodies.

'But you'll be seeing them soon, I hope.' Fay was polishing rapidly and stacking glasses back in the cupboard. 'It's ages since you came to stay with us.' She flashed a teasing smile. 'I suppose Joey's too great an attraction now.'

Tina shook her head vehemently, not betraying even a trace of a blush. 'I don't know why everybody persists in trying to pair me off with Joey. He's so juvenile!'

'And what are you?' Fay assumed her big-sister expression. 'Joey's a nice boy, just right, I'd say, for your first play at the field.'

'What do you mean? My first play at the field?' Tina

25

asked indignantly. 'What do you think I've been playing since you left three years ago? Old Maid?'

Fay laughed happily. 'How do I know? Although I do remember my mother teaching you to play that when you were so tiny you couldn't hold all the cards in your little fist. Happy days!' Her pretty features lit suddenly with mischief. 'Come in with me tonight and then you can tell me the full ghastly account of your love life since I've not been around to look after my adopted sister.'

Nothing loath, Tina agreed eagerly. Often, in the old days, she'd stayed with Fay while John Raimond was away for any reason, or Fay had come over to keep the young girl company so that she did not have to spend a lonely night in the big bungalow. Now it seemed like old times to curl up in the spare bed in Fay's former room and whisper confidences across the darkness to the girl in the other bed. She had very few secrets from Fay, and despite her earlier boast few illusions about her youthful love life. Certainly none about Joey.

'He's more interested in art. He's hoping my father will persuade his parents to let him go to art college instead of business studies. That's the entire extent of his interest in me.'

'By the way he looked at you tonight I'd have said otherwise,' Fay teased. 'I overheard him offering to help you look after the studio the next few weeks while your father's away.'

'Huh, he fancies himself as a salesman.' Tina wriggled further into her pillow. 'He's hoping to impress Father with the number of paintings he's flogged to the tourists.'

There was nothing feigned about Tina's indifference to the subject of Joey, or a couple of other boys Tina's own age who had been present at the party, and for a little while Fay lay silent. A faint light flickered through the screens, probably from a campfire along the beach, and somewhere a guitar was being strummed beside the sighing sea. Tina's eyes closed, then opened as Fay said suddenly:

'What a pity you couldn't have had your birthday a day later, then Pierre would have been here for it.'

Tina's fingers closed more tightly over the edge of the coverlet. 'How could I? My father would have been away. How could I have any celebration without my father?'

'Mm, I suppose so.' Fay's agreement was sleepy. 'But it's a pity, all the same. It would have made a good start for Pierre's return.'

'Father couldn't stay another day. He has to be in 'Frisco tomorrow night, ready to start his lecture tour. He's doing a real coast-to-coast this time, and then he's stopping over at Honolulu on his way back. There's going to be an exhibition of his work and a special opening party in his honour. I could have gone, but I don't want to be away from the studio as well because there's a big cruise ship due in that day and we might make some sales. We need some cash,' Tina added matter-of-factly.

'What about your tame salesman, Joey?'

'He'll be away by then.'

There was silence again. Tina heard Fay turn over and settle down, and her fingers relaxed the grip they had unconsciously maintained on the light coverlet. The subject of Pierre was safely avoided—the one secret even Fay had never shared. Tina gave a soft sigh and prepared to give herself up to sleep, then Fay's voice came thoughtfully:

'I'm surprised you're not showing much interest in Pierre's return. In fact, you've positively clammed up every time his name has been mentioned today.'

'I haven't!'

Fay chuckled in the darkness. 'Oh, yes, you have. I suppose you've forgotten the thing you used to have for my handsome brother-in-law.'

'I never did!' Tina was thankful for the dark that hid her flaming cheeks. 'I've never had a thing for any man, and what's more, I don't intend to.'

'Famous last words! Darling, you haven't even started yet!'

The indulgent amusement in the older girl's voice stung Tina. 'I mean it. I'm never going to let myself care so much for a man that it hurts.'

'There's no other way of loving a man, my pet.'

'Isn't there? The Tahitians don't love like that. They simply enjoy an affair without getting all emotionally involved. They're far more sensible about it—and happy—than we are.'

'But you're not a Tahitian.'

'I was born here, so that makes me Tahitian by birth, if

not by blood,' Tina said stubbornly.

'Never.' Fay turned over and propped herself on one elbow to stare at the dim outline of the younger girl. 'Your heritage is English, and any other influence is French, so don't get your ideas mixed up at this stage. And don't ever imagine you can play around with sex without getting emotionally involved, or you will get hurt.'

'I've no intention of that, either.'

'I'm glad to hear it.' Fay subsided against her pillow. 'You'll fall in love one day like anyone else, and I hope to goodness that the man, whoever he is, is a strong enough character to knock those silly notions out of your head.'

'Oh, stop being so bossy!' Tina flung herself over and wriggled down in her bed. 'You're only three years older than me. Just because you're married and got two babies it doesn't mean you can shout down everything I say.'

There was a sharp movement across the room, then Fay pattered on light feet to stand and look down at the petulant little figure lying hunched there.

'Tina, we're quarrelling!' Fay said incredulously. 'I'm sorry—I never intended to shout you down. Whatever gave you that idea?'

'You said my notions are silly.' Tina knew in her heart that she was being childish, but some inner resentment made her go on doggedly: 'You make me feel like an infant again. I wish people would let me grow up.'

Fay's usually gentle mouth compressed with wry humour. 'The trouble with you, Tina, is that your father's spoilt you. And so have we. We've always tried to protect you, to make up for ...' Fay sighed and left the words incomplete. 'It's quite true what you say; three years isn't so much, but marriage and motherhood can bring a maturity that years just can't measure.'

She fell silent, and Tina bit her lip, knowing that Fay spoke the truth. 'I'm sorry,' she said at last. 'I don't know what got into me. I——'

'Forget it.' Fay pressed her hand on the slender shoulder that had shrugged remorsefully. 'Put it down to over-excitement. It's been a hectic day.'

Tina nodded, glad to seize the proffered excuse, even as she knew it wasn't true. How Fay would laugh if she knew the real reason! Well, not laugh. Fay was never unkind, she was too good-natured ever to be that, but she would have teased, never guessing how teasing could wound ... She smiled tremulously, ready to say goodnight, but Fay remained standing there, her face taking on its thoughtful look.

'You will come and stay with us, for a long visit, as soon as your father gets back. Promise,' she said slowly. 'You know that my mother will look after him and see that he eats occasionally.'

'Of course.' Tina was a shade puzzled by the earnestness of the request. She knew that she had a genuine open invitation to visit Fay and Paul whenever she wished, in the same way that she and her father would be very disappointed if Fay and her husband failed to look in at the Raimond home whenever they came over to the main island.

'And I'm going to tell you something that, even if it doesn't banish any silly notions of not being a big girl now, should give that sensitive little ego of yours a big kick,' Fay went on with a return of her teasing tone. 'As I left home Paul reminded me to fix up a definite arrangement about having you to stay with us for a while. Do you know what he said?'

Tina shook her head.

'He said, "If Tina can't jolt Pierre out of his doldrums I don't know who can." ' Fay grimaced. 'Nobody ever handed me a compliment like that!'

Tina's mouth had parted. 'You mean ... Paul said that I ...? Oh, no, I couldn't,' she stammered, dismay engulfing her like a warm tide. 'I——'

'Nonsense. You always had a thing about Pierre, even though he used to tease you unmercifully.' Fay paused, her expression growing serious. 'Paul's terribly worried about him, after all this upset of Madeleine. We couldn't believe that the marriage was finished for good. But Pierre wouldn't even consider trying for a reconciliation, even though her people as well as Pierre's begged them to try again. And now he's going to settle with us.'

Tina nodded wordlessly. She was sorry for Pierre, but she didn't even want to think of him, let alone see him again. It would unleash too many humiliating memories.

'And there isn't exactly a surplus of glamorous diversions on Kaloha, apart from Corinne, who isn't Pierre's type at all, and the tourists, who really don't count, most of them are comfortable matronly types on the feminine side, I'm afraid. So far we don't attract the young gilded set. But somehow we've got to lay on some feminine talent for poor old Pierre and try to salvage some of his battered pride,' Fay ended wryly.

'I'm afraid it's no good expecting me to fill the bill.' Tina lay back and stared up into the darkness. 'Anyway, it's nearly three years since we last met. I was only a kid. Pierre may not even recognise me—if he even remembers I ever existed,' she added bitterly.

'Nonsense.' Fay straightened and pattered back to her own bed. There she paused and glanced back at the silent Tina. 'But tomorrow will settle that question. You don't imagine that he'll still remember the little squabble you had just before he left, do you?'

'What squabble?' *Was that what he'd told Fay and his brother?*

Fay shrugged and climbed back into bed. 'Whatever it was that left you looking like a thundercloud that last morning before he left.'

'What a super memory,' Tina scoffed.

'Haven't I?' Fay returned calmly. 'Maybe if you hadn't clammed up and glowered at Pierre every time you saw him that last day, refusing even to come with us to see him off, it might not have stuck in my super memory. What did happen, anyway, to upset you?'

'I can scarcely remember—my memory isn't as good as yours.' Tina pretended to yawn deeply. 'Heavens! let's get off to sleep or it'll be morning before we do.'

'I doubt if it's worth going to sleep now.' There were the light sounds of Fay composing herself for that state. Then she said softly: 'You *are* coming with us tomorrow to meet Pierre, aren't you?'

'I suppose so.'

With the unwilling response she could do nothing else but make Tina closed her eyes and tried to shut out the knowledge she had been able to forget all day during the excitement of her coming of age; that Pierre was coming back to the islands. To help his elder brother run the hotel on Kaloha, to stay there for at least a year.

Once she would have been delirious with joy at the very

thought of seeing him again, but now she felt only the cold foreboding of dismay. Pierre meant only a memory of unhappiness, of the moment when she betrayed the tender poignancy of first love and found only humiliation and disillusion. A day she would never forget as long as she lived.

No, she had no love now for Pierre. She never wanted to see him again.

Fortunately there was such a rush next morning to get her father packed and organised for his journey that Tina had little time to think of the meeting she dreaded. John Raimond was a superb artist, but faced with a suitcase of things to pack and the rounding up of such trivialities as passports and travellers' cheques he became a fussy, excitable man in a hassle who took the combined efforts of his daughter and Aunt Wynne to ensure that he was lined up in the departure hall at the right time and complete with essentials like his razor and a toothbrush. And then, manlike, he was full of last-minute rejoinders to his daughter. That whatever happened she wasn't on any account to sell the Maupiti landscape or the copra children. No matter who offered what. And she hadn't to forget to collect his linseed oil—he was right down on it. And would she answer that letter from those magazine people about the Gauguin article —he'd completely forgotten about it in the rush ...

She assured him that she'd tie up every end, reminded him to get a new supply of his special allergy pills while he was in the States, and at last the goodbyes and kisses were exchanged and John Raimond joined the file of passengers for the plane. By the time Tina got back to the house and helped Violet, their domestic help, to clear up the whirlwind of debris left behind by the previous evening's festivities and John Raimond's departure, she was exhausted.

Fay and Paul had gone to pick up some shopping and see the travel representative who arranged their block bookings, and though they had invited Tina to join them for lunch she had refused, knowing how rarely they had an opportunity of a little time to themselves. Instead, she had a roll and some lemonade, then after a shower to freshen herself she cycled down the coast road to the outskirts of the town and the somewhat ramshackle building which served as her father's 'showroom' and studio and where the more traditional aspects of his work were displayed. These were the pictures the tourists wanted, and—more important—bought, to take home along with the other souvenirs of their holiday cruise. In the back part of the building, behind the palm partition which aided the right atmosphere to a Tahitian artist's studio, were what he called his 'real' paintings. Here he entertained serious clients and visiting artists, and it was his boast that he could distinguish the genuine art-lover from the souvenir collector, regardless of their appearance, the moment they walked in the door.

Yes, her father knew his art, and his customers, Tina reflected, but he was hopelessly impractical in other ways. Only when he was away was she able to have what she called a whisk around. Basically she had a tidy nature, along with a flair for making an eye-catching display of Tahitian craft, carved bowls, spears, *tiki* worked in wood and ivory or bone, drums, baskets woven of pandanus, and the inevitable necklaces of shells. Now she whisked round, collecting the painting debris that her father left like an ebbing tide, sorting his colours and getting out fresh tubes to replenish his box, removing the most hideous of his paint-rags—which he hated parting with—and finding replacements; everything must be ready for him in case he was itching to work when he returned. It all depended on his mood ...

The day was quiet, as far as customers were concerned. There was no ship due that day, to bring a surge of sightseers who might want to buy a Gauguin print, if not an original by a modern, living artist, and Joey did not turn up, somewhat to her surprise. But Tina did not mind being alone. She had plenty of jobs she wanted to do, and this would be a marvellous opportunity to whitewash the studio and make a raid on the ants. Unless one made regular, ruthless onslaughts they got into everything.

But the thought of the coming reunion with Pierre would not be banished. Useless to tell herself that she was no longer a gauche fifteen-year-old who'd been foolish and naïve, and that Pierre had probably long since forgotten the child-woman who had betrayed her heart and his disillusion. Somehow she could not dismiss the premonition that

32

Pierre would reopen the book of unhappiness again. But how could he? She had no lingering feeling for him, no nostalgic curiosity to see him again. Oh, she was being stupid and fanciful.

She finished her self-allocated stint for that day and lit the Primus to make herself a cup of tea. She knew that some strange instinct was making her delay, so that she would scarcely have time to get back home and shower and change in time to meet Fay and Paul.

At last she got up and rinsed out her cup, then, defiantly aware of her somewhat grubby self, she locked up and wheeled her bike out on to the road. Maybe they'd have given up and gone without her ...

With the thought, she saw the old Dyane coming round the curve and slowing to a stop. The door opened and Fay got out, immaculate in a sleeveless cream silk dress with a bandeau of black velvet holding her sleek blonde hair. Fay stared at Tina's skin-fitting old pink jeans and the flowered island cotton shirt knotted casually to betray a portion of Tina's slender midriff, this last adorned with a smudge of dirt.

'What on earth have you been doing?' Fay demanded. 'We've been waiting ages for you.'

'I've been clearing up—the place was in such a mess.' Tina leaned on the handlebars and suppressed a secret sigh of relief. She couldn't go to the airport like this! 'I'm sorry, Fay, but I forgot the time. You'd better go without me.'

'Nonsense!' Paul's dark head was tilting out of the window and his eyes held amusement. 'What is wrong?'

'What's wrong?' Fay looked exasperated. 'Look at her! Oh, Tina, you are the limit.' She glanced at her watch, then at her husband. 'Have we time to go back?'

'Non!' Paul was laughing. 'I like my sweet little sister's natural look. You look as beautiful as ever, *ma petite*, except ...' He whipped out a spotless handkerchief and leaned out of the car to dab at the smudge on Tina's firm, tanned midriff. 'Stand still, *ma belle*—I *am* your adopted brother-in-law, which makes it perfectly permissible for me to do this. Especially while my wife is looking on!'

Tina giggled. She adored Paul in a special way that was totally innocent, and she knew Fay understood this. 'Spit on it,' she suggested, grabbing the handkerchief and suiting

33

action to the suggestion. 'Thanks, Paul. I can run a comb through my hair in the car.'

She refused Fay's offer of a lipstick and contented herself with combing out her long hair vigorously until it hung in a silky smooth swathe to her shoulders, its natural ripple making it turn under into a lovely flowing curve that followed the slender hollows of her neck. She caught Fay's eye and looked away, slightly shamefaced; she should have left time to go back and polish up. Fay looked gorgeous, and Paul as handsome as ever in a spotless white shirt and grey, hand-sewn denims. Then abruptly Tina's mood changed again. What did it matter? Wasn't it *pas à la mode* these days to be formal, in dress or behaviour, or anything?

She smiled wryly to herself. Three years ago she would have spent the entire day getting ready for this occasion, rejecting everything in her wardrobe as hopeless, layering her face with make-up, and endeavouring to avoid her father's disapproving eye. He had objected very strongly to any experiments with make-up in those days. What an idiot she'd been at fifteen! Now she couldn't care less what sort of an impression she made on Pierre.

All the same, she was tense and wary by the time they reached the airport. They had scarcely minutes to spare, and as Paul parked the car they could hear the flight arrival announcement being made. She hung back a little when the passengers began to disembark and the ripples of excitement began to surge through the groups of people waiting to meet friends and visitors. Then she saw Pierre and caught her breath, half prepared to find her heart would play her false and give a great lurch of emotion. But there was nothing. Nothing to disturb the small set smile of politeness she had assumed for Fay's sake.

There was very little change in him. He was still slight of build, not quite as tall as Paul, and the three years had made no noticeable difference to his appearance—except that the little one-sided smile which had once turned her heart over was there no longer. His smile seemed almost forced as he greeted his brother and kissed Fay. Someone bumped Tina with a suitcase as they pushed past, and then as she turned back Pierre was catching her hands and drawing her to him.

'Tina—it *is* Tina! But you have grown, *ma petite!*'

'I haven't really.'

She turned her cheek, letting him kiss her, and a slow surge of relief was welling within her. It was true. She was immune. She could return his kiss, make all the trite little exclamations people made at a reunion like this, forget that once she——

Suddenly she stiffened. Everyone seemed to be talking at once. Paul was picking up his brother's cases, and Pierre was still holding on to her hands, but everything seemed miles away. Over Pierre's shoulder she saw a cold grey gaze, sharp grey eyes that were staring at her, almost as though they knew her. Their tall owner wanted to be past. He was murmuring something, and shouldering past a group of tourists, but still his gaze held Tina.

Abruptly she pulled her hands free of Pierre's, and in that moment she recognised the stranger. Three years rolled away, and she was fighting this stranger on a lonely beach, hating him because he saw her tears, because he saw her hurt, because he hurt her again with brutal, arrogant strength ... And he had recognised her now.

His gaze had shifted to Pierre, missed nothing, and now returned to her, to take in her grubby shirt and pants, the shabby sneakers on her bare feet, the strained young face bare of make-up. She thought he was going to speak, and her lips parted to whisper a soundless acknowledgement. But before the words formed in her throat he had gone, thrusting past with long strides, and as she turned her head she saw only the broad dark outline of him threading his way through the clusters of travellers. She did not hear Fay's voice until her arm was caught and tugged.

'Tina! Have you seen a ghost or something?'

'N-no.' Tina found her voice and shook her head, as though to bring herself back to cold normality. It seemed that Pierre wanted to dine out that evening before returning to Kaloha, but Fay and Paul, though tempted by the celebration to round off the day, were doubtful. It would make them terribly late getting back to the hotel.

'But nothing will have gone wrong,' Pierre exclaimed. 'What could go wrong? You always swear that Jules and Rosa are such treasures. Do you not trust them out of your sight? Or is it that this brother of mine is not to be trusted

35

to navigate the way home in the dark?' he added tauntingly to Fay.

'Paul's a jolly good sailor,' Tina defended. 'Better than you.'

'Ah! So you remember. I think you still do not trust me,' Pierre teased. He sighed deeply. 'Oh, it is good to be back. So let us have our freedom tonight—before Paul puts on my shackles and begins my term of toil.' He slipped an arm round Fay and Tina and guided them towards the exit, leaving Paul to cope with the luggage.

In a short while they were back to Fay's old home, where Aunt Wynne waited eagerly. She had never been able to resist Pierre, and now he lavished coy compliments on her, and Tina seized the chance to escape.

Darkness had come as she crossed the lane to the bunga-low, and the sudden emptiness of the house closed round her as she entered. It was always like this when her father was away, and suddenly she was glad that the day was to be extended and that for the next three weeks she would be staying at nights with Aunt Wynne.

Quickly she showered and changed into her jade green lace Josephine dress. They were all the rage among the younger set just now, and the long flowing lines from the tight, high-waisted little bodice with its low-cut neckline accentuated Tina's youthfulness even as it lent a hint of sophisticated coquettishness. She took special care with her make-up, and when she studied the result in her dressing table mirror her jade-shadowed eyes looked back at her with a sparkle of mischief in their depths. If her feminine instinct was right Pierre was more than ready to flirt with her; very well, it might be fun to let him—on her terms this time. He would discover that it was no naïve fifteen-year-old he was amusing himself with now!

The thought brought satisfaction, and Pierre's reaction when they came to collect her seemed to prove her in-stinct well founded. He was especially attentive to her, with that indefinable air of gallantry which the Frenchman has made his own, and the moment they entered the restaurant Tina began to enjoy herself. All the colour of Tahiti was here; the flower girls with their garlands, the thrum of guitars, the cabaret hulas, and the warm magic of the tropical night. Tina knew it was all a garish façade

36

donned for the tourists, but tonight she was going to suspend belief and pretend she was one of those wealthy gilded girls who came ashore from gilded yachts, to nibble at heart-of-palm salad and sip champagne with the same carelessness as she downed Coke and a banana.

'You've grown up,' Pierre whispered as they danced. 'I'm going to wear out the strip of Pacific between here and Kaloha.'

'I thought you had a broken heart,' she responded flippantly.

'So I have. Are you going to help me mend it?'

Her mouth curved with a trace of bitterness. 'I'm better at breaking things than mending them—or so my father says.'

'I don't believe it.'

'Maybe I'll prove it before long.'

'*Mon Dieu!*' He drew her closer. 'I hope not. Once in a lifetime is enough for any man.'

'Then don't take the risk,' she said coolly.

He slowed their steps and looked down searchingly into her face, the darkening of puzzlement coming into his eyes. 'You *have* grown up, my little island Luana,' he said at last.

'Time doesn't stand still, Pierre.' She met his gaze levelly and disengaged herself as the music came to its close. 'And maybe I'd better make it quite clear that I don't answer to Luana now. My name is Tina.' She smiled at his startled face and walked back to their table, her heart beating a little faster, but this time with triumph.

She was conscious of that puzzlement lingering in his expression several times as the evening wore on, but she was determined not to give him a single inkling of encouragement or the slightest cause for believing that she was ready to provide balm for his bruised heart. *If he has a heart*, she reflected, still surprised by this new ability to see Pierre as he really was; a facile charmer, a philanderer to whom any girl was a challenge.

That her unexpected attitude might be proving a very potent challenge, far more so than if she had met him with either her former innocent adoration or hurt reproachfulness, never occurred to her. When, a while later, a Polynesian business man with whom Paul was friendly joined the party, Tina once again accepted Pierre's invitation to

37

take the floor. But this time he remained silent and withdrawn until the dance was almost over. Then he said
suddenly:

'There is something I have to say to you, *ma petite*. Let
us find a quieter and cooler spot.'

Without waiting for her assent he drew her from the
crowd of dancers and scooped aside the bead curtain which
masked a doorway to the Oleander Garden. The garden was
a feature of the place, and several other couples walked or
talked along the scented pathways among tropical shrubs,
while lanterns strung overhead cast soft pools of rose
radiance in the darkness. Beside a fountain that cascaded
rainbow spray Pierre stopped. He faced her and stared down
intently into her face, as though choosing what he wanted
to say.

'Well?' she said at last, impatiently. 'What is this world-
shattering secret?'

'Oh, my dear!' His shoulders expressed a rueful shrug.
'How you have changed!'

'You've already reminded me of that,' she returned,
giving him a cool little smile. 'For that matter, so have
you.'

'In what way?'

'I'm not prepared to put you wise to that.' She held his
gaze, her own very direct. 'Did you really expect me to be
the same naïve child of three years ago?'

'Of course not! But I did hope you would have forgiven
me.'

'Forgive you?' Tina turned away and held one hand
under the cool rainbow drops. 'What do you mean, Pierre?'

He reached out and caught her hand, looking at the
sparkling splashes that lay on it. 'You haven't forgiven me,
I can see. Tell me, *chérie*, what do I have to do to earn that
forgiveness?'

She withdrew her hand. 'You don't have to do anything.'

'No penance?'

Tina began to lose patience. 'Oh, for goodness' sake,
forget it. It's silly, talking round in circles like this.' She
began to walk away, not bothering to glance back to see if
he followed.

Before she had taken three steps her arm was seized.
Pierre pulled her round to face him, and now the banter had

left his expression. It now held a bitterness and an intensity that shocked her with its force.

'Very well. If you are not prepared to let me say what I have to say in a civilised manner, then I must find other means to make you listen,' he said harshly. 'I am well aware that you bear me a grudge for the way in which we parted three years ago. As I am well aware of what your feelings were towards me then. And do not pretend you have forgotten!'

'No, I haven't forgotten.' She attempted to keep her voice low and steady, as she sought to free herself from his grip. 'But I don't think there is anything more to be said about that childish episode, three years ago. Now please leave go of my arm, Pierre.'

But her plea might have been unspoken, for Pierre's face darkened and his other hand went to her shoulder, making her a prisoner between his hands. 'Perhaps it was a childish episode to you, but do not try to deny that you felt a special affection for me, one you had felt for no other man, and which I doubt if you have felt since, despite your cool English assurance. But what did you expect me to do? Go ahead and seduce you? A fifteen-year-old child?'

'You did make one effort in that direction,' she accused. 'Or will you start saying my memory is at fault?'

'No, your memory is no more at fault than my own.' The grip of his fingers had tightened, and she saw the glint of white teeth between his grim lips. 'Perhaps it will give you satisfaction to know that I too regret what happened, and I have never forgotten.'

'You are trying to tell me you still cherish sentimental memories of an adolescent's first rave on you?' Tina's mouth twisted with scorn. 'I don't believe it. A Frenchman sentimental! I thought it was only the English who were reputed for their sentimental approach to love, *monsieur*.'

His eyes narrowed with darkening anger. 'It would not occur to your small adolescent mind that I had no option than to behave as I did. To flirt, to tease, to laugh at you. For otherwise I might have been tempted beyond endurance to take what I read in your eyes, *chérie*.'

'You really believe that! But I believe you do!' she cried. 'Was your ego so vain that it couldn't resist any conquest? Even a naïve kid? Thank heaven you *did* go away. And thank heaven that I was only a gauche schoolgirl at the time!'

'What do you mean by that?'

'I mean that I can look back and be thankful that I wasn't older—old enough to be really hurt. It means that I can look back and know that I'm free of the silly childish crush which you seem to remember with such satisfaction. And now,' she pushed her hands against his chest, 'I'm going back to the others.'

For a moment Pierre stared at her small furious face as though he did not believe what he saw. Then with an exclamation of anger he pulled her roughly against him and before she had time to protest he kissed her with hard, violent force.

Instinctively Tina struggled, a flare of hatred making her desperate to escape that fierce invading mouth. But her struggles seemed only to make Pierre tighten his bruising grip even more.

At last she dragged her mouth free and beat at his chest. 'Have you gone mad?' she cried. 'Let me go! Do you hear? Let me——'

'You heard what the lady said. Just do that.'

There was a gasp from Pierre as the quiet voice spoke behind the struggling girl. 'Who are you, *monsieur*, to interfere?' Pierre blustered.

'It doesn't matter who I am.' The voice was still quiet and controlled, but there was a deadly ring in its deep tones. 'Let her go.'

Surprise already had slackened Pierre's hands, and Tina seized the chance to slip free. She turned, a cold dismay beginning to well through the anger Pierre had evoked. Without looking, she knew the owner of that voice, if not the identity, and she wished the ground could open and engulf her as she met the cool, scornful gaze.

The stranger sighed. 'You take a long time to learn your lesson, don't you?' His mouth compressed as he placed himself between Tina and the now discomfited Pierre. 'I should have thought that once was enough.'

He raised one hand and pointed to the lights spilling from the terrace windows. 'I suggest that you return to your friends—and remain with them. I may not be around the third time.'

For a dumbstruck moment Tina stared at the lean, dispassionate face of the stranger. Why did it always have to be him? Looming like some omnipotent guardian presence to witness her humiliation.

She swallowed hard, and whispered, 'Thank you—but there certainly won't be a third time.'

'Won't there?' His mouth curved ironically. 'Like to bet?'

That smile brought the bitter tears of humiliation springing to her eyes. 'No,' she choked, 'I wouldn't,' then pressed her hand to her mouth and fled.

CHAPTER THREE

TINA awoke next morning with an odd feeling of excitement, as though something momentous might occur that day. Why this sense of expectancy should be present defied analysis, though, because all the excitement was over and there was absolutely nothing she could think of that was likely to happen.

Fay and Paul had gone home, taking Pierre with them, of course, and it would be several days before she could expect to hear from her father. Then Aunt Wynne had the new fund-raising sewing project on at church which would occupy her spare time for the next couple of weeks, so it was back to the everyday routine, Tina reflected as she got up and turned back her bed to air. There was the studio to look after, and Joey and Rena and the crowd when she was free. Swimming, and mooching along the harbourside, coffee and Cokes at their favourite dive of the moment, and the new disco at night if inventiveness failed to produce more original amusements. No, Tina made a face, there wasn't anything extraordinary in the offing to get steamed up about. Except . . .

What had made Pierre turn all amorous last night? And then fly into such a stupid temper because she refused to fall for his Gallic blarney?

Remembering the scene the previous evening brought the glints of anger back into Tina's eyes as she showered and dressed. For a man supposed to be suffering from a broken heart Pierre had displayed a most unconvincing picture. And then to cap it all by making her look an all-time fool in front of that man, of all men. Twice in her life she had encountered that stranger, and both of those occasions had made her feel an embarrassed fool. And all through Pierre; each time!

The slightly pleasurable feeling of excitement had changed now, and it was in a mood of vexation that Tina got out her bike and cycled down to the studio.

Who was he? When had he come back? Was he back at the vanilla plantation on Kaloha?

The unanswered questions plagued Tina all that morning. Why hadn't she asked Fay last night? Because Fay would know the identity of the big dark man. Kaloha wasn't big enough to keep secrets—it was difficult enough to keep secrets anywhere in the Islands, let alone a tiny spot like Kaloha where everybody knew everybody else. Yet a strange reluctance had kept her silent last night when she rejoined the others, along with a somewhat disgruntled Pierre, the same reluctance that had kept her silent over the long years since that day on Kaloha. As though some barrier were preventing her voicing her curiosity.

Tina closed the studio at lunch time and went home to shower and change before going across to Aunt Wynne's for lunch. Then, refreshed and cool again, she lingered in the quiet room, kneeling on the old carved wood chest that held her personal treasures and looking across the infinite blue with reflective eyes.

Once, during a visit to Fay before the twins were born, she had wandered along the beach on Kaloha till she reached the boundary of markers. She had gone in a mood of secrecy, her heart beating in a stupidly disturbed fashion, and carrying a small rolled bundle under her arm. For some reason she had put off the journey several times, until this particular day when she had told herself not to be so utterly silly and quickly rolled up the carefully washed and ironed blue cotton shirt and slipped from the hotel before she could change her mind. She had to take the man's shirt back, hadn't she?

No prints but her own marked the warm white sand, and the shadowy groves were silent, only the rustle of the trade wind's passing and the sound of the sea breaking the silence. When she reached the foot of the steps she had paused, listening, for a few moments, before she stole on up

42

the steep path that wound its way to the bungalow.

The place seemed deserted when she reached it, and again she had stopped uncertainly, fighting a ridiculous impulse to throw the shirt down on the veranda and run. But she fought the craven impulse and walked steadily along the creosoted boards. The lounger was still there, and the same white cushions, and Tina looked down at them, wondering if the stain was still in where she spilled her coffee ... With the thought she was reaching out to turn over one of the cushions, then a gruff voice behind made her start violently.

'And what's your business, young woman?'

She spun round and met the suspicious stare of an elderly thickset man. He had come silently up the path from the garden, and now he barred her way.

She had felt fright and stammered in French: 'I'm sorry, I didn't mean to intrude. I—I was looking for someone else. The—the other man.'

'What other man?'

'The—the owner,' she said defensively.

'I am the owner.'

'Oh ...' her mouth parted and she stared at him in some bewilderment. 'But I thought ...'

'Permit me to introduce myself,' the gruff-voiced man said unsmilingly. 'Henri Latour. Now what can I do for you, young lady?'

'I'm Tina Raimond.' It was difficult not to quail before the fierce questioning survey. 'I wanted to see the other man—I don't know his name, but I'm sure he lives here. He said it——' She had faltered into silence, hearing the echoes from the past. *This is my beach you're weeping all over* ... How could she explain to this unsympathetic old gentleman?

'No one lives here but me—and my houseboy. Are you sure you've come to the right place? My name is definitely Latour, and I can assure you I've lived here more years than you could remember.'

'Yes.' She sighed and turned away. Perhaps she *had* dreamed it all. Perhaps her man of mystery had never existed. But he did, she told herself fiercely. How could she have dreamed all those details? The white cushions, the boy called Kim, even the blue bucket in which he had brought the ice ... They were real enough, as were the mementoes she still possessed, and the faded blossom the stranger had put in her hair. *You're too young to wear the flower of love* ... No, it had been no dream.

She had become aware of the uncompromising presence of the real owner and looked up. 'I'm sorry—maybe I did make a mistake. I'm sorry to trouble you.' He gave a shrug, and she had been conscious of his gaze following her all the way down the path to the beach ...

Tina came back to the present. It had been right enough. Henri Latour did own the Kaloha Vanillery, at least he had held the lease for many years, as Fay and Paul held the lease of Akaia. His name had cropped up that very evening at dinner back at the hotel. Capitaine Roulier and his daughter Corinne had been present, and someone had asked if old Henri ever heard from his son these days. The answer had seemed to be in the negative, and after a tacit agreement that it was all very sad, and now that his wife had passed on it was very unlikely that the old rift between father and son would ever be healed, the subject of Henri Latour had lapsed. Tina still didn't know the full story of the Latour family rift, and it did not occur to her to ask questions; to do so might involve explanations she had no wish to make.

At that time she was still extremely sensitive about the whole business that had precipitated her into Henri Latour's home, even though he had not been present at the time. And the fact that a stranger had been present, a self-possessed man who had conveyed a marked air of proprietorship, would have caused sufficient sense of intrigue to warrant a good deal of teasing from Fay and family.

Eventually Tina had come to the conclusion that the stranger had been a visitor, perhaps a buyer, or an agricultural inspector, or even old Henri's lawyer or someone like that. His visit had been too brief to leave much impression of interest among the community on Kaloha, and it had amused him to tease a distraught, impressionable young girl who had crossed his path during that short time. So she came home, shoved the blue shirt down into the depths of her treasure chest (as her father usually termed it) and resolutely banished all thought of Pierre and the arrogant stranger from her mind.

44

And now they were *both* back.

Tina stood up, rubbing at the pattern imprinted on her knees by the carved rosettes that bordered the top of the chest, and lifted the lid. A wry smile curved her mouth as she delved into the assortment therein and came up holding the crumpled folds of blue cotton. She shook the garment. Had he ever missed his shirt?

It was just too bad if he had. After all, if the arrogant brute was so cagey about his identity he could hardly expect to have his property posted back to him, could he? Anyway, judging by the quality of the evening gear he was wearing last night, the loss of one old cotton shirt wasn't going to break him. With a scornful little smile at herself for giving the thing house-room all this time, Tina held it up against herself and struck a mocking attitude. Despite everything, she had experienced a moment of traitorous softening the day she had laundered and carefully pressed the shirt, fully intending to return it to its owner next time she visited the island. The thought occurred that after all he had tried to be considerate and perhaps she had allowed the whole incident to get out of proportion. Even if his autocratic male ego had not allowed an exactly sympathetic approach he had fed her, administered first aid, given her a lift back, and it had been rather nice of him to think of lending her a covering. To say nothing of the magnolia for her hair ... Too young to wear the flower of love! Typical male cheek! As though she were a babe in arms. As if she wanted to sport a pagan display of availability!

A faint smile, part rueful, part reminiscent, curved Tina's mouth. Then abruptly it vanished. Last night was enough to wipe out any feeling of gratitude. Pierre was enough to cope with, without——

'Tina! *Here* you are—where have you been?'

The voice made her start with shock. She spun round, to see Pierre framed in the veranda doorway.

He put out his hands with a little Gallic gesture that was placatory. 'Did I startle you? Forgive me, *chérie*, but you did not answer my knock, though I was certain I should find you here. Listen, *ma petite*,' he began to move forward, 'I do not have much time and I——'

'Pierre, you had no right to walk in like that.' Tina found her voice and backed towards the door. 'This does

45

happen to be my bedroom.'

'Ah, yes, I am aware of that now.' He flashed a whimsical smile with a glance about him that seemed to heighten the intimacy of the room, then shrugged. 'But I have already said I am sorry. Please, little one, I must talk with you. To make my regrets for last evening. When I awake this morning ... I think it must be the jet-lag. Oh, my head!' He tapped his forehead with a long, slender expressive finger and flashed that appealing smile again. 'I have no other excuse, *chérie*, except that in my eagerness to renew our interrupted friendship and make amends for our last unfortunate leavetaking I—I—— What is it that you say in English? I crashed in where the angels fear to walk.'

'Tread,' Tina corrected automatically. She stared at him, some of the dismay she felt showing in her eyes. He was looking back at her, his gaze eager and almost comically concerned, and Tina was aware of weakening, against her will. She had forgotten how charming Pierre could be when he wanted to. She gave a helpless little shake of her head. 'You didn't need to come rushing back straight away.'

'But of course!' Confident now, he moved towards her, with the obvious intention of setting a more definite seal upon the reconciliation. 'And if it hadn't been for the interfering Mr Thornton last night I am sure the evening might have ended very differently. For I——'

'*Who* did you say?'

Pierre's brows drew together. 'Thornton. That intrusive Englishman who thought to play the gallant knight. You must know him, *chérie*. He——'

Tina controlled herself. 'Yes—that is, I recognised him, but I—— What is his name, Pierre?'

'Thornton. Max Thornton.' There was surprise in Pierre's tone and expression, as if he were unsure of her reaction. 'You have not yet met our objectionable new *propriétaire*? Although I am not surprised. He arrived only yesterday, practically incognito. To survey his newly inherited estate, I presume, and have the advantage of a preliminary spy-out of his tenants before they become aware of his identity,' Pierre said acidly. 'But he is unlucky. One cannot keep a secret like that in the Islands. I happen to know that the clerk in Maurragne's office told Delphine in Quinns, and Delphine told her husband, who told Alphonse, with whom

46

we do car-hire business, and he told me. So now everyone will know that the new owner of Kaloha has arrived—to stay,' Pierre concluded on a note of satisfaction.

'You mean that Max Thornton—the man last night—*owns* Kaloha?'

Pierre nodded. 'He is planning to run the plantation himself, I gather.'

Tina subsided on the edge of her bed, the blue folds of the shirt that still, strictly speaking, belonged to that new owner of Kaloha falling forgotten across her knees. 'But I thought that was all forgotten about ages ago. I mean, I know that Kaloha was leased, years and years ago, and passed to some old Scotsman who never even bothered coming to the islands. All because his grandfather sailed the world in a windjammer and fell in love with them, in eighteen-hundred-and-something, and bought the lease of Kaloha for a bag of nails and a crate of tools. Unfortunately, he went native and the mosquitoes got at him. But as far as any of his heirs coming and ruling the island . . . it's quite ridiculous. Sure the story hadn't been embroidered by the time it got to you, Pierre?'

'No.' Pierre's lips snapped together on the negative. 'There is nothing of embroidery about Mr Max Thornton, I assure you.'

Tina refused to be convinced. 'I don't think he can make much change. Unless he collects the cowries himself each year!' She began to giggle. 'I remember how we laughed when Fay and Paul were negotiating for the hotel, and Monsieur Maurragne explained about the old leasehold and told them it was quite legal but no one was likely to interfere with any plans they made, as long as they paid the handful of shells each year on January the first.'

'The equivalent of your peppercorn rent.' Amusement flickered in Pierre's eyes. 'I always knew the English were mad, *chérie*. All the same, it is not right that an Englishman should still own that ridiculous lease. The islands are French, and Kaloha is one of the Islands, small though it is. It is not right,' he repeated with a flash of anger.

'But they were not French then.' Tina had an urge to tease. 'The first protectorate dated from 1842 and Polynesia didn't become a colony until forty years later. Anyway, it never made much difference as far as Kaloha is concerned.

47

Certainly it's never bothered the inhabitants. After all, the New Hebrides are jointly governed by England and France and it seems to have worked out very happily. It's only in Europe that countries seem unable to be civilised about these matters.' She stood up. 'I'm sure Mr Thornton will continue to allow the Anglo-French alliance to go on as it has done all these years on Kaloha. Do you think he is going to challenge the gendarme to a duel or something?'

'You are quick to spring to the defence of Monsieur Thornton.' Pierre's mouth compressed. 'A total stranger, who had the effrontery to interfere last night with a matter that was no concern of his. I do not understand you, *chérie*.'

Tina took a deep breath. 'I thought you came here to say you were sorry,' she reminded him. 'Not to pick another quarrel.'

'Oh no!' Pierre expressed shock. 'Nothing was farther from my thoughts. But it was just that . . .' he shrugged and looked at her appealingly, 'you seemed to be on his side.'

'I'm not on anybody's side.' Tina folded the shirt and dropped it carelessly into the open chest. She slammed down the lid and decided it was time to change the subject. 'What are you doing here today? I thought you were going to help Paul.'

'But I am!' Pierre assumed an injured expression. 'Paul is actually entrusting me with the clients! This morning I brought six of the ladies across in the hotel launch. They leave tomorrow, and they decided they wished to spend their last day in Papeete, shopping and sightseeing. That is why I do not have much time—I have to meet them in an hour's time to act as guide.'

'I hope you haven't lost one.' Tina side-stepped him and made for the door. 'Have you called on Aunt Wynne?'

'Yes—I went there first to seek you.' Pierre followed her into the hall. 'Please, *chérie*, before you rush away . . . say you are not still furious with me.'

Tina sighed. What could she say, except the negative he demanded? She shook her head. 'Of course I'm not. Now, Pierre, we both have jobs to do. At least I have.'

She picked up her bag without waiting for any further blarney, and he, perforce, had to follow her out and across the track to Aunt Wynne's. But he refused to leave until he had extracted her promise to accompany him a couple of days later and help him show the new party of tourists round the island.

'After all, you know Tahiti so much better than I do,' he wheedled.

Later, she did not really regret giving her promise. Meeting strangers from other parts of the world was exciting, and she truly loved the rich Polynesian island which was the only home she had known. Despite her English parentage, England remained a name, familiar it was true, but nevertheless a not quite visualised country known only by pictures painted in words by her father in his occasional moods of reminiscence and books she had read. She knew she had relations in England, on her mother's side, but contact since her mother's death had diminished to the annual card at Christmas with a stiff message of greeting. They had never approved of John Raimond, and Tina, with the fierce loyalty born of love for her father, had long since ceased any effort to make the fragile link any stronger.

No, if they thought John Raimond, a then penniless young artist, not quite good enough for their daughter, then they could go on freezing in their cold wet northern climate, large country mansion or no, Tina would tell herself in those occasional moments of retrospect. Their letters had always made her darling mother sad when they came, for reasons which the child Tina had not been able to comprehend; now, in possession of the sad facts of the rift between her mother and her family so far away, the adult Tina saw no reason for any softening of the heart towards the grandparents she had never seen. She never wanted to leave the islands, the incomparable sea with all its moods, the colour and smells and fascinating life of Tahiti, well named the Pearl of the Pacific.

She knew all the famous spots, Point Venus, Vahipahi Waterfall, the Gauguin Museum, the scenes where the film of *Mutiny on the Bounty* were shot, and many others not so well known. Somewhat to Pierre's surprise, she proved an able and natural guide, with a vivid way of recounting history that instantly caught and held the interest of her listeners.

After the second trip that week she suggested to Pierre that they hire outriggers so that the more adventurously inclined sightseers could explore the wilder, less known parts of the island, only accessible by water from where the highway eventually gave way before nature's formidable obstacles. The idea proved a great success, and Tina was both embarrassed and amused when one of the departing tourists pressed a very generous tip into her hand just before he climbed into the launch and Pierre headed to sea and Kaloha.

'Keep it, *chérie*, you have earned it,' Pierre grinned three days later when he arrived with another party. 'It will save Paul having to put you on the salary list.'

Tina was not so sure. He was now leaving all the talking and arranging of schedules to her, but at least he seemed to be satisfied for the moment with the resumption of their relationship and the strictly lighthearted, careless approach she had set.

Another thing for which she was thankful was that he appeared to have forgotten his pique concerning Max Thornton. He never mentioned the man Tina still thought of as Mr Mystery, and she restrained any impulse to inquire casually what impact, if any, the newcomer might be making on Kaloha. But she was often aware of a curiosity that prompted her to break her resolution. Where, for instance, was Max Thornton staying? For accommodation was, to say the least, limited on tiny Kaloha. There was only the one hotel, that which Fay and Paul had worked at so hard to build into the success it was rapidly becoming. Surely Pierre would have mentioned the fact if Max Thornton had moved in there. And she certainly couldn't imagine him staying with Capitaine Roulier, or rooming above the *tinito*'s—Kaloha's only store. He must be staying with Henri Latour, she decided. For wasn't this where she first encountered him? Perhaps he was another recluse! In which case he and the notoriously unsocial Henri would get along famously.

She checked herself. She must not forget that Henri Latour had his family troubles too, if rumour and gossip told accurately. The thought was enough to evoke sympathetic insight in Tina and make her think more kindly of the irascible old planter. Families could break one's life in twain, if one loved them dearly; she had only to remember her mother to realise that. Anyway, why should she be wondering about Max Thornton's whereabouts? It was unlikely that their respective social circles would ever overlap —as a man he was totally off her wavelength. In any case, he'd probably gone again, after a brief look round his domain.

Tina banished both Max Thornton and curiosity from her mind. The days flew by, stretching into three weeks, then a month, this fresh involvement helping to bypass the restless loneliness she would normally have experienced while waiting for her father's return.

John Raimond rarely wrote letters, but his progress across the States was punctuated by a series of cards, postmarked by the cities in which he had alighted to deliver his lecture before taking off for the next stop in his crowded agenda. Then one morning, exactly a month after his departure, Tina received an airmail letter bearing a Chicago postmark.

Excitement coursed through her; he would be home any day now. Chicago was his last but one stop before he returned to the east coast. Then there was only the stop-over at Honolulu, and home!

She was smiling as she slit the envelope, but almost instantly a sobering realisation struck her; the postmark was six days old. He should have been home by now.

A few moments later Tina's oval face was a study in disappointment. She put the letter in her pocket and gave a sigh of resignation. She might have known! For wasn't predictability one of the least of her father's attributes?

'What's the matter?' asked Aunt Wynne, when Tina went across to break the news.

'He's not coming back.' Tina slumped despondently on a chair and stared at the crystal sparkles on the lagoon.

'What do you mean—he's not coming back?' There was a flash of concern on the older woman's placid features as she seated herself and lifted the mesh cover off the bowl of salad. 'Fruit juice, dear?'

'Thank you.' Tina accepted the glass mechanically. 'I've just had a letter. He's met an old friend, Crewe Gordino. He came here once, oh, ages ago. The American artist. I didn't like him very much. He was too hearty for worlds.'

Aunt Wynne forked salad on to her plate. 'A big burly man, with a habit of slapping folks on the back and almost felling them ... Yes, I remember him. But it must be all of five years ago.'

'He's coming to the Islands, on a sailing holiday. He suggested that Father join him. Apparently Father has a commission to do a series of seascapes for a shipping firm's palatial new offices and thought it a marvellous idea. Here,' Tina fumbled in her pocket, 'read it.' She passed the letter over and reached for the salad.

There was a silence, and then Aunt Wynne gave a small chuckle. 'Oh, Tina, you do still take things to heart. At first I got the impression that your father wasn't coming back at all!'

'But it'll take *weeks*!'

'The time will pass quick enough.' The older woman looked at the disappointed young face with affectionate eyes. 'Besides, why shouldn't he have a break? It'll be good for both of you to have a long spell away from each other.'

Tina looked at her as though she couldn't believe this heresy. 'Isn't a month long enough?'

'It isn't a question of time.' Aunt Wynne's expression grew thoughtful. 'You have to give back independence to your father, in the same way that he has to recognise the fact that his daughter is no longer a child.'

'What are you trying to say?' Tina's eyes widened. 'That I'm a possessive daughter? Oh, come off it, Aunt Wynne.'

The older woman shook her head. 'Because of circumstances, losing your mother when you were so young, and having no brothers or sisters or other family here, your father and you have had a much closer relationship than many other fathers and daughters. But it can't go on for ever. You'll marry, and who can tell? he may remarry one day. He's still a comparatively young man.'

Tina was silent, partly with surprise and partly with being faced with an aspect which had never even occurred to her to ponder its possibilities. To hide the sense of disquiet she was abruptly experiencing she nodded soberly. 'Point taken. Who are we going to marry him off to?'

'I'd leave that to him.' Aunt Wynne laughed wryly. 'Meanwhile, what's wrong with taking his advice?'

'Which advice?'

'Didn't you read his postscript?'

'No!' Tina squealed, and grabbed the letter, turning it

sideways to decipher the p.s. scrawled in the narrow margin. She read aloud slowly: 'Suggest you shut up shop and inflict yourself on Fay until I get back. If she'll have you, that is! Love. J.R.'

'Well, why not?' exclaimed Aunt Wynne. 'It's a very sensible suggestion. After all, they'll be quite a while, and there's the stop-over for the exhibition. And we can keep an eye on things at this end.'

Tina hesitated, doubt clouding her eyes. 'I know you would, but I don't want to impose on you for such a long time. Actually, I might as well close the studio, we're so down on stock and Daddy always does the ordering. That's one of the reasons why I was hoping he'd be back this week.'

'Well, he's obviously not very concerned about that,' observed Aunt Wynne bluntly.

'No, because he'll be feeling wealthy after his tour and getting this new commission.' Tina's smile was wry. She knew her father too well, despite her love for him. 'He'll relax after it, until another hard-up spell comes along, then he'll start painting like mad and pushing business for all he's worth.'

Aunt Wynne smiled and forbore to add further comment. Then her face sobered. 'I wish you would go to Fay, though. I'd like to know you were with her for a while. She's had such a strained look about her lately. I think she's feeling the strain of the last two years—she and Paul have worked so hard—and now the twins are at their most exhausting stage, running all over the place and getting into everything. They're a full-time job in themselves. I've often wished I dare offer to help, but it's so difficult. Not for worlds would I give Paul the impression I was going to be an interfering mother-in-law. And now they've got this new arrangement for these package deals . . .'

Tina nodded thoughtfully. She was aware of the particular difficulties to which Aunt Wynne referred, and understood her concern. Paul and Fay had just learned that the hotel had been chosen by South Pacific Airways as an accommodation base for their new three-centre islands holidays. S.P.A. were one of the top airlines operating across the southern hemisphere and their standards were extremely high. It was a tribute to Fay and Paul to be selected as the Polynesian base for these expensive and de-luxe packages, which were to cater for the discriminating holiday-maker who wanted luxurious and exotic destinations without the drawbacks of mass tourism.

As Pierre had remarked, they wanted a real desert island with glorious unspoilt nature all around, but they also wanted flush loos and shaver points, not forgetting a chef's cuisine and an adequate wine list. Kaloha, and Fay and Paul, could supply the lot, plus a fast launch to take them over to Papeete if they felt the urge to sample the more commercial fleshpots. It was going to mean a more certain financial future with the recognition of their hard work for the young couple, but it would also mean a great deal more responsibility. For though they were fortunate in having a first class chef and receptionist in Jules and Rosa, the rest of the staff sometimes caused uncertainty. The four island girls, while cheerful and willing enough, were no exception to Polynesia's famous *fiu*, the traditional mood of 'who cares?', which meant that suddenly, without any warning, they remembered some urgent business that demanded their presence elsewhere. It was something the European simply had to accept as part of the capricious, sun-loving islander's character, and to protest was useless. A smile or shrug, and the inevitable '*Aita péa péa*,' would be the only response. This had accounted for much of the widespread employment of Chinese labour. The serious, industrious Chinese never suffered the inconvenient mood of *fiu* . . .

Tina forgot her initial disappointment at the news her father's letter had brought. There was quite a lot she could do to help Fay, take the twins off her hands for part of the day if nothing else. She thought of the picturesque tangle of coral and limestone buildings which formed the main part of the hotel, the cool palm-thatched chalets for those who wanted to live the pagan way, the lovely beach gardens that Paul had designed, ablaze with scarlet and pink and white blossom and crowned by a magnificent coral tree which was worthy of any ancient Babylon, and the swaying reflections of the palms by the lagoon pool. In her mind's eye Tina saw it all against the glorious backdrop of Kaloha's hills, and the long curling tongue of silver beach that stretched down past the casuarina groves, to where the scent of vanilla came to drift on the air . . .

She looked up at Aunt Wynne's waiting expression and exclaimed softly: 'I'll send a note with Pierre tomorrow.'

Her voice gave no hint of the sudden little surge of excitement that had welled up at the thought of spending the next week or so on Kaloha.

Somehow, Kaloha had never seemed more inviting...

CHAPTER FOUR

'IT's terribly sad, really. And he's so wonderful with the imps.'

Fay sighed and lay back, closing her eyes in one of her rare moments of relaxation from her hotel responsibilities. Beside her, Tina murmured agreement as she watched the tall figure of Pierre ducking under the joint splashing attack of two determined toddlers. The plump little twins bounced up and down in the shallow ripples, gurgling delight as Pierre pretended to lose his balance and then toppled back into the water.

'Help me! I am being drowned by your terrible infants!' he shouted.

'Help yourself,' Tina called back, laughing as the twins proceeded to jump on their victim. She adjusted her sunglasses and reflected that it was true; Pierre *was* wonderful with his baby nephews. His patience seemed endless and his energy unlimited as he devised new games with which to amuse them.

Tina was surprised. Somehow she had never imagined the elegant young Frenchman as a family man, and after hearing Fay's more detailed confidences regarding the break-up of Pierre's marriage to the beautiful Parisian girl called Madeleine she saw no reason to change her impression of Pierre as that of an irresponsible charmer.

'To be truthful,' Fay mused, 'I can't blame Madeleine. To start with it was an arranged marriage, and Pierre is still a typical man who believes that it's okay for him to have a flirtation on the side, but not for his wife. She did try, but she couldn't help falling in love with another man, and the family pressures didn't help matters. There were suggestions that it was time a family was started—as if that would miraculously mend a marriage halfway to the rocks on the wedding day.'

'And Madeleine's being a career girl would make her much more independent in her outlook,' said Tina.

Fay nodded. 'It's what Women's Lib is all about, but of course Pierre couldn't see it that way. We've tried to convince him that if he hadn't tried to play the heavy-handed husband it might still have worked out, for as far as we can gather Madeleine did try to make it work. She gave up her job, and I believe she was a superb cook and hostess, but she found out about one of Pierre's little affairs and the balloon went up. She walked out on him, met this other man and fell hopelessly in love, and that was that. So of course Pierre decided to have his freedom. It's his pride that suffered most of all, but he won't admit—André! Stop that!'

Fay scrambled up and ran into the water, to put a firm maternal stop to André's attempts to push his brother's head under the water. There was an indignant wail, laughter from Pierre, and then another wail as Jacques decided he had been most unfairly attacked by his mischievous twin. Fay swept up the squawling pair, one under each arm, and bore them towards the hotel. 'Definitely time for their nap,' she panted as she stumbled past Tina. 'But no need for you to move, my pet.'

'No—I'll come with you and give you a hand.' Tina jumped to her feet and relieved Fay of one wriggling infant. She was aware of a strong reluctance to be left alone on the beach with Pierre.

Tina had been on Kaloha for four days now, and though she was loving every moment of it she was becoming very wary of Pierre. Like Fay, she had very strong suspicions regarding the true depth of Pierre's supposed heartbreak. And like Fay, she was pretty sure that Pierre was suffering from damaged pride more than anything else. Now he was looking for fresh conquests to appease the battered ego.

He had haunted Tina ever since the moment of her arrival, and she was beginning to dread being alone anywhere, for without fail Pierre would soon discover her whereabouts.

She heard his footfalls on the crushed coral path, sensed his presence about to come between herself and the sun's brilliance, and then felt his hand close round her waist. If only he didn't have to be touching her all the time!

But there was little evasive action she could take at the moment. André had wound chubby little arms about her neck and leaned a trusting cheek against her shoulder. He was almost asleep already, and all Tina's developing instincts of womanhood responded to the child in her arms. He smelled delicious; of sun and sea and sand and warm baby. Not for anything would she quicken her step and disturb him before the twins were indoors and popped into their airy cots for their afternoon nap.

Pierre's fingers slid up and down against her skin, making a caress that demanded her attention. 'Shall we swim?' he asked. 'As soon as you've settled the imps.'

'You promised Paul you'd type out next week's menus,' Tina reminded him quickly.

Pierre made a face. 'I'll start on them tonight—it's much too hot to sit typing this afternoon.'

'Perhaps you should have a siesta, until you're acclimatised,' Fay suggested as she walked up the two shallow steps into the shade of the palm veranda.

'You are joking, my sweet sister-in-law,' Pierre grinned, pushing the swing door open for her. 'Do you think I am going to allow Tina to be lonely while she is here?'

There wasn't much fear of that! Tina thought ruefully as she slipped into a fresh bikini, ready to join Pierre for a cooling swim. She was becoming more and more aware of a thwarted impulse to take a long leisurely stroll along the shoreline—alone! So far the opportunity had not arisen. She sighed; perhaps tomorrow . . .

But it seemed that for once fate was going to indulge her whim. It was an extremely warm afternoon, cloudless, and with very little breeze to temper the sun's power. Most of the guests had chosen to laze about in the beach garden where the palms and shrubs made cool shady awnings, or cool off in the lagoon pool. Tina and Pierre had scarcely emerged before a couple of the men approached Pierre with a request for a fishing trip early the following morning. Pierre returned to reception to make the necessary note, and almost immediately he was stopped again, this time for information on the easiest route to the *marae*.

Fay came out at that moment. 'You'd better take them,' she said. 'It's quite a climb and there are several tracks.'

'Can we make it this afternoon and get back before darkness?' one of the guests asked.

Fay nodded, adding a warning that they would need strong footwear to traverse the rough mountainous path which climbed steeply to the temple.

One of the ladies looked slightly nervous. 'Is this one of those places where they made sacrifices? *Human* sacrifices?' she whispered.

Pierre gave her a reassuring grin. 'I rather think the old Polynesians were more concerned with feasting and other amusements,' he said tactfully. 'Provided they weren't warring with invading warriors from other islands, of course.'

'You see, Millie, you've nothing to worry about,' the nervous lady's husband said ironically. He hitched at the cord of his camera and made an impatient gesture. 'Well, if we're going, we'd better go, folks.'

Pierre did not look very pleased when Tina excused herself from accompanying the little expedition, but he could not very well protest or cajole too pointedly. At last Tina was free, to follow the impulse that beckoned along the deserted shore. She gave a small sigh of thankfulness. Pierre was becoming much too possessive, and while she could feel a certain sympathy for him she had no intention of allowing herself to be inveigled into any more situations which might get embarrassingly out of hand. Twice was quite enough, she told herself ruefully.

She encountered no one on her journey, and when she reached the boundary markers she paused, a reflective light entering her eyes; was Max Thornton still as autocratic as ever about 'his' beach? Maybe he had a point, she conceded reluctantly as she moved on. He was not to know who might thoughtlessly invade his island once a tourist centre got established. He was probably only ensuring that it became properly understood that parts of the island were still private. Tina halted again, and shrugged at her thoughts. Why should she be making excuses for Max Thornton? He was obviously quite capable of managing his own affairs!

She looked up the incline towards the bungalow. It had not changed at all. Obviously old Henri did not worry about the occasional fillip of a new colour scheme in paintwork or renewing curtains. The place had a slightly neglected look, as though its owner had ceased to care. But

58

then Henri Latour hadn't anyone to care for, or to care for him, she thought with a flash of compunction.

Her mood had changed now. The impulse had vanished, to be replaced by an impatience at her irrational whim. What was she going to say if she did climb the path and knock at the door? Her previous encounters with Max Thornton had not been exactly encouraging. A wry little smile curved her mouth and she turned away. At least she had had her stroll with self-commune!

She had taken only a couple of steps when she heard the cry. She stopped, wondering if she had imagined it, or if it was a bird noise. But the sound came again, a groan this time, and definitely human. It seemed to come from directly overhead.

Tina turned and ran swiftly up the steep curving path to the house. As she passed the end of the windbreak and sighted the veranda she gave a gasp of alarm. Henri Latour was sprawled there, lying awkwardly across the veranda steps, one hand clutching his side, the other grasping the rail. She hurried to him, seeing with dismay that his face was grey and distorted with pain. Perspiration beaded his brow and upper lip, and at first glance she thought he was unconscious. Then his eyes flickered open as she bent over him anxiously.

He struggled to say something, the effort making him groan afresh, but Tina could not distinguish the painfully slurred words. Instinct told her that he was seriously ill, and she touched his shoulder quickly as he made an attempt to move.

'Stay still—I'll get help.'

'No one——' He slumped back as she darted towards the door and thrust it open.

It took only seconds to discover that the house was deserted. Hastily she snatched cushions from the living room and ran into the nearest bedroom to seize the coverlet off the bed.

The heavily built form had not moved. She put the cushions under his head, easing one under him to pad the edge of the step, and tucked the coverlet round him. She crouched down. 'Is Kim out? Just nod.'

'Yes ... at the drying shed ... Max ...'

The weak voice trailed away, and Tina gave him a tremulous smile which was intended to be reassuring. 'I'll find him—promise you won't try to get up till we're back?'

A groan of pain was the only answer, and she didn't waste any more time. She hurried through the house, and at the gate by the track her mind recaptured those moments so long ago when she had climbed on to the pillion of the moped. Max had ridden to the right, and they had passed through only plantation land, so the drying sheds must be somewhere in the opposite direction. Trusting in her instinct, Tina set off swiftly along the well trodden track.

It descended in a gentle gradient for several hundred yards, and just as she was beginning to feel the onset of panic lest she was miles away from help the trees thinned out and she glimpsed sea and a large clearing. There were the drying sheds. With a gasp of relief she quickened her speed towards a group of youths who were loading crates aboard a truck.

They stared at her, and even as she began her urgent request she caught sight of the tall, unmistakable figure at the far end of the shed. She darted on, and almost cannoned into him as he turned abruptly in her direction.

His face betrayed surprise, and little pleasure. 'What the devil——?'

'It's Monsieur Latour! He's ill! Back there—I found him.' By now Tina was out of breath. She gulped air, and started again. 'Please—hurry up! I think he's——'

She found she was explaining to space. Max Thornton was already hurrying on long loping strides in the direction of the house. She started forward, then stopped. She would never keep up with *that* pace!

She stood still, getting her breath back and looking curiously around. The last of the spring harvest was dried now and the workers, mostly Chinese boys and some women, were preparing it for export. One group of girls nearby were busily lining containers with paraffin-waxed paper, and at the long benches farther down the open shed Chinese boys and women sorted the long, treacly-dark vanilla pods, checking their quality before packing them into the ready-lined boxes.

The heaviness of vanilla aroma hung in the air, rich and cloying, but Tina lingered, aware of curiosity. Although she had spent all her life in the islands this was the first time she had actually been in a vanillery and she experienced a sudden surge of interest in the process behind the familiar smell that pervaded most of the islands, a rival in pungency to the ever-present copra and the sensuously heady perfume of *tiare*.

But this was no time to indulge her curiosity, she thought with a pang of guilt.

Max Thornton was already out of sight. She hurried back, to find Monsieur Latour almost exactly as she had left him. Max Thornton had packed more pillows and cushions round the elderly planter to make him as comfortable as possible, and now his strong fingers encircled Monsieur Latour's wrist while his frowning gaze checked the second hand of the watch on his own wrist. Tina stood by silently, until Max glanced up.

'I'm glad you didn't move him. He ...' Max paused, then straightened and turned to her. He lowered his voice. 'I'm afraid it's a coronary. I want to get him to hospital as quickly as possible. Is the hotel launch out?'

'Not when I left—do you want me to——?'

'No, I want you to stay here with him. I'll be as quick as I can.'

'Yes ...' She divined his plan, to hurry to the hotel, get help, an improvised stretcher, the new, high-powered launch, and get the stricken planter transferred across to Papeete and medical aid as quickly as possible.

'What do I do?' she asked.

'Nothing, except keep him calm and still. His pulse is very slow. Don't give him anything to eat or drink but try to keep him reassured. Okay?'

She nodded, and when he had gone she sat down on the top step and looked compassionately at Monsieur Latour. He was quiet, huddled back against the pillows, and his breathing seemed steadier. After a moment or so he stirred. He passed his hand feebly over his damp brow and took a shuddering breath.

'*Mon Dieu!* What happened?' He stared. 'Who—who are you?'

'I'm Tina.' She smiled. 'Are you feeling any better?'

'I—I think so. But that pain! Like a knife ...' Again he stared. 'Haven't I seen you before, somewhere?'

'Once, a long time ago.'

The effort to remember seemed too much for him. 'Where is Max?' he asked weakly.

'He's gone for the doctor.'

'There's no doctor on Kaloha, little girl. I don't need one, anyway. I'll be all right ... when I've had a drink.' He moved, obviously a feeble preliminary to getting to his feet, and Tina put out an alarmed hand.

'No ... Max—Mr Thornton made me promise not to let you move till he came back. He won't be long—please be patient.'

He seemed about to argue, then subsided back, something like fear in his eyes. 'I've had this pain before, but never so bad.' His hands moved fretfully. 'This would happen, just when I——'

'Please don't fret,' she broke in. 'I'm sure it's going to be all right. But please don't take any risks—for my sake!' she appealed wryly. 'I promised I'd look after you, and I'll really be in trouble if I don't.'

'From whom?' A glimmer of amusement broke through the lines of pain. 'I wasn't aware that Max had found himself a *petite amie* already.'

Tina felt an uncontrollable surge of colour enter her cheeks. 'I'm not Mr Thornton's *amie*, Monsieur Latour, nor am I likely to be.'

'But perhaps you would like to be.' Monsieur Latour was still above all a Frenchman. The amusement flickered again. 'There is still time, *mademoiselle*. He is going to be here for a while, this time.'

'But I am not.' Tina's mouth compressed. 'Now please, Monsieur Latour, don't talk, and don't get excited. I'll go and get a cool sponge for your forehead, to bathe away that perspiration and make you feel more comfortable.'

She knew it was more to give herself something to do, to avoid the embarrassing turn the conversation had taken. Though why should it be embarrassing? And why did she have to blush like a schoolgirl simply because an elderly stranger had decided to tease? She found a sponge, wrung it in cold water, and went back to her charge. She was thankful to see that his colour was not so deathly pale now, although the hint of blueness still lingered in his lips. He demanded a drink again, and as tactfully as possible she refused. He grumbled, but perhaps he had some inkling of

62

Max's suspicion and he did not protest very forcibly. She sat down by him, to wait out her vigil, and about twenty minutes later she saw the launch cutting across the lagoon.

Paul had come, and also two of the guests, a Canadian business man and his wife, who fortunately had been a nurse before her marriage. She took over calmly and capably, complimenting Max and Tina on doing the right thing in not moving the patient, and supervised the transferral of Monsieur Latour into the launch. She insisted on going over to Papeete with them, and Tina was left with the Canadian businessman to walk back along the beach to the hotel.

It was several hours before his wife and Paul got back. The doctor had confirmed Max's suspicion; Monsieur Latour had indeed suffered a coronary, and would have to stay in hospital for some time. Max was remaining in Papeete for a couple of days, until there was more news of Monsieur Latour's condition, and suddenly everything seemed very quiet. Pierre returned from the trek to the *marae*, expressed conventional sympathy when he heard the bad news, then said abruptly: 'What were you doing along there, anyway, *ma petite?*'

'Just walking. Any law against it?'

'None at all!' he placated. 'But I did not think you were so anxious to renew acquaintance with our arrogant suzerain!'

'Oh, Pierre, you idiot!' Fay laughed, but Tina could not join in the amusement. During the following two days she was unusually restless, and unwilling to admit to herself that Max Thornton had anything to do with the cause of that fidgety state. When the mailboat arrived at Kaloha's tiny port the next day, she made herself refuse to accompany Pierre down to the harbour office to collect the mail. With this unfamiliar knot of impatience tight inside her, she had to wait until someone asked the question: 'Was Thornton on it? Any news of old Henri?'

'I do not know,' Pierre replied, untying the small packet of post. 'Thornton was leaving as I arrived. But Henri must be all right, otherwise the place would have been buzzing.'

Tina gave a sigh of relief, but found it did nothing to lessen her taut frame of mind. When lunch was over and the twins were settled for their afternoon nap, she went to her room to shower and change, and give in to a slightly audacious impulse which had come to her the previous evening. Fortunately Pierre was not about when she emerged, and she slipped quietly out of the hotel and made her way down to the beach.

Well, she had a good excuse, hadn't she? she whispered to herself as she set off along the shore. And—a soft chuckle of mischief bubbled from her—would Max Thornton recognise his property?

She reached the foot of the path to the bungalow and hesitated for a moment. This was sheer foolishness, but she was going through with it just for the fun of it. If he was at home, of course! With deliberate steps and an airy nonchalance she ascended the path, swinging her straw hat by its strings and humming a lighthearted little melody. She did not look at the house until she was actually at the veranda stairway. Only then did she glance upwards, and with a tremor of shock wondered how she could have failed to sense being watched.

Max Thornton was leaning on the rail. Dark sunglasses hid his eyes, and his mouth was enigmatic. He stayed unmoving as she came up the steps, and when she reached the top he drained the last of the liquid in the tall glass he held before he said unsmilingly, 'Hi.'

'Hi,' she returned. 'How is Monsieur Latour?'

'As well as can be expected.'

'Oh, I'm glad.' Tina's mouth pursed on a tiny sigh. He wasn't exactly forthcoming! She stood her ground, waiting for a comment which surely must be forthcoming. After all, she *was* wearing his property! And to her mirror it had looked very casual and attractive, just showing a tiny strip of her brief white shorts below the hem. But her mirror had not told how sexy the carelessly donned garment looked on her slender body, its loose long line emphasising the thrust of her young breasts against the thin blue cotton material.

He moved lazily, and suddenly she was tense under a long speculative assessment. 'This for my benefit?'

'Of course not!' She felt deflated, yet some stubborn little impulse made her add, 'Do you know, I once made a special journey along here, for the sole purpose of returning your property.'

'Really?' The level gaze did not flicker behind the dark

shades. 'You must be a very conscientious girl.'

'I never take anything for granted,' she said stiffly, turning the big circle of straw round within restless fingers.

'And now you've made a second journey. How very commendable.'

There was a brief silence, then he reached out and took hold of the lapel between finger and thumb. He stroked the material. 'That shirt cost me twelve quid in London.'

'Rather expensive for a casual garment.' The light pressure and warmth of his hand were invoking an unexpected tremor. 'I did notice the shirtmaker's label when I laundered it.'

His mouth flickered at one corner. 'Well, am I to reclaim my property?'

'What?' She blinked. The strong tanned fingers were hovering over the top button. 'Now?'

He did not seem to notice the shock in her voice. 'Isn't this the purpose of this visit?'

'It is not!'

His brows went up. 'You've decided to add it to your own wardrobe?'

She brushed his hand away. 'I do happen to be wearing it at this moment.'

'Oh.' The infuriating little twitch flicked at his mouth again. 'I thought perhaps you'd just slipped it on—that you had a bikini underneath.'

'You thought wrong.'

'Intriguing. My apologies.'

'Don't mention it!' She settled the lapels and assured herself that all the buttons were indeed still secure. 'I'll bring it along next time.'

'Is there going to be a next time?'

'Any reason why there shouldn't? I did remember the other thing.'

Again the dark brows went up, this time in query.

She groped in the pocket of the shirt and brought out a handful of shells, scooped up during her walk along the beach. She held them out on the palm of her hand, and he glanced down at them, his expression betraying puzzlement.

'My rent—for being on your beach.'

She saw the amusement tugging at his mouth, and sheer,

delirious laughter trembled within her. Then he looked up. 'I don't remember drawing up any agreement for payment in shells in this particular case.'

'No, this is in advance.' Triumph was beginning to tingle through her veins. She had actually succeeded in driving a tiny wedge into his immunity. 'I've no intention of being caught out a second time.'

'For what?'

She shrugged. 'A forfeit for trespassing.'

'I remember no forfeit.'

'Maybe not.' Tina was enjoying herself. 'But my memory's pretty good.'

His teeth glinted whitely in a brief smile, then the enigmatic look snapped back. 'Throw away those shells. You've given me other ideas.'

'Oh! Such as?'

'Are you trying to flirt with me?'

'Flirt?' She gave a scornful gesture. 'What an old-fashioned word, Mr Thornton.'

'So is a forfeit—but it's still a good idea!'

'What do you mean?'

'You know perfectly well, my innocent.' He took a step forward, and Tina took one back. It brought her against the veranda rail, and Max Thornton's hands captured her by the shoulders.

'Tell me something,' he said in dangerously quiet tones, 'is this the way you behave with Lover Boy?'

'Pierre?' The delicious amusement in her eyes changed to sparkles of outrage. 'It most certainly is not!'

'I'm relieved to hear it. Otherwise I'm not surprised that you fail to keep him at arm's length.'

'Practice is making me perfect at that art now,' she returned coolly.

'Is it? At cost of your expertise in the opposite direction?'

'I haven't a clue what you mean?'

'I think you have.' His grasp grew perceptibly firmer and his expression somewhat grimmer. 'I'm not a safe bet in the flirtation stakes, you little pagan.'

'I never thought you were.'

'Nor am I prepared to be a bulwark every time Lover Boy becomes a trifle too much for you to handle.'

'You won't need to any more.' Tina flashed him a brilliant smile that was meant to conceal a certain ebbing of her defence reserves. Max Thornton was a master—but for a novice she had not acquitted herself without honour. She stood up on tiptoe, and in a second had planted the most transient of kisses on his chin and twisted out of his grasp like elfin quicksilver.

'There's your forfeit—tell Henri I was asking after him.'

She sped down the veranda steps, paused at the foot to wave, and with a final audacious gesture scattered her handful of shells like a rain of pearls. She reached the curve in the path without once looking back.

The exhilaration of her encounter with Max Thornton returned every time she thought of it during the next few days. But as the week drew to a close she was aware of encroaching disappointment. In retrospect, she had to face the fact that she had indeed deliberately tried to flirt with him, and even the stubbornly held excuse, that she *had* to find out if he was human where she was concerned, couldn't cancel out the truth.

For the first time it occurred to her to wonder if he had thought her cheap. Pride recoiled from this possibility. Didn't the feminine half of the species always enjoy a mild flirtation with an attractive member of the other half? Tina agonised over the problem, trying to convince herself that he'd probably forgotten it by now. Oh, why was it so important to prove that he did like her a little bit ... ?

Fortunately there was plenty to occupy her time that week. A new crowd of guests had arrived. The twins were as demanding as ever, and Fay decided to have a gala night on the Saturday. Capitaine Roulier and Corinne were invited, along with some friends from Papeete, and suddenly, on the Thursday night, Paul said: 'I think we should ask Mr Thornton.'

Pierre gave a groan, but Fay looked thoughtful. 'I think so too. I don't believe he's as anti-social as they say. I think he's just busy. Capitaine Roulier was saying that he's taken over the complete running of the plantation for poor Henri. Apparently he once did this before, while Henri took his wife back to Europe, just before she died.'

'Yes, but old Henri and Max Thornton's father were wartime cronies, in the Resistance or something,' Paul said.

'Well, I'm going to ask him. I've always had my doubts about Kim's cooking,' Fay declared firmly. 'The odd times I've been along there the place seems to be in a shambles and poor old Henri doesn't seem to care. Of course men on their own seem to lose heart.'

'Then we will invite our new suzerain,' Pierre grinned. 'Perhaps our fair Corinne will charm that so-British dourness.'

Tina frowned suddenly, and a pang of dismay replaced the pleasurable sense of excitement aroused by Fay's proposal. Tina had never taken to the languid daughter of the Capitaine, with her faintly supercilious manner and her constant running down of Kaloha for its lack of social life. Fortunately, they did not see a great deal of her, and they would see even less soon, once the negotiations were complete for the lease of the little shop in Papeete where Corinne was planning to open a new fashion boutique. But that was a few weeks away, and until she got into her apartment over the shop she was spending most weekends with her father. The thought of her with Max Thornton was distinctly perturbing.

'Will you slip along with the invite first thing in the morning, please?' Fay looked at Tina.

'Of course.' Tina hoped she sounded casual. 'Anything else I can do to help?'

'I will come with you,' Pierre announced, getting up and moving to stand behind Tina's chair. 'I do not trust this Thornton man.'

Tina wriggled under the possessive hands curving round her shoulders and Pierre's lips brushing against her hair. She longed to retort: 'I think it's the other way around,' but she forced a smile and said briefly, 'Don't be silly, Pierre.'

'Me? Silly? When all I wish to do is protect you! Oh, I am disillusioned, *ma petite*.'

'Well, if I don't come back tomorrow you can send out a search party,' she said flippantly. 'But give me time to try the Corinne act myself.'

Pierre gave a gasp of mock horror. 'You wouldn't!'

'Why not?' She disentangled herself and stood up, conscious of Paul's amazed gaze. 'I'm free.'

Paul chuckled and shook his head at his younger brother. 'Never try to argue with a woman; it is a long and tedious waste of time.' He cast a mischievous glance at Fay. 'I have discovered there are subtler and more pleasing short cuts to victory.'

Fay was not prepared to let this challenge go, and under cover of their amicable wrangling she made her escape before Pierre could prevent it. Certainly she had no intention of submitting to Pierre's intention of accompanying her the next morning; if he was so determined he could deliver the invitation himself. She could wait another day to see Max Thornton again.

But once again fate seemed to be working for her. Pierre had forgotten that he was due to pick up supplies for the hotel, and Tina set off on the beach walk alone. This time she carried the blue shirt in a neatly folded package, and she looked cool, fair and poised in a crisp, shell-pink slip of a dress with a tiny matching bolero. The thought had crossed her mind that Max Thornton might be elsewhere when she arrived at the villa, and she was prepared with an informally written note from Fay should this be the case. But she was not prepared for the downward plunge of her spirits when she found only Kim in possession.

Ruefully, she delivered the note, and on impulse decided to leave the villa by the gate that led to the track. She might as well walk back to the hotel by the inland route.

She found it shady but not very cool under the trees. They cut out the hot sun but also broke the refreshing shore breeze and trapped the moist heat. Before she had covered half the distance Tina was beginning to feel hot, sticky, and somewhat less soignée than she had felt an hour ago. And she wasn't working, she thought guiltily, noticing how busily the plantation girls were engaged at their tasks along the avenues of vines that sloped up the gentle incline to the left of the track. Some of them looked so young, little more than children, to be working so industriously. They scarcely spared her a glance as she passed, and she wondered if something was wrong with the plants in that sector, for a little farther along the avenues were almost deserted. The next moment she forgot the wondering thought as she heard the put-put sound of an approaching

69

moped. It appeared almost immediately, and she side-stepped off the narrow track to wait until it had passed. But it slowed, and braked to a halt. Max Thornton looked at her.

'Lost?'

'Not at all.' She eyed him unsmilingly. 'Actually, I'm playing postman.'

'Postman?' His head tipped to one side. 'Without the knock?'

'Without the knock,' she agreed solemnly. 'I've just delivered an invitation to dinner tomorrow—to Kim.'

'Oh. For Kim—or me?'

She pulled a face. 'Ask a silly question ...'

The first hint of a grin broke gravity. 'Okay, I asked for that. Like to come back for a drink?'

'I'd *love* to,' she drawled.

The hint of a grin vanished. 'Social inanities do not become you. Say yes please and hop aboard.'

'Yes-please-and-hop-aboard.' Maintaining indifference, she settled herself on the pillion, coolly tucked her arms round his waist, then gave way to a happy little grin he couldn't see.

Suddenly the day had become a delight. The long iced drink he fixed for her tasted like nectar, the lounger on the veranda seemed the most desirable spot to be, and all existence seemed heightened, more vivid, more vital.

'How long are you staying on Kaloha?' he asked idly.

'Probably until the end of the month.' She sipped her drink and explained about her father's lecture tour and his sailing trip home with Crewe Gordino. After a pause she said impulsively: 'I'm glad you're helping Henri.'

He shrugged. 'It's little enough to do.'

'Not if it stops something going wrong. Like blight or whatever attacks the vine.'

'Heaven forbid!'

She set down her glass. 'I saw the girls were terribly busy in one section, just before you came along. They were working as though their lives depended on it. That's why I wondered if there was something wrong.'

To her surprise he began to chuckle. 'For a local, you don't seem to know much about vanilla, little one.'

She shot him a glance of affront. 'They mine coal in

Newcastle and gold in Johannesburg, but that doesn't mean every inhabitant there knows mining from A to Z.'

Max stood up, unperturbed by her indignation. 'Another drink?'

'No, thanks.'

'Then we'll do something about your sadly neglected education. Come on.'

'Okay.' She pretended a sigh, but she was too happy to maintain a show of indignation as she followed him through the house and out to the gate. Once again she climbed aboard the pillion and experienced the sweet satisfaction of folding her arms round that strong waist. When they reached a point near the place where he had met her an hour previously he stopped and they dismounted. He led the way along one of the avenues and Tina followed, her steps feeling soft and muffled in the thick layer of humus that lay on the ground. He stopped beside a vine heavy with rachis in full blossom.

'See anything wrong with that?'

She shook her head after a quick inspection. 'It looks healthy enough to me.'

'It is healthy.' He moved on, to where a tiny slim Chinese girl was working, her fingers seeming to fly along the lower side of a flowering rachi.

The Chinese girl flashed him a smile, not ceasing her task, and Max said, 'Annette is our pollination expert. She can do nearly three thousand flowers a day.'

'And I am not going to break my own record today if you stand over me, making me nervous, Mr Thornton,' Annette exclaimed, deftly parting a blossom and inserting pollen on the tip of a splinter of bamboo.

Tina noticed that Annette ignored the uppermost flowers along the branch, and Max explained that this was because these would result in a misshapen bean of poor quality. 'And those underneath don't?' Tina looked puzzled.

'Law of gravity,' Max said solemnly. 'The flowers along the underside drop a long straight pod which is far easier to grade and pack later, after the drying.'

'Fascinating. Tell me more.'

'The flowers have to be pollinated as soon as they bloom. That's why we have so many girls working on them. Every vine has to be checked every morning while the flowering

71

season lasts.' Max drew her on, explaining that the vanilla in this section of the plantation was Tahitensis, indigenous to the islands, but farther on Henri had introduced plani-folia, commercially the most important species. 'It belongs to the orchid family, and the Aztecs used vanilla for flavouring and healing purposes long before it was known in Europe. One of Cortez's officers is supposed to have been very curious about the recipe for a rich chocolate drink served to Montezuma, the Aztec ruler, in a golden goblet. Apparently it was a closely guarded secret, but eventually Diaz succeeded in discovering the source of the special flavour, which of course was vanilla. After that the Spaniards began importing the beans to Europe, where it soon became one of the most popular culinary essences. Now,' Max sighed, 'unfortunately for the plantations, much of the vanilla flavouring sold is of the synthetic kind.'

'I didn't know it had medicinal uses.' Tina reached up to grasp a leaf and exclaimed as Max caught her wrist sharply.

'Like many plants and herbs it has its place in folklore, but I'm afraid it has other propensities which outweigh any healing qualities it might possess.' He drew her hand to-wards him and looked at the slender wrist. 'The sap and the leaf can raise blisters from contact with the skin.'

'I didn't know.' She turned to glance at him, then down to where her hand still rested within the firm warmth of his grasp. She felt strangely reluctant to withdraw from that contact, but at last she did so and murmured, 'Thanks—I don't think I got stung.'

'No.' He moved aside, glancing at his watch. 'I'll run you back to the hotel.'

Somehow, Tina knew that he was going to slow and stop a little distance from the hotel and her instinct proved true. Under the swaying leaf-frond patterns of that same *bourao* he sat astride the moped and regarded her with enigmatic eyes when she had clambered off the machine.

He gave an almost imperceptible shake of his head. 'No, I'm not coming in.'

A sudden fiery colour flooded her cheeks. 'Do you still hold my juvenile gaucherie against me?'

'Not at all—as long as you've left it behind you.'

She bit her lip, painfully conscious that where he was concerned those youthful failings were not forgotten or escaped as easily as she wished. She said slowly, 'Let me make amends—come and have a drink.'

With irrational disappointment she saw refusal forming in his face, then unexpectedly his mouth softened. 'I haven't time, little one.'

She shrugged, trying to regain her earlier mood of piquant self-assurance. 'Another time, perhaps. But you will come tomorrow?'

'I wouldn't miss it. Salaams!'

She watched while he revved the machine into action and swung into a wide loop, giving her a mocking salute before he headed back to the plantation. The sounds died away and she turned to walk the short remaining distance to the hotel, unaware of the little smile, half dreamy, half retro-spective, lingering on her mouth. There was something strangely sweet in the realisation that all trace of her previous antipathy towards Max Thornton had vanished. And not only had it gone, but it had been replaced by a strong desire to further her acquaintanceship with him. A memory flashed back of an article she had read recently in some magazine. She'd smiled at the time, at the pseudo-psychological advice offered to the feminine sex on the im-portant subject of attracting a man, but the closing pearl of wisdom now seemed to take on a certain significance: *'Remember, a man will take a girl on her own valuation!'*

Tina frowned, pondering an interpretation of this state-ment. It didn't only mean the obvious, that a girl who be-stowed her favours over-generously was likely to gain a lightly held reputation, it could also apply to her whole attitude. Take her own brief experiences. At her first meet-ing with Max she had angered him; at the second she had plainly disgusted him, even though it had been no fault of her own—how could she have predicted Pierre's be-haviour? But Max was not to know of her lack of encour-agement to Pierre. But today had been different. And Max had been different—his jibe at her 'social inanity' had held no real iron. Oh, she *was* looking forward to tomorrow!

She crossed the side terrace, still wrapped in her musing, and did not notice Rosa, the hotel receptionist, staring at her with an expression of shock. Rosa took an abrupt step forward, her lips forming Tina's name, but before she could speak Fay appeared. Tina reached the terrace doors at the

73

same moment as Fay, and the dreamy little smile was wiped from her lips as she saw Fay's white, distraught face.

'Oh, Tina ... we've been looking all over for you! We——'

'Fay, what's the matter?' Alarm flared in Tina's eyes. 'Are the twins——?'

'They're all right.' Fay gulped, as though she did not know how to put into words what she had to say. 'It's—there was a message. An hour ago. Your father. He——'

'What!'

A shadow fell across the terrace and Paul's arm went round Tina's shoulders.

'You are frightening her,' he said to his wife. 'Tina, chérie, they have lost radio contact with the yacht. But please try not to think the worst. Capitaine Roulier brought the news, they——'

'The yacht? You mean my father——!' Tina pulled from Paul's steadying arm and whirled to face him, seeking to break the spell of horror that was overwhelming her. 'No —it can't be! You don't mean——'

'Come and sit down, chérie. Fay, get her a drink.' Paul took Tina's ice-cold hands and drew her firmly to a chair. 'Try not to panic—it may not be as bad as you think.'

Numbed with shock and fear, Tina let him press her into the chair and stared fearfully at his concerned face. 'What happened? When——?'

'There was a very bad storm at sea two days ago,' Paul began gently, 'in an area noted for its calm disposition. But when there is a convergence of the trade winds from north-east and south it can cause very serious conditions indeed. Your father and Mr Gordino encountered this storm and as far as we can tell suffered some damage to their craft. During their voyage they had kept radio contact with the U.S. Weather Bureau, but this contact ceased at the time of this storm. That same night a Peruvian cargo vessel reported a Mayday distress call from that area. Unfortunately the bad conditions and static made reception so difficult they were unable to collate precise bearings or make any further contact. Mr Gordino's wife and family are extremely worried, which is natural, and a search of the area is being made. But the Pacific is a very large ocean,' Paul said sadly.

74

Tina was so silent and unmoving that Paul looked at her with alarm. Fay knelt down beside the chair and touched Tina's hand. 'Darling, I know it's frightening, and it's easy to say there is every hope,' she whispered. 'But it's true. That distress call may not have come from the yacht. Obviously their radio has given up, but that doesn't mean the yacht was wrecked.'

Tina shook her head wordlessly.

'They could be worrying about you and Mrs Gordino worrying about them,' Fay urged. 'And if they've gone off course, hundreds of miles from landfall, they've no means of making contact.'

'Not until they can hail another vessel. That is true, *ma petite*,' Paul said consolingly. He put his arm round the slender trembling shoulders and above Tina's bowed head he looked at his wife with despairing eyes. 'All we can do now is wait and hope.'

CHAPTER FIVE

WAIT and hope!

After the initial shock wore off Tina wept, and the release of tears swung to an almost hysterical mood of disbelief. Of course it couldn't be true; she had to believe Fay and Paul. She had to hope. She read and re-read her father's last letter, desperately seeking the tiniest scraps of information on which to base reassurance.

After all, Crewe Gordino's yacht was a luxury one, motorised and therefore not entirely dependent on the vagaries of sail. It was equipped with the latest radio gear and Crewe Gordino was an experienced sailor. And as Paul said, in his efforts to prevent her giving way to total despair, the fact of Crewe Gordino being a well-known sporting personality accounted for much of the concern which had arisen. Had he been an unknown, the news might not have broken until he actually reached port and recounted the story.

But Tina's brave hope was almost quenched during the days that followed. The disappearance of the yacht made headlines round the world. It seemed that every vessel, under every flag, was looking out for it or signs of survivors, and after two days living for the news bulletins from Radio Papeete, Tina was possessed of a dreadful restlessness. She decided to return home, and resisted all attempts at dissuasion from Fay and Paul. The dinner party to which she had looked forward so much had been cancelled, and Tina knew that she was casting a cloud over the hotel, despite Fay's vehement denials of this. Max had called once, quietly offered his sympathy and any help he could give, but it was Pierre who insisted on taking her back to Papeete.

There, enfolded in the motherly comfort of Aunt Wynne, she did not have to pretend a brave morale she was far from feeling. She haunted the maritime office, hoping against hope that the new day would bring the news for which she prayed in every waking hour. But the days dragged by, and hope ebbed. The newspapers and the news bulletins from Radio Papeete ceased to hold any mention of the missing yacht and its occupants, and Tina's eyes grew more shadowed and her small features more pinched with despair. She no longer rushed down to the maritime office after breakfast; she now felt a reluctance, almost a dread, to enter the door. She could not bear to see the pity in the young clerk's eyes, giving its message before she could voice her desperate little request.

Pierre and Fay came over twice to see her that first week, and her friends rallied round, endeavouring to cheer her and sustain hope. But as the second week dawned Tina began to avoid their well-meant solicitude. She dreaded the awkward silences that would come, and the pity glimpsed in unguarded moments. She began to make excuses, and took to setting off on long solitary rambles away from the town, subconsciously seeking the haunts favoured by her father, the places he had taken her in her childhood days, the places where he had painted while she had played or idled or watched his brushes make their magic. She walked and swam, and repeated mechanical, unnecessary tasks in the bungalow and studio, trying to tire herself out before the long lonely hours of darkness when there was no escape in physical activity. And at night, uninvited, Max would invade her thoughts.

Somehow it added to her sense of loss that he had failed to make any further contact. He must have been over to see Henri, who was still in hospital and likely to be there for some time still. Yet he had not called, not even sent a message.

But why should he? she asked herself sadly. Their acquaintanceship was of the briefest, too casual yet to be thought of as friendship. At least he had inquired after her, once, so Fay had said, but that was all. And Fay had not mentioned him again. Tina tossed restlessly in the narrow bed in Fay's old room where so many youthful exchanges of confidences had taken place. How vital and intense some of them had seemed at the time, and how unimportant they were recalled now in retrospect, as unimportant as this silly heart-aching because Max Thornton had failed to offer the comfort she so desperately needed. And yet, from nowhere came the strange little thought, her father would have liked Max Thornton ...

She wakened as always just after six, when dawn broke over the Pacific in all its glory of pearl and apricot. She lay for a little while, then showered and dressed before she made the morning cup of tea Aunt Wynne loved and took it to her bedroom. But the older woman was listless and pale as she sat up and smiled at Tina.

'I feel headachy today—I expect it'll pass off,' she said, when Tina commented on her pallor.

'You always say that, and it never does,' Tina rebuked her gently. 'Why don't you stay in bed? I'll bring you a light breakfast?'

But she knew the uselessness of it as she spoke. Aunt Wynne hated giving in. She would insist on getting up and carrying on with her plans for the day, and she would finish up prostrated with a blinding migraine. Today proved no different. After the departure of the two visitors she had been expecting for morning coffee she sank into a chair and pressed her hand to her eyes. 'Of course you were right, Tina,' she sighed. 'But there wasn't time to put them off. And I wanted to do some shopping today.'

'And why couldn't you ask me to fetch it?' Tina brought the tablets and a glass of iced water. 'Now take these and go and lie down. I'll get back as quickly as possible and make the lunch.'

'Not for me.' Aunt Wynne shuddered at the thought of food. 'Don't rush back, darling. I shall try to sleep it off.'

She let Tina shepherd her into her bedroom, darken the room and leave a drink by the bed. As Tina was on the point of leaving Aunt Wynne called her back. 'I nearly forgot ... will you call at Cécile's and see if the rose crochet silk I ordered has come in?'

Tina nodded and dropped a light kiss on Aunt Wynne's hot forehead before she departed with the note of the shopping requirements.

They did not take long to collect, and she left Cécile's till last, knowing the elderly Frenchwoman would be disposed to gossip and at that hour business would be slack. She would exclaim distress on hearing of Aunt Wynne's indisposition, and there would be helpful suggestions as to remedies and inevitably several small news items to impart. Cécile was widowed and lonely. She had an income from her late husband's estate and ran the little drapery business to occupy her days, and sooner or later most of the senior ladies from the community found their way to her shop to seek the leisurely attentiveness and selection of goods not always available in the more brash boutiques patronised by youth. Today was no different. The order had just arrived with the previous day's boat. She hadn't yet got it all unpacked, but the new crochet silks were in the consignment.

Half an hour later the silks had emerged. And so had the surprising news that Cécile had been to the hospital to visit Henri Latour.

Tina felt a twinge of guilt. In her own distress she had forgotten Henri. She should have gone to see him, she thought, resolving to go that very evening.

'So sad that this should happen just when his son is coming home, after all these years,' sighed Cécile as she counted out the skeins of silk. 'Let us hope that Henri continues to improve. It would be so sad if he is still in hospital when Alex arrives.'

'You know Monsieur Latour's son?' Tina said with some surprise.

'Ah, yes.' A rather secretive little smile touched Cécile's immaculately rouged lips. 'But it was many years ago. I never thought he would return.'

Tina was silent. She knew only the common gossip that Henri Latour and his son had become estranged, that the family quarrel had never been healed, but she had no knowledge of the cause.

'It was the letter which brought on the attack, or so the doctor believes,' Cécile went on, smoothing out a sheet of tissue paper. 'It must have been a great shock just to hear from Alex, but to learn the reason . . .' Cécile paused in her wrapping action and leaned forward. 'Alex was in a car accident last year and it left him with a lame leg. Now it seems that there has been a delayed after-affect, something to do with the nervous system. It's quite a rare condition, Monsieur Latour told me, but unfortunately there is no cure. They can alleviate it for a while, and that's all. Actually, they think it could have been developing slowly, and the accident triggered it off much more severely.'

Cécile completed the neat little parcel, and in her silence Tina read the rest; Alex Latour was coming home to make his peace with his father, in case . . . She began to count out the coins while a surge of unutterable sadness swept over her. Why was life so cruel? And so futile. All those wasted years between father and son, probably over some proportionately minor cause, and it took disaster to bring about a reunion. Tears stung at her eyes as her own father's features, never very far from memory now, swam into her mind and she saw his presence as though he actually stood at her side. How often had she argued with him, sulked if he had rebuked her or refused her some petty whim. How often had she failed to express all the gratitude and love she owed . . .

'We'll certainly see a change in Alex—after all, it must be all of fifteen years and none of us are getting any younger. Ah, he was a handsome young gallant.' Cécile handed over the package, a wistful expression coming to lurk in her still sparkling black eyes. 'He was always in a scrape, usually over a girl. He couldn't resist a pretty face. And he couldn't settle to a job, certainly not on the plantation. Poor Henri used to despair. It isn't surprising that he lost patience with him at the finish. Henri had a hard streak in him in those days.' Cécile chuckled and patted the fluffy wisps of abundant black hair that was as artlessly styled as that of any girl. 'That's why I wouldn't marry him.'

'Monsieur Latour?' Tina stared.

Cécile nodded. 'Oh, yes, I have had my day, *ma petite*, although you might hardly think so to look at me now. But I chose my dear Emile, and never regretted it.' Cécile crossed herself fervently, then abruptly became brisk again. 'Now if the *couleur* is not satisfactory, *chérie*, do not be afraid to return it. *Oui? Merci.*'

Cécile smiled and prepared to shut up shop before lunch. Tina wandered out into the brilliant sunlight, debating mentally whether to return straight home or have a cool drink and an ice first. She was so very thirsty. She stowed the little package in the carrier on her bike and was about to mount when a voice exclaimed: 'Tina!'

The bike wobbled and she turned awkwardly, a tremulous exclamation of surprise escaping her as she looked up into Max Thornton's face.

She was almost glad when he gave her a direct look and said: 'No news yet?'

She shook her head, finding it easier to return a simple 'No,' than answer the awkwardly phrased inquiries so many of her friends made. They worked round to it so cautiously in their efforts to avoid hurting her, little knowing that it brought more hurt than the plain outright question.

He said, 'I thought not—you're looking too peaky.' He paused, his mouth unsmiling. 'Is there anything I can do?'

'I don't think so—but thanks all the same.' She bit her lip, wanting to keep him talking but unable to think of anything to say.

He glanced at his watch, then back to her face, and his expression subtly changed, as though he perceived the mute desire. 'Are you in a hurry?'

'Not particularly.'

'Come on, then, I'll take you to lunch. But I've to meet someone in ten minutes.'

The glimmer of pleasure died instantly in her eyes. 'In that case I'd better not ... I mean, you don't want——'

'I doubt if you know what I really want, little one.' His mouth betrayed a quirk at the corners. 'But we'll have to get a move on.'

'Oh ...' She remembered her bike, and a small frown of uncertainty returned between her brows. Did he have a car? Or...?

'I'm on foot,' he said calmly, once again discerning the unspoken query, 'but if you don't ride Tour de France style I reckon I can keep up with you okay.'

For the first time since that fateful day two weeks ago Tina felt a lifting of the black tension of despair. She cycled along slowly, weaving a steadily undulating course with which Max's long strides kept pace easily, and made no attempt to force a casual conversation. It was enough to have his company and the sudden intuitive knowledge that he did not wish her to make any pretence of a cheerful sociality she did not feel.

When he escorted her to a table in the new Reef Grill-room and excused himself for a few minutes she sat there quite contentedly, her chin on one hand, and watched a high-spirited group of obviously newly arrived tourists at another table. One of the men was still wearing his *lei* and jovially resisting the ragging of his comrades. One of them raised a camera, the man with the *lei* ducked, and a smile came to Tina's mouth. She had watched similar scenes so many times before, then beyond the noisy group she saw Max returning, and the little smile vanished as she saw his companion. It was Corinne.

It did not occur to Tina to analyse her disappointment. When Max had mentioned meeting someone she might have realised that it was a fifty-fifty chance on the appointment being with a woman. But he had not elaborated, and she had never dreamed that it would be with Corinne.

The tall blonde French girl was slim and svelte in dazzling white matelot pants and a scarlet top with dark blue thonging at throat and hip. The outfit looked as though it had been poured over her, and the bantering tourists were suddenly silent. Corinne pretended not to notice their turning heads. Slightly in front of Max, she advanced towards the table where Tina waited and flashed a brilliant smile.

The smile, and her 'Tina! How are you, *chérie*?' expressed nothing but surprise and concern, but Tina knew instinctively that the other girl was anything but pleased at this unexpected gatecrashing on her lunch date.

Corinne settled herself, then directed a sympathetic glance at Tina. 'And what have you been doing since last we met, my dear?'

Tina shrugged. 'There's little I can do, except wait.'

'No, I did not mean that.' Corinne switched her glance to Max for a moment. 'I meant to occupy yourself this sad time. We were just talking about you last night, over on the island, were we not, Max?' Again the flicker of the blue gaze to him. 'And he agreed with me that perhaps you would be better to return to your friends, where you would have the children for distraction. And of course Pierre,' she added.

'I prefer to be at home just now,' Tina said quietly.

The arrival of the waiter and the choosing of the menu interrupted conversation, and Tina hoped that Corinne would not resume her no doubt well-meant advice. For a while the subject of Tina's welfare was dropped, and when Max inquired how the new boutique venture of Corinne's was progressing it seemed that this would monopolise the conversation throughout the meal.

Tina had no objections. She would have liked to talk to Max alone, but as this was not to be she preferred the discussion to exclude herself. In any case, she thought wryly, she shouldn't have been present. Corinne, however, had not forgotten. She scooped up the last spoonful of delicately tinted lime icecream, touched her lips with her napkin, and said firmly: 'I have an idea.'

Max murmured, 'Oh . . .' and Tina bent again to her own ice dessert.

'How would you like to help me for a few days, *chérie*?'

'Me? In what way?' asked Tina, after a moment of surprise.

Corinne leaned forward. 'The alterations are complete now, everything is finished. But there is not much time to arrange all the special displays I have planned for the opening next week. And all the stock . . .' she gestured with slim, expressive hands. 'There is so much to do still. I have seen the attractive little displays at the studio, which I understand you usually arrange, so why not come and help me?'

Tina was silent, still a little surprised at this unexpected request. What exactly did Corinne want? Did she want a salesgirl? For surely Corinne would have her own very definite ideas on displaying the trendy clothes she would doubtless be vending.

'Of course if you do not have the time . . .' Corinne's

slender shoulders rose slightly. 'But I think it would be good for you. After all, *chérie*, there comes a time when one must face facts and realise that life goes on. Perhaps that sounds hard, and you may think me unfeeling, but in time you will realise that what I say is true. However,' she smiled and reached over to touch Tina's hand, 'think it over and let me know as soon as you can. In the meanwhile I will struggle on alone.'

She turned an expression of wry self-pity to Max, and added: 'I should never have managed without your help, *mon ami*. So many things to deal with ...'

Her tone and her expression conveyed a sense of intimacy as well as fervent gratitude, and Tina experienced a sad little feeling of being shut out. So Max had been deeply involved with the preparations for the new boutique. He must have spent quite some time here during the past week or so, yet he had not once made any attempt to contact Tina, even though he was so near ... Tina sighed and reached for her bag. What did it matter ...?

She straightened and found herself looking straight into his eyes.

'I think Corinne's right,' he said. 'Why not consider it?'

In her heart Tina realised all too well the truth of Corinne's suggestion. No matter how hard it was to admit it she would have to face up to it sooner or later. Only the previous day Aunt Wynne had asked gently what she was going to do about the studio; was she going to re-open it? Tina had shied away from the thought but she knew she could not postpone a decision indefinitely. If she was going to continue running it in her father's absence she would need to order new stock, decide on which prints to continue, and which of the remaining originals of her father's work she was going to keep ... At the moment she knew she could not bear to part with any of them, but the time would come when she had no option but to sell. She would also have to find a way to support herself. The little money she had would not last much longer ...

Aware of his questioning gaze she said unsteadily, 'Yes, I will—but I'd like to talk it over with Aunt Wynne. I'm not sure what arrangements she may have made for the next few days. If I let you know tomorrow ...?' She glanced at Corinne uncertainly.

Corinne said that would suit her fine, and a few minutes later Tina was making her way home alone, only realising as she reached the house that she had forgotten to thank Max for her lunch. She sighed to herself as she let herself in; it couldn't be helped: she would have to remember to thank him next time she met him.

She found Aunt Wynne sound asleep. Tina put away the shopping things and then a little while later she made a cup of tea and took it in to Aunt Wynne, finding to her relief that the headache was better and the older woman was feeling more like herself again.

After she had recounted her meeting with Max Thornton and the subsequent lunch with him and Corinne, Tina was not surprised when Aunt Wynne instantly sided firmly with Corinne's suggestion.

'But please yourself, of course,' Aunt Wynne concluded, 'you don't have to do anything you don't want to as far as I'm concerned. But I think you will be glad later if you do.'

Tina thought it over and decided to make Aunt Wynne's advice the deciding factor. Next morning she got ready immediately after breakfast, putting on a touch of lipstick for the first time in two weeks, and made her way into town to Corinne's boutique.

She found Corinne already there, looking slightly bewildered amid the smell of fresh paint and an array of packages and enormous cartons.

Corinne gave her an unexpectedly warm smile. 'I hoped you'd come. *Mon Dieu!* Where do we start?'

Tina looked round, at the gleaming empty shelves and new showcases, and the piles of boxes everywhere, and said dryly: 'You'd better tell me.'

'*Certainement!*' Corinne beckoned. 'Help me open this one.'

Tina went to hold steady a large carton while Corinne strove to remove the heavy metal staples which secured the top. As they struggled with it Corinne explained that she had obtained the exclusive agency for La Belle Camille perfumes and cosmetics. 'Heaven knows how much I shall sell of this lot at the price they are,' she confessed ruefully, 'but I'm hoping the display will add a certain *cachet* to the place.'

Tina began to forget her earlier reserve regarding

Corinne, and as the carton yielded up its treasure trove of fragrant delight the two girls were united in an essentially feminine rapport of discovery.

There was a complete range of make-up, as well as various skin-care preparations and bath toiletries, all in the attractive ivory and gold packages with the distinctive Camille cameo embossed in pale satiny blue. Then they came to the perfumes.

'Where are the testers?' Corinne delved eagerly, giving a cursory glance at the volume of glossy coloured literature which described the products. 'Which shall we try first? *Etude?* That's the heavy one—for stunning a man! Or *Nocturne*—to mystify his senses.' Corinne giggled and dug her finger nail into the sealing film that enclosed the glass stoppers of the black glass flacons.

Tina picked up one of them, and Corinne said impatiently: 'That's the floral one. Here, try this! *Ballade!* Whispers to him the secret you are too shy to tell!'

'I have no secrets to tell,' Tina smiled wryly, watching Corinne draw out the glass dropper and take a long, experimental sniff at its fragrance. 'Mm,' the French girl nodded and leaned forward to touch the dropper to Tina's wrist, 'I like it.' She applied some to her own throat and wrists, waiting until the warmth of her skin brought out the full sensuous depth of the scent. Then her eyes sparkled with something like curiosity. 'You'd better wear some of this next time you meet Pierre.'

Tina began to make a neat stack of the packages which were now strewing the floor. 'Why Pierre?' she said quietly.

'You like him, don't you?' Corinne looked surprised. 'He has quite a yen for you, *petite*. I know that.'

'But I don't happen to have a yen for him.'

Corinne sat back on her heels. 'But he's very attractive.'

'Then maybe you're the one who should wear *Ballade*,' Tina returned.

The amusement had gone from Corinne's eyes. 'I think not. There is only one man for whom I should wear it, and frankly, I do not think I will need a perfume to whisper my secrets for me—when the time comes.'

There was open challenge now in the French girl's eyes, as though she divined the name that had instantly sprung

85

into Tina's brain. Tina clenched her hands, impatient with herself. Maybe Corinne did have a certain yen for Max Thornton, and she also possessed quite enough élan to set about making that yen into something a little more tangible, but it's nothing to do with me, Tina told herself. With some difficulty she returned Corinne's open stare and shrugged. 'Leave *Ballade* for the girls who need it, then. Now hadn't we better make a start?' she added with a commendable lightness.

Corinne nodded agreement and scrambled to her feet, and the subject of perfume's aid to romance was allowed to lapse. But despite this the thought of Max continued to hover in Tina's mind. Was he attracted to Corinne? From Corinne's remarks the previous day he appeared to have been involved in her negotiations concerning the boutique, which suggested a strong degree of friendship, if nothing else. And somehow, from the little she knew of her, she felt certain that Corinne would miss no opportunity of furthering that relationship should she so desire.

It was a disturbing thought, and strangely depressing. It also brought back the sensation of youthful immaturity which she thought she had shaken off long ago. Only Max had succeeded in evoking it again, that evening of Pierre's return to the islands. But during her few more recent encounters with Max she had been pleasantly aware of a new assurance, and eagerness to put youthful inanity firmly where it belonged, in the past.

With a sigh Tina attempted to banish the musing sadness and give her full attention to the job in hand.

It proved the start of a full and busy week. By the end of that first day the two girls had evolved a rough order out of chaos. They unpacked most of the stock, putting the clothes on to hangers in the stockroom behind the shop and setting the boxes of small goods aside to be dealt with later. Corinne was planning to carry a wide range of articles, some jewellery, a selection of accessories like belts, handbags and straw goods as well as the trendy luxuries like the huge mother-of-pearl-framed sun-glasses on a stick like a quizzing glass and the silk parasols which opened out like big gold sunflowers. Every day Corinne changed her mind about where to display what. The La Belle Camille range began in the little side window, moved to the centre of the main window, gave way to orange and straw beachwear and went into the display cabinet just inside the door, then finished up back in the side window. The same with the undies. The delicious rainbow pastels of the briefs, slips and bras changed rota in the fittings almost as many times, and a particularly luxurious set of silk and French lace did the grand tour of windows and showcases until it found its home in an alcove above the range of glass-fronted shelves along one wall.

At last Corinne pronounced herself satisfied, and the eve of opening day arrived. All the invoices had been sorted out and checked, everything was priced, and as Corinne observed, all that remained was to await the customers. She gave a last look round at the results of their work and turned to Tina.

'Will you come and help me tomorrow?' she asked. 'If only to give me moral support for the first day?'

'I was hoping you would ask me,' said Tina. 'Not that I think you need the moral support.'

Corinne did not laugh. 'You're a strange girl, Tina,' she said abruptly.

'In what way?'

'You've worked here every day for a week and never once hinted about any payment. And now you are ready to give up another day the moment I ask.'

'You asked me to help you, not come and work for you,' Tina said, hiding her surprise. 'And you were right; I've enjoyed this week.'

As she spoke she knew it was the truth. The days had been full of interest, and despite her initial reservations a curious, if guarded friendship had sprung up between herself and Corinne. It was unlikely to have occurred but for the chance meeting the previous week, and she realised that she would have been both disappointed and suddenly at a loss if Corinne had not made this new request.

'I'd like to take you on permanently,' Corinne said suddenly, 'but at present it just isn't possible. I don't know if it's going to pay that kind of profit, and I've a large debt to pay off before I dare permit myself the luxury of staff.'

Tina could understand this. She shook her head. 'You don't owe me anything, and if you need me you just have to say.'

'Thank you.' Corinne bit her lip, seeming for once at a loss for words. Then she swung round impulsively and opened one of the showcases to take out one of the white and gold packages containing perfume. She looked at it, and gave a sudden little laugh as she put it back and drew out another. 'Yes, it shall be *Ballade*, despite your objections. And you must wear it tomorrow evening.'

Impervious to Tina's protests, she pushed the expensive gift into Tina's hands, 'I hope you are not going to refuse an invitation to our little celebration tomorrow evening.'

'I didn't know you were planning one.' Tina looked down at the ornate package with the crystal flacon of perfume nestling beneath the transparent lid.

'Oh, it was Max's idea! Only last night.' Corinne laughed excitedly. 'He thought it was a pity to allow the occasion to pass unmarked. Nothing wildly elaborate, just a few friends for a meal—and champagne.' Corinne paused, her gaze suddenly speculative as it searched Tina's face. 'Naturally I suggested to Max that he bring Pierre—for you, *chérie*.'

There was a silence. The warm little glow that had lit Tina's eyes suddenly died, vanquished by the same dispiriting sense of disappointment as in the restaurant the previous week. 'It's very kind of you,' she said at last, her voice toneless, 'but I'm not sure if——'

'Such short notice?' Corinne's red lips assumed a rueful moue, then parted. 'You are not worrying about what to wear, I trust? For we can take care of that!' She waved her hands expansively to encompass the boutique and went on before Tina could reply, lowering her voice confidingly: 'You know, *chérie*, that we must be a good advertisement for my boutique. So shall I help you to choose something very special? After all, it is the least I can do to repay you for your assistance.'

Tina felt the smoulder of increasing anger as she listened. Did Corinne think she lacked both wardrobe and the taste to refurbish it? How dared she talk about being a good advertisement for the establishment, as if Tina might let her down? And how dared she link her with Pierre this way? Before she could stop herself Tina put down the perfume and said abruptly: 'Thank you, but that won't be necessary. I have other arrangements made for tomorrow evening.'

Leaving Corinne staring, Tina turned and walked out of the boutique before the other girl could make any reply.

Tina spent that evening alternating between angry satisfaction at her impulsive exit and the beginning of something like remorse as her anger gradually cooled. She began to wonder if she had been too hasty and misjudged Corinne. Had she read disparagement where none was intended? After all, she herself had offered assistance without the remotest intention of expecting any return, whether monetary or in kind. Had the circumstances been reversed might she not have reacted the same way? Offered gifts, impulsively, as Corinne had done? Shouldn't she try to see things from Corinne's angle, remembering that Corinne had a very businesslike approach to her new project? Wasn't it logical to wish to appear in public as a soignée, attractive representative of the fashion wares one hoped to vend?

In her heart Tina knew this was true, and that she had been hasty, if not churlish in her rejection of the perfume and her refusal of Corinne's invitation. But she could not subdue the instinct that insisted otherwise. It told her that Corinne was one of those girls who could be sugar-sweet and affability itself when it suited her purpose, but all of this masked a Corinne who would display a somewhat different façade should her personal interests ever be threatened.

Tina went sadly to bed. It was too late now to retract. She would keep to her promise to help Corinne during the first day, but nothing would induce her to go back on her refusal of the invitation ...

If Corinne was surprised to see Tina the following morning she gave no indication of it, and the first few hours of business allowed little chance of retrospect. Papeete came in force, to crowd round the attractively dressed windows, to nudge and giggle, to inquire and admire, and sometimes to retreat with shaking of heads at the price of fashion— for the Tahitians would not demean themselves to bargain. Secretly, Tina sympathised and considered that many of Corinne's prices were too steep, especially for the younger girls. It was all very well to gear up to the inflated level of the tourist snares on the Quai, and that of Papeete's wealthy section of residents, but many of the locals were still happiest when browsing and milling among the little streets that converged on the old market. Still, it was Corinne's affair, and if she could make a success of a new, exclusive establishment then good luck to her.

They closed the new cream and blue-crested shades at eleven-thirty, shutting out the last customer and the sun, and took advantage of the lengthy lunch and siesta break to take stock of their morning sales. Corinne pronounced herself fairly satisfied, although Tina sensed a trace of disappointment over the Camille sales. The other cosmetics, beachwear, and a particularly attractive range of printed cotton dresses had gone well, so had jewellery and lingerie, but the special, exclusive lines dear to Corinne's heart had lagged behind. However, it was too early to start judging, as Corinne observed when the first day came to a close.

She had still made no reference to the evening ahead when Tina began to gather up her bag and light jacket prior to departing, but she put the perfume down in a conspicuous place and said casually: 'You forgot it last night.'

Tina said awkwardly, 'Yes ... I'm sorry I left so abruptly, I——'

The little hesitation lengthened, then Corinne said lightly: 'No need to explain, chérie, I know that my offer caused you some offence, although it was not intended.' She gave an expressive shrug. 'You are still very English, are you not? Stubborn and very proud. But let us not quarrel about it—I am much too grateful to wish that.'

There was a silence. It, and the slightly hurt expression now on Corinne's face, made Tina feel as though she was completely in the wrong. She bit her lip and slowly took the perfume. 'Thank you—this is more than enough. More than I wished.'

Corinne gave the same little shrug of slim shoulders again, moving after Tina towards the door. 'My pleasure, chérie—and you have not changed your mind about the other?'

The ambiguity of the question hung in the air, telling Tina quite plainly that the invitation was not being repeated, merely her previous refusal being confirmed. She said quietly, 'Thank you, no, but have a good time.'

Corinne's, 'Ah, I will, I'm sure—shall I give your regards to Pierre and Max?' stayed in Tina's memory all the time she rode home and cast a sad little cloud over the prospect of a lonely night in front of her. Aunt Wynne had gone to visit friends across the island and would not be home until late, and the wreath of light aglow like a cascade of diamonds along the edge of the lagoon, beacons of the town awakening enthusiastically to the night, seemed to underline the silence of the quiet suburban villa.

Tina made herself a light meal, cleared it away, set the tray ready for the late night drink when Aunt Wynne returned, and then, unable to find any further time-consuming chores, took a magazine and her radio on to the veranda. Somewhere down there, among that wreath of dancing will-o'-the-wisp radiance, Corinne would be gilding her attractive self, confident in the knowledge that she was to have two eligible escorts in attendance. Champagne, music, dancing, gaiety, and Max . . .

Abruptly Tina turned up the volume of the radio, as though to shut out her own thoughts. It was her own fault; she *had* been invited, and she had let pride dictate her decision. It would be better to forget the matter, not waste time in such silly speculation. She would only have been paired off with Pierre, which was the last thing she wanted . . . Tina flipped over a page, read the first couple of paragraphs of the short story, and almost jumped out of her chair as a voice said:

'So this is where you are!'

Max was standing on the veranda stairs, a scarce three paces away.

Tina felt the magazine slide from her hands and skid to the floor. Max came forward, the veranda light catching the sheen on his dark head, and Tina's heart was caught in a curious constriction. She said throatily: 'You!'

'Yes, me. Why aren't you ready?'

The grimness of his tone did not seem to augur any social mood, and instinctively she took refuge in pretence of misunderstanding. She picked up the magazine. 'Ready for what?'

'You know perfectly well.' He towered above her, his mouth an unsmiling line. 'I never dreamed when I got over

91

a few minutes ago that ... Why not?'

'If you're referring to Corinne's party, I'm not going.'

'For what reason?'

'I don't have to give one to you.'

'Oh, but you do.' Anger glinted in his eyes. 'Especially as your excuse of other arrangements appears to be totally false. Which is precisely what I expected,' he added grimly.

'How do you know?' she demanded.

'Because I do. Now,' he glanced at his watch, 'I'll give you ten minutes.'

Tina's mouth compressed. 'I'm not going. Now hadn't you better get back to town? I doubt if Corinne likes being kept waiting.'

She gave a gasp as the magazine was snatched out of her hands and a set of fingers like steel fastened round her wrist. He yanked her upright, till her stubborn little mouth was only inches below his own.

'Why do you persist in making me angry?'

'You're making yourself angry! I'm not!'

'Don't you know it's for your own sake?' he hissed. 'Why do you think I suggested the party in the first place?'

For a moment she stared at him incredulously, then she tried to wrench her wrist free. 'Because you're sorry for me? You don't need to be! Just leave me alone!'

'Tina, don't try me too far! Nobody's sorry for you! And short of carrying you there, or keeping you on a handcuff, I can't make you, but I'm prepared to try.'

'What! You wouldn't dare!'

'Wouldn't I? Corinne seems to think you've nothing to wear. Shall we inspect your wardrobe and *I'll* decide what you'll wear?'

Tina's lips parted. 'You mean she actually——'

'Oh, for God's sake! Women and their claws!' he groaned. 'I don't know what happened between you, but I can hazard a fair guess.'

'Can you? I doubt it,' she said bitterly.

'Tina, I've been around long enough to recognise a few examples of basic feminine behaviour. I've also met several of the world's Corinnes, so don't make the mistake of underestimating my ability for perception. There'll always be girls who have to be the mainspring of attraction—and who are quite prepared to take advantage of someone less self-assertive. Someone who can be as infuriatingly stubborn and childish as you are at times, Tina,' he added angrily.

She drew a furious breath. 'If that's the effect I have on you I fail to understand why you're wasting your time here and now.'

His mouth compressed in a sardonic curve. 'I doubt if you're old enough or wise enough to judge any effect you might have on me, and I suggest you reserve your estimates until you are. Now, for the last time, do I shove you under the shower, haul a garment over your head and bundle you outside into my car? Or are you coming in a more conventional way?'

Suddenly Tina could feel her own heart thudding as she faced him, the lean implacable lines of his features telling her he meant every word of his threat. At last she whispered faintly, 'I believe you would.'

'Yes, I would. But I doubt if it would lead to a successful party.' His voice had imperceptibly lost some of its force, and something almost like resignation had softened his mouth. He released her wrist and put both hands on her shoulders. 'Tina ... if I say I especially want you to join us tonight, will you take that tight little grimace of battle out of your mouth and let it relax? It doesn't go with the hurt look in your eyes.'

'I—I wasn't aware of either,' she said stubbornly.

'You're not standing here.' Without warning he bent his head and very lightly touched his mouth to hers.

Her lips parted under the light pressure, more with astonishment than anything else, and abruptly he straightened. His hands squeezed her shoulders briefly. 'Go on—that ten minutes is almost up already.'

In a state of haziness Tina found herself turning towards the doorway. The transition from anger to something very like tenderness had disarmed her, and all she was conscious of was the soft quivering sensation left by the touch of his mouth. The desire to argue had fled, so had all memory of Corinne, and there was only the automatic bidding of habit to guide her through the motions of showering, drying, talcuming, and sorting along the dresses in her wardrobe. Only as she took down the same little jade green lace dress she had worn the evening when Pierre returned did the dreamlike haze begin to dissolve. Tremors of excitement stirred in her, and a delicious sense of anticipation, as though something were coming alive in her again. In front of the mirror, she looked at herself, meeting that dark, tremulous glow in her own eyes as she quickly applied pale rose lip tint and silvery jade shadow above her long lustrous lashes. Tina had never been vain of her appearance, and never realised how beautiful were her big serious eyes with the deep smoky depths within their blue. Now she felt a sudden doubt about the eye-shadow; it matched the dress, but was it right for her colouring? Somehow it had never occurred to her to worry, but tonight it seemed to matter that her appearance should be absolutely right.

She glanced down at the jumble of little make-up containers on the dressing table tray, and she saw her father's photograph.

In a moment the thought of eye-shadow fled. A feeling of guilt rushed over her, heavy with remembrance. She picked up the photograph, and the small war of conflicting emotions tugged at her heartstrings. She wanted desperately to go with Max ... and yet ...

Outside, beyond the shutters, his step creaked on the veranda, and then he called: 'Tina, are you nearly ready?'

She set down the photograph and went to slide the screens aside. He came into the rectangle of light and looked down at her troubled face.

'What's the matter?' he asked.

'It's—my father. For—for a few moments I'd forgotten.' Her mouth trembled and she swallowed hard as she looked up at him. And then suddenly it seemed the most natural thing in the world to move against him, into his arms and cling to him. Against his shoulder she murmured: 'I wanted so much to come with you, to feel happy again ... now I feel guilty, because ... it's wrong to, when ...'

Max's hands were strong and steady on the slender shoulders. He shook his head. 'No, not wrong, Tina. It's only wrong to desire happiness at the expense of another's. I doubt if your father, were he here, would agree with your reasoning.'

'But it seems disloyal,' she whispered.

'Do you think your father would wish you to renounce happiness for the rest of your life?'

'No, but . . .'

'You have to go on living, Tina. Some day you will fall in love. I hope with the man who wants to marry you and take care of you, and I'm sure that your father would wish you that happiness and fulfilment more than anything else.'

'I can't imagine myself married,' she said in a low voice, wanting to be convinced yet still tormented by the guilt that had overtaken her in those moments by the dressing table. 'Oh, I've thought of it at times, but pushed it aside. I was so happy; there was never anyone to think of—I mean as seriously as marrying. Anyway,' she laughed shakily, 'nobody ever asked me.'

'They will. And now,' he held her a little away from him, 'are you ready to take that first step?'

She nodded, her eyes very wide and luminous, and intent on his unsmiling features. Suddenly they seemed very dear, very strong, and very reassuring. She whispered unsteadily, 'Thank you—I'm sorry I always seem to fly off the handle at you and make you angry. I don't mean to.'

'Don't you?' His mouth curved at one corner. 'I'll try to remember that.' For a moment he studied her, then for the second time that evening he bent his head and let the firm pressure of his lips rest on her soft, unresisting mouth.

It was the kind of kiss her father might have dropped on her cheek in passing; it made no demand, nor lingered long enough to arouse any awakening of either response or revulsion in Tina. Yet its memory stayed with her, awakened anew each time she met his glance, danced with him, spoke with him during the course of the evening. It did not occur to her to try to analyse any reason for this sweet, persistent little memory; she knew only that he had brought comfort when least expected and helped her to come to terms with a reality that had to be faced. For this alone she would always be grateful to Max Thornton.

That night, after Max, Corinne and Pierre brought her home and departed after a brief nightcap with Aunt Wynne, Tina lay in bed musing over the medley of small incidents that had made up the evening. The party had been a tremendous success. Corinne had looked stunning in a glorious white creation, and somehow the original number of eight had grown to nearly three times that number before the party finally broke up. Pierre, despite Corinne's averred reason for his invitation, had seemed unable to take his eyes from her and spent most of the night trying to fend off determined competition from two other smitten males equally bent on monopolising her favours. Corinne had basked and glowed in all this adulation, and Tina had been perfectly happy to watch; it was Corinne's night, and she deserved her success.

At last Tina's eyes closed, and for the first time in weeks she fell asleep without the dread numbness of despair to cloud her dreams. Tomorrow was a new day . . .

But the new day brought the letter.

CHAPTER SIX

THE letter bore an English stamp, above the strong, erect black writing that indicated a hand which would brook no nonsense.

Tina knew that writing, and even before she could bring herself reluctantly to slit the thin blue envelope she felt her spirits darken, as though they would match the mood of the grey rain clouds that had swept across the island that morning from a squall-tossed sea, to shroud the mountain tops and transform the lagoon into a seething expanse of foam-flecked lead. A fitting harbinger to the missive from those far-off northern shores.

England. Was it to be her new home? Her future? All the rest of her life?

Every instinct recoiled from the idea. Yet her grandmother appeared to take it for granted that the proposition outlined in those precise black sentences would prove instantly acceptable. As comforting as the chill, formal condolences which opened the letter. That Tina should prepare herself immediately for the journey; the journey to the home which her grandparents were prepared to offer her—in England.

Tina paced the room, still unable to take in that completely unforeseen proposition, then sank down on the sofa. She rested her chin on the faded chintz arm and stared dully across the veranda. The rain squall which had sprung up so quickly an hour ago was settling now, and the sun was escaping in brilliant shafts through the fleeing clouds, lighting a myriad sparkling crystals across the garden. Tahiti was smiling again after her brief tantrum, and the raindrop diadems merely enhanced the beauty of her vivid tropical glory. The view from the veranda was one on which Tina had looked countless times, but now she saw it as though through new eyes. The rich pagan enchantment took on a fresh dimension, one suddenly very precious, and she imagined closing her eyes, then opening them to an unknown vista, alien, chill ... amid strangers ...

A great lump of grief swelled in her throat, and tears stung in her eyes. As though in sympathy with her troubled spirit the spiky pink star-flowers under the trellis drooped sadly, shedding their delicate petals with each flurry of breeze, and the tamarisks swayed like mournful feathered ghosts by the white picket fence that bounded the garden. How foolish she had been last night! To begin to believe that life was holding out new hope. Now that was all over, she thought desolately. Nothing would ever be the same again. But England ... so far away ... Panic closed round her at the thought. What was she going to do?

But beneath it all was the true fount of grief; the dread that the letter meant the end of hope, of acceptance she could not face, that she would never see her father again ...

The impulse to take refuge in tears was almost overwhelming, but she fought it down and went to bathe her face in cold water before seeking as always the comfort and advice of Aunt Wynne.

'What am I going to do?' she asked unsteadily, when the older woman had read the letter for the third time. 'How can I?'

For once Aunt Wynne had no answer. She shook her head and looked at Tina with troubled eyes. The fateful letter still in her hand, she crossed to the window, then turned and came back to where Tina sat.

'Don't try to decide yet. You don't have to write back immediately, do you?'

'No, but ...' Tina needed a much more reassuring response than this.

'Thinking it over,' Aunt Wynne said slowly, 'it may be the best thing that could happen.'

'What!' Horror widened Tina's eyes. 'You mean you think I should *go*?'

The older woman sighed. 'Life does not stand still, my dear. Some day you must start looking to your future. Your father would be the last man to deny that.'

Almost exactly Max's words last night. Tina braced her slight shoulders. 'I know. But I still can't accept that—that he——'

'I know,' Aunt Wynne broke in quickly. 'It takes time. That's why I'm wondering . . . if the complete change, the journey, and meeting them, might not be for the best, after all.'

Tina's gaze was drawn to the letter. 'I never dreamed that they'd suggest—I never thought they'd even bother to write. But to go to England . . .'

'It was bound to come, you know,' Aunt Wynne said quietly. 'It isn't such a surprise to me. In fact, I should have been shocked if it hadn't.'

'You would?'

'Well, they're your only living relatives, my dear.'

'They're no real relatives of mine,' Tina retorted, anger tightening her mouth. 'They hated my father, and they never cared a jot about us after my mother died.'

Aunt Wynne shook her head. 'That isn't strictly true, Tina. Admittedly they disapproved of your father because they considered a penniless young artist and self-confessed Francophile a poor match for their only daughter, and he quarrelled bitterly with them when they wanted to bring you up in England, their way, and he refused to let you go. But disapproval is a long way from hate, Tina.'

'I never needed them to bring me up.' Tina stared with sombre eyes at the flaunting scarlet of bougainvillaea against a vivid blue sky flecked with soft little white clouds, and wished the island enchantment would lay its balm on her bruised heart. 'I had everything I could wish for—except Mummy . . .'

'Yes, but isn't it time to start forgetting old bitterness?'

Tina made no reply, and the older woman looked down at the slender, woebegone figure crumpled up in the chair. Aunt Wynne sighed. She did not need to close her eyes to go back in time, or forget that during the past two or three years Tina had subtly matured into a very beautiful young woman. Studying the tumble of soft, now untidy hair with its bright honey sun-streaks that owed nothing to a hair stylist's aid, and the tender rose flush on the sun-bronzed oval cheek, she saw the child of yesteryear with vivid clarity. Then, as now, Tina had curled up in this same chair and summoned tears as her weapon against the threat to uproot her from everything she knew and loved. Then, as now, it had been the question of her future, when the distraught widower had been torn over the decision he had to make; whether to send his beloved child home to her grandparents in England, or indulge his own longing to keep her with him on the island. What was the best for Tina? he had asked Aunt Wynne, and she had not known how to answer.

Tina herself, with a blend of tears, temper, childish cunning and her very real sorrow at the loss of her mother, had finally swayed his decision the way they both, in their hearts, wanted. Tina had stayed, despite the anger and protests of Elizabeth Kingman, the grandmother she did not know, to be mothered and spoilt by Aunt Wynne, and adopted by Fay as the sister neither girl possessed. But courtesy aunt or no, there was no blood tie, and the older woman felt the stirrings of conscience; how could she use her influence to sway Tina in the making of this same decision?

It was so difficult. Tina was a child of the islands, born to the sun and the carefree, idyllic freedom of Polynesia. It seemed unthinkable to uproot her and transplant her to far-off England's cool green realm. Yet technically, she was now an orphan. The autocratic old couple in their ancient manor in Hampshire were her own kin, and surely held some claim to her. And there was another point which seemed to have escaped Tina; it could have proved dismaying if they had chosen to ignore her existence. For there wouldn't be much money when John's affairs were wound up. When there were no more pictures to sell the studio would have to be closed, and what then? Few could compete with the Chinese business interests on the island, and John Raimond's careless, impractical failure to provide a standby training for a career suitable for his daughter now took on an ominous look. Once, when Aunt Wynne had suggested he consider the matter, he had brushed her concern away easily; Tina had himself to look after, he could provide for her, couldn't he? And she would get married ... But Tina was eighteen now, had given no indication of even thinking of marriage, and now she stood alone to face the hard, economic facts of living that hid behind the paradisical face of Tahiti.

Aunt Wynne sighed heavily and stood up. 'You can't decide at once, Tina,' she said. 'But you must think it over very carefully.'

'I don't need to think it over,' Tina cried. She snatched up the letter and unfolded it. 'Listen, does this sound loving and inviting?

'*The distance and circumstances prohibit our coming out personally to deal with the matter, but it should not present undue difficulty. Presumably your father dealt with someone of legal repute in Papeete, who will be acquainted with his affairs; instruct them to sell everything as soon as possible and make arrangements for your passage to England without further delay. Your grandfather and I both feel that your education has been sadly neglected and no time should be lost in preparing you for a suitable career in England. It is all too easy for young people to drift into a shiftless existence these days, particularly in the part of the world in which your father chose to rear you. Naturally we regret your sad loss, my dear, but feel confident you will soon settle down here once you are free of the somewhat bohemian atmosphere in which you have been brought up. We see no reason why you should not be here by the end of next month and are making suitable preparations to receive you. Until then, your affectionate grandmother, Elizabeth Kingman.*'

Tina paused for breath. 'Does it?' she demanded.

'It sounds the chilliest invitation I've ever heard—not one I'd accept in a hurry,' said a light lilting voice from the doorway.

Tina leapt up. 'Fay!' she cried joyfully, and launched herself across the room.

The two girls clung together for a moment before Aunt Wynne hurried to kiss her daughter and exclaim: 'This is a surprise—I didn't expect you at all this week.' Abruptly her smile sobered. 'There's nothing wrong, is there? The twins?'

'They're fine,' Fay reassured her hastily. 'No, I had the chance of an early lift over so seized the opportunity to do some shopping, and see you, of course. Pierre will come over for me this evening.'

'But where is he now?' Her mother looked puzzled.

Fay laughed. 'Oh, Max Thornton brought me over. He called this morning, very early, to say he had business to see to for poor Henri, and did we need anything. So I suddenly decided to come over with him.' Fay looked at Tina. 'I hear you had a very good night last night.'

'Yes.' Tina forgot the letter for a moment. Max couldn't have had much sleep. By the time he got back to Kaloha... Why hadn't he stayed overnight instead of ...? Suddenly she felt a strange sense of relief. After he had left last night she had wondered if he had stayed, perhaps continued the celebration a little longer with Corinne ... But he hadn't. She became aware of Fay speaking, of his name being spoken again.

'There's some doubt if Henri will be able to manage the plantation again, not without a lot of help. He's had a very bad coronary, it seems, so Max may be staying here for good.' Fay turned to the silent Tina and reached out for her hand, to draw her down on to the sofa. 'You know, it must have been a premonition I had about you this morning. Now what's it all about? I came in at the shiftless existence bit. What did I miss?'

Tina handed over the letter and sat silent, watching Fay's expression as she scanned the fateful letter. When Fay looked up her usually sweet mouth was taut. 'I'll never mistrust my instinct again. You're not going, are you?'

'I don't know.' Tina shook her head despairingly. 'They *are* my grandparents. They seem to want me, and it's kind of them to want to help, after everything in the past, I suppose, but I can't bear even to think of leaving here.'

Fay frowned. 'Well, nobody can make you. You're of age. And I don't care for their peremptory suggestion that you sell up everything. It seems too drastic. After all, I feel there's still a chance that your father may not be—be lost. I mean, he could have drifted for days, perhaps been picked up by a long range schooner without radio. You know as well as anyone about the ramshackle old cockles that ply the Pacific, defying every maritime law in existence.' Fay hesitated. 'Maybe I shouldn't say this, raising a false hope again, but these things do happen. I don't think you should take this step, Tina.'

'But, Fay . . .'

Neither of the two girls heeded Aunt Wynne's troubled protest. Fay's words held the sentiments Tina desperately wanted to hear, and as though in answer to the unspoken plea, Fay went on: 'It isn't a decision you can make instantly. Of course, it depends on how badly you want to be remembered in their will,' she added flippantly.

'Fay!'

Her mother's shocked rebuke could not be ignored this time, and Fay looked momentarily ashamed. 'I'm sorry, I shouldn't have said that. But after all, they're supposed to be loaded. There's no mention of how she's going to raise the fare to Britain, and I can't say I remember them showering her with love and generosity during these past years.'

'Yes, but it must have been very difficult in the circumstances . . .' Aunt Wynne strove to be impartial. 'You know how it was.'

'Yes, and now they're offering charity and expecting her to be grateful.'

'I don't think they mean it that way,' Aunt Wynne objected. 'It's probably been just as difficult for them to make the approach.'

'I don't agree,' Fay said in stubborn tones. 'Personally, I consider that letter little short of callous. They're proposing to uproot her from everything she knows and loves, and I can't see the slightest promise of love and affection when she gets there! As for the bit about her education,' Fay went on disgustedly, throwing the letter aside, 'I think it's insulting. They sound as though they think she's a little savage, or something.'

Tina gave a soft sigh in the silence which followed. She could feel only relief that Fay had the courage to put into words her own fears and instinct regarding her grandparents.

'Fay, is this wise?' Aunt Wynne broke in. 'Tina's upset and unsettled enough as it is.'

'She'll be even more unsettled if she goes there and isn't happy,' Fay returned flatly. 'Face it; you know as well as I do why they want her. Not for her sake, but because in some obscure way it will appease their bitterness at the way Tina's mother, their only daughter, defied their wishes.

Oh, maybe they don't consciously realise their motive, but I think that the resentment is still there, and if they can have some say in managing Tina's life it'll help to cancel out that bitterness.'

'And that's why I think Tina should consider their offer very seriously,' Aunt Wynne said firmly.

'Yes, but not at the speed they expect,' Fay retorted. 'It'll take every sou she can raise for the fare. A one-way ticket. How does she get back if it doesn't work out?'

There was no real answer to Fay's blunt question; it held too great a modicum of fact and sense. Aunt Wynne moved at last. 'I'll make a cup of tea ...'

Tina raised a ghost of a smile. Twenty-five years in the South Seas had not quenched Aunt Wynne's love of a cup of English style tea, nor her belief that it was the antidote to all ills of the emotions. When she had gone from the room Fay turned to Tina.

'There's another thing. I really came here to see if you could help out for a while.'

For the first time Tina noticed the faint lines of strain around Fay's eyes, and she remembered Aunt Wynne's concern a few weeks ago, just before her previous visit to Kaloha. Tina forgot her own troubles. 'What is it?' she asked. 'You know I'll do anything.'

'It's Rosa. She's pregnant, and she's being so dreadfully sickly with it. Of course she won't give in, she says it will pass, but Jules is worried about her, and so are we.' Fay sighed. 'I just can't allow her to overdo things, and she's going to have to ease out of the hotel work for a while in any case.'

Tina could well understand Fay's concern. Rosa, wife of Jules, the hotel chef, was an extremely efficient receptionist and would be a considerable loss. Fay had come to rely on her a great deal during the past year or so, as the hotel had gradually built up into a successful concern. 'What can I do?' Tina asked. 'Just name it.'

'Come over to us for a few weeks, until I can rearrange my staff. Take over the reception desk each morning, and then be prepared to float wherever you're needed. I've found a little island girl who's a treasure with the twins, but how long she'll stay is anyone's guess. You know what they are,' Fay sighed.

Tina nodded. Staffing problems seemed to be a major headache for hoteliers the world over, and no different on Kaloha. She was beginning to experience the relief of thankfulness that Fay had brought the answer to her own particular problem. Only one thing nagged at her. She said abruptly, 'You're not just making this an excuse to help me?'

Fay gave a rueful laugh. 'If you're not convinced, just come and see poor Rosa. There's nothing imaginary about her state! I'd have asked you before, offered you a permanent job—why not?—you're bi-lingual, articulate, and I've no doubt that you'd very quickly fall into our routine. But Paul wondered if it would offend you.'

'You should know me better than that!'

'Then it's settled,' said Fay. 'We'll find you plenty to keep your mind occupied, and we'll write a nice letter to your grandmother, explaining quite truthfully that you have a job with us, that you can't leave until Rosa's baby arrives, but you'll keep in touch.'

And so it was settled. Tina went down to the studio, had a check over, and closed the shutters. Although she had toyed half-heartedly with the idea of trying to keep it going on her own she knew that it held too many poignant memories. A much longer time would need to elapse before that idea became possible. By the time Fay returned from her shopping trip Tina had packed a case and was ready to depart with her as soon as Pierre arrived.

The sun was falling behind the wild black peaks of Moorea as Pierre set course for Kaloha Isle. The island sunsets are fabled, but on this particular evening it seemed that Nature was endeavouring to outdo her usual six o'clock spectacular. Gold and crimson flames streaked across the sky, dripping liquid amber fire-crests over the rim of the ocean and cutting a flare path of copper through the darkening waves, while the purple veil of night stole in from the eastern horizon. Brilliant stars began to stud the veil, and it was as though some heavenly artist suddenly laid down his brushes and slowly drew his cloak of sequinned velvet across his wondrous creation.

Tina sat by Fay's side under the canopy of the launch and watched the spume of their wake fan out like a swathe of silvery lace on the dark water. Spray flecked her face and bare arms, and the freshening breeze of the open sea tugged at her hair, and gradually a strange sense of timeless detachment took possession of her; she felt as though this warm sea night could enfold her for ever in its wonder.

This was the enchantment of the islands; how could she ever leave it?

She was awake long before dawn next morning and fully dressed when the saffron and flamingo tints melted the purple veils and the dawn breeze raced up with the sun. A new sense of purpose was displacing uncertainties and after the letter had been written last night she had felt as though a weight had been lifted from her. Here on Kaloha there was a sense of security, she felt as though she belonged.

Once the initial strangeness wore off she found the duties of receptionist neither onerous nor particularly nerve-racking. Much of it depended on keeping cool and using her common sense, as Fay had forewarned. Guests mislaid their keys, their cameras, their books, their spectacles, their cardigans, almost everything except—fortunately—their money. They ran out of toothpaste, aspirins, notepaper, sunburn cream, stomach powder, laxatives and anti-laxatives, and invariably there was the odd awkward customer, who, having specifically chosen a holiday spot genuinely 'away from it all', suddenly wanted to know how to get to Tahiti, Moorea, Bora Bora, Huahine—or even Pitcairn!—for a day trip. And they all wanted to know if the stories they had heard about the South Sea Islands were true!

Tina had a good knowledge of history and custom, and she was able to answer most of their queries in this line as well as advising on other small problems. After the early lunch, on Paul's insistence she and Fay rested, and then she helped Fay deal with correspondence, requests for brochures, and confer with Jules over the next day's menus, after which it was Pierre's job to type them out.

Pierre's attitude had subtly changed towards her during the past few weeks. He no longer haunted her so insistently, although he still adopted a possessive air towards her in company, and for this she was profoundly thankful. Her previous visit had held many moments embarrassingly difficult through his unwanted attention, but it seemed those times were over. For good, she hoped, knowing that her youthful infatuation for him was completely dead.

It was not until the following weekend that she began to notice something.

They had an unexpected visitor in the elegant shape of Corinne. Her father was entertaining visitors and ostensibly Corinne was spending the weekend with him to act as hostess. But she appeared quite late on the Saturday evening, imparted an account of the boutique's progress, and managed to spend a considerable portion of the Sunday in the vicinity of the hotel, swimming and sunbathing with Pierre. After a sundowner, during which she casually mentioned that Max was joining her father and his friends that evening, she departed for her father's villa and took Pierre with her. He did not return until long after Tina had gone to bed in the cool blue room in the private wing of the hotel.

She heard the hotel runabout crunch to a halt on the drive below her window, and the soft, melodious little whistling that was characteristic of Pierre when he was alone. Tina looked at her watch on the bedside table; it was almost two in the morning. They had made quite a night of it, she reflected, and experienced a surprisingly sharp pang of jealousy; Corinne certainly seemed to gather up the men. Had Max stayed there all this time? Probably he had. She turned over to settle down again, trying to dismiss the silly feeling of hurt. She didn't care if Pierre was attracted to Corinne, and it would be strange if Max did not socialise occasionally. But he had not been near the hotel once all that week. He must have heard that she was there . . .

It was an oddly unsatisfying thought on which to sleep, and Tina made up her mind to take a stroll along to Henri's villa. Why not? Max had betrayed signs of mellowing a little of late. And why shouldn't she admit, if only to herself, that suddenly she wanted very badly to see that unpredictable man again? Just as long as she remembered not to make him angry!

But fate intervened in her plan, in the form of the twins. Little Jacques took a tumble the following morning and got a coral cut. Fay was well aware of the danger of coral poisoning, and, rather than take the risk of this setting in, she insisted that Paul or Pierre take Jacques and herself over to the mainland to have the doctor examine and dress the foot.

It was a deep cut and bled profusely, causing something very like panic stations. Actually, the small victim was very brave; it was André who screamed at the sight of his twin's blood-covered foot and refused to be pacified. This in turn upset Jacques and made him decide that there must be something fearfully wrong with him after all. He began to wail.

It was just as well that Fay gave way to her instinct, for the cut proved severe enough to warrant a stitch, but the double journey and an unforeseen delay meant they were away the best part of the day. It was late afternoon before they got back, and to Tina had fallen the task of keeping André placated during their absence. He refused to allow her out of his sight, and she began to wonder if there was not a great deal of truth in the belief that twins separated were aware of any harm or pain that befell the other. By the time the overwrought toddlers were at last settled for their long-overdue afternoon rest it was nearing sundown and Tina felt as exhausted as Fay looked.

She and Fay sat down to a cup of tea, and she realised her intention of going to see Max would have to be postponed until another day. She felt a mixture of disappointment and relief. She had not realised how much she had looked forward to seeing him, and yet a fear had worried her that he might greet her advent with coolness or impatience, or even that touch of arrogant derision present in his manner on previous occasions. But why should she fear this? Surely the night of Corinne's party had cleared the air. Hadn't that second sweet kiss set a seal on a new peace . . . ?

Tina's heart quickened with the memory, and she did not notice Fay sit up rather sharply, as though she had just remembered something, and reach for her bag.

'I almost forgot—there was some mail.'

Fay drew out the bundle of letters, still in their string, and untied them. There were several airmails, and even as Fay looked at the top one for a moment before she held it out Tina felt the chill of foreboding.

'Oh, no!' she whispered, reluctant to take it from Fay's hand.

'Oh, yes, I'm afraid,' Fay sighed.

Her grandmother must have written almost by return post. The letter was not lengthy, but it was very much to the point. Tina's grandfather knew someone at Lloyds. He had made exhaustive inquiries in an attempt to discover if anything further had been heard of the Gordino yacht. The response had been a negative, and Tina's grandmother felt the time had come to face facts. She had suddenly realised that she knew nothing of Tina's present circumstances financially, and so she had already made arrangements for a bank draft to be transferred to the Papeete bank for Tina. The sum would cover her air fare and sundry travelling expenses, and it was felt that there should be no further delay in making the necessary arrangements.

Only in the last paragraph did the impersonal tone relax and a note of warmth creep in. Mrs Kingman concluded: *'We fully realise, my dear, the distress and uncertainty you must have suffered during the past few weeks, and understand your reluctance to leave your friends. But you are still very young and we feel sure that in the future you will come to realise that this is by far the wisest solution. We look forward to making your acquaintance very soon, please wire details of your flight arrival as soon as possible...'*

It was as though a cool, unemotional woman had endeavoured to add a persuasive note where she feared reason would most certainly fail.

Tina sat as though stunned. The hard-won fragile tranquillity of the past few days had fled, leaving the problem she had believed solved looming as large and unsurmountable as ever. Plainly her grandmother had no intention of taking no for an answer; by sending the money for her fare she was forcing Tina's hand.

Unheard, Pierre had just walked into the room. He stood looking down at the two girls, cleared his throat dramatically, then demanded: 'Now what is the matter? Not *another* crisis!'

Both his tone and his expression were facetious, and abruptly Tina jumped to her feet. At the moment she could not face another discussion with herself and her future at the centre of it. She had to be alone, to think this out, try to decide what she was going to do. Oh, if only people would stop tugging at her, would let her have time to adjust and make her decisions in her own time . . .

She exclaimed, 'I'm just going out—it's so hot—I must have some air,' as she almost ran from the room. Pierre made a movement to follow, but Fay put out her hand and caught his arm, shaking her head at his surprised expression.

'Let her go,' Fay whispered, holding him back until Tina had made her escape.

Tina did not bother to collect a bag or anything. She ran out of doors in the brief halter sun-top and thin white cotton shorts she had worn all afternoon while amusing André in the garden. Instinct was dominating her actions now, carrying her on hurrying feet down the path to the beach and along the warm amber sand to the marker stones. The sinking sun cast a weaving latticework of black from the thick canopy of palm leaves, and the heavy scent of vanilla lay on the breeze, beckoning her the way she must go.

The path up to Henri's villa seemed achingly familiar, and as she glimpsed the old lounger and the same old white cushions on which her youthful clumsiness had once tipped coffee she knew a flash of longing to be back in time; even though that day so long ago had been fraught with anguish at the time it now paled in intensity compared with the problem she faced today.

Kim was visible through the open door as she crossed the veranda, and even as he saw her and came forward inquiringly she knew with a stab of despair that her journey had been wasted. Max was not there.

The houseboy could not tell her where Max could be found, except that he was somewhere in the plantation, and she turned away. The plantation covered a big, sprawling area; he might be anywhere within it, and suddenly she felt timidity make her reluctant to ask if she could wait a little while to see if he returned soon.

She came out on the track and looked along its green shade, resignation in her eyes. She was being foolish, anyway. What could Max say or do to help, save by mustering the same arguments and advice as put forward by Fay and Aunt Wynne? She might as well return before night fell.

The plantation was silent. Its workers had gone, and even the birds seemed to have departed, perhaps on the last forage for food before the long tropical night descended. There was nothing here, yet Tina felt reluctant to turn her steps towards the hotel. In this sudden mood of uncaring she walked slowly along the track, until she reached a rough pathway that wound its way up the hillside. The island held many old pathways, most of them overgrown now with disuse, and during her many visits to Fay she had explored several of them. But she had never followed this one, mainly because it branched off from Henri Latour's plantation and she had been diffident about trespassing. Now, however, she began to wander up its incline, ducking where the creepers looped low overhead. Sooner or later it would meet a path leading down to Akaia village —she couldn't get lost; Kaloha was scarcely big enough for that.

She had been climbing steadily for a while, caught in this lonely refuge of indifference to her surroundings, when she noticed that the vanilla vines no longer wreathed their supporting trees and the undergrowth was dense and uncultivated. Outcrops of rock and basalt loomed ahead, and there was a subtle change in the quality of the silence. Tina, who was acutely sensitive to atmosphere, paused, looking about her, and suddenly realised where she was heading. The plantation was left behind and the path led up to the *marae*, the ancient temple which very few islands lacked.

Here, long ago, the priests invoked the gods to bestow their blessings, that the crops might be fruitful, the warriors triumphant, and the ocean yield up its living harvest. The islanders would offer prayers and gifts to evoke the vital *mana*, and after the rites there would be feasting and revelry, and dancing climaxing in the wild sexual abandon which had so horrified the first missionaries who stepped on Polynesia's shores.

Now the ancient slabs of stone stood desolate, the last of the sun striking its rays of dark fire across the time-blurred surfaces as Tina reached the site. She walked to a fern-edged stone, instinctively touching its surface before she sat. If a stone held moisture, warmth, it still lived, *tapu* ... So claimed superstition, and no islander would touch a sacred object. Still less would a Tahitian girl be here alone after nightfall.

110

Tina shivered. She should not have come this far. Already the sun was falling over the edge of the ocean, making the lagoon into a great mirror of glowing bronze far below, a bronze which would rapidly dim like the embers of a dying fire. She would be stumbling back down the path in the darkness, and Fay, knowing she was upset, would be starting to worry. Possibly she would send Pierre out to see if there was any sign of her. But nobody would think of looking up here . . .

Yet still Tina sat, unable to make the move that would break out of this strangely comforting limbo. Here she was free, to watch the red-gold miracle of transformation from day to night. The island was spread beneath her in a pattern of black silhouetted on copper, and across the lagoon the ring of rose-tinted surf pounded and frothed against the reef, making its strange wild music that rarely ceased. In a few minutes the lights of the evening fishermen would sparkle like glow-worms on the water, and the sound of guitars would strum their island serenades. It all added up to a magic that could never pall. Then there was a sharp sound, rough, like a falling stone, and Tina gave a start.

The spell was broken, and she shivered as a breeze curled round her bare shoulders. Wasn't it time she gave up being so impressionable? Life was too full of reality to escape for long. She got to her feet, hesitating as she wondered whether she should return the way she had come or take the other track down to the village. Then she remembered the rough-hewn steps, about twenty of them, and decided to take the plantation path. It would take longer, but there were no steps . . . She moved carefully across the now dark plateau, then froze as a deeper shadow wavered in the depths of the path below.

The shadow stilled, and she blinked, then it moved again and a white, faintly luminous blur swam into her vision. Tina gave a small gasp of fright and recoiled. Suddenly all the ancient lore of the islands, of rock spirits, of the dreaded *varua ino* and the *tupapau*, no longer seemed something a European would be reluctant to admit to his belief. Tina fought down the spasm of fear, told herself it was imagination, and took a determined step forward. Then she almost screamed aloud as a voice exclaimed sharply:

'Tina!'

With a sense of relief that made her go weak, she recognised the voice. The shadow and the white luminous blur of a silk shirt resolved into the figure of Max Thornton. He came towards her, and the timorous smile fell from her mouth before it had time to form as she distinguished the grimly startled lines of his face.

'What the devil are you doing sitting up here in the dark?' he demanded.

'Nothing,' her shoulders drooped and she turned away, 'I just came up to be alone, and think.'

'Not exactly the ideal spot for meditation, I'd have thought.'

'Maybe not.' She shrugged. 'I was just leaving, anyway.'

'Is something the matter?'

'Everything's the matter,' she returned tonelessly.

'Was that anything to do with your call in search of me a little while ago?'

'Oh ...' she glanced at him. 'Did Kim tell you?'

Max nodded. 'He also watched you take the hillside path.'

Tina considered this, and experienced a faint lightening of her mournful spirits. 'Is this why you—why you came up here?'

He looked down at her and avoided the inference. 'Is it urgent?'

She sighed. 'I don't know what to do. I came to ask your advice, but really, no one can decide but me.'

'Do you want to tell me about it?'

'I had another letter from England ...' Tina sank down on a dark stone, still warm from the departed sun, and in a flat tone recounted the contents of the second letter from her grandparents. 'I thought I'd settled it after the first one,' she added miserably.

'First one?'

The note of puzzlement surprised her, until she realised that he knew nothing of the previous letter. She said quickly, 'I forgot—I haven't seen you since the night of Corinne's party. The first letter came the next morning. I wrote back straight away to say what they suggested wasn't possible. I thought that would be the end of it. But it isn't—they must have written back the moment they got

112

my letter.'

There was a brief silence, then Max said quietly, 'What's wrong with going to see them? A trip to England could be the best thing in the world for you. Take your mind off all the unhappiness and uncertainty of these past weeks.'

'To leave here! Go to England!' Tina looked at him as though he'd suggested a trip to Mars. 'But the cost! Even if I wanted to go. Do you know what the air fare is from here to England?'

'I've a reasonably accurate idea,' he said in equable tones. 'I flew out myself not so long ago. And I gather they've already got that in hand,' he reminded her.

'Yes, but that's on the assumption I'm going to *live* with them! What if I hate it there? How would I get home again?' she cried. 'Oh, no, I couldn't bear to leave my home. Least of all on a one-way ticket.'

Max was silent. He drew a deep breath, then slowly seated himself at her side. 'There is a way,' he said at last.

'How?' she whispered despairingly.

'Be independent. Borrow your fare from a neutral source.'

'A neutral source?' she repeated. 'I don't understand.'

'People do, you know.'

'I can't see the bank lending me that sort of money—to leave with.'

'I wasn't thinking of the bank.'

'Where, then? I couldn't—wouldn't ask Aunt Wynne or Fay. And I'm not selling my home, not for anyone or anything.'

'Try asking me.'

The words dropped into the stillness with astounding clarity. 'You!' Her eyes rounded with amazement.

'Yes, me.' He smiled slightly.

'But——'

'Hear me out.' He put his hand over her wrist to quell her protest. 'Why not accept your grandparents' invitation, on the understanding that you are free to return to Tahiti after, say, three months? And I will arrange with my London banker to cover the cost of your return. That way you're safe. And it may make two elderly people very happy.'

For a long time she was silent. Coming as it had, totally unexpected, his offer had amazed her and now she did not know what to say. At last she turned and stared at him through the veiling darkness. 'Why are you offering to do this for me?' she whispered.

His expression remained unchanged, unreadable. 'I shouldn't try to dig into my motives, little one,' he said lightly. 'Just think it over.'

'Are you sorry for me?' she persisted. Suddenly it was of vital importance that she knew.

'I'd be inhuman if I weren't.'

'But I don't want you to feel sorry for me.'

His shoulders moved. 'Why not? You've had a rough deal.'

'I—I don't know what to say,' she sighed.

'Don't say anything. It's unnecessary.'

'But it is!' She felt his movement away from her and saw him get to his feet. Again there was that imperative sense of need, now coupled with urgency. Without pausing to check her own motives she sprang up and seized his hands. 'Max, it's terribly kind of you—I appreciate it, more than I can say. But I don't want you to feel that you have to—because you're sorry for me, and—and——'

Her voice tailed away, and she looked at him imploringly, scarcely realising that her hands were clinging to him and her body was pressing itself close to his tall, hard strength. Nor did she notice a sudden tensing of his shoulders and that there was no warmth of response in the hands within her urgent grasp.

He said evenly, 'You don't have to get worried about it, Tina.'

'But I can't help worrying. How can I accept all—all that money? I mean——'

'Yes, you mean what?' He was unmoving.

'Oh, I don't know!' With a mute gesture of despair she bowed her head and rested her forehead against his chest. 'One can't put some things into words. At least I can't.'

'No, I see that.' At last he moved, and with a deliberate movement he freed one hand and put it under her chin, forcing her to raise her head and look at him. He said coolly: 'Tina, what do you want me to be to you?'

She trembled, and drew back uncertainly. 'I—I don't understand. I don't know what you mean, Max.'

'I think you do.' His eyes were searching her small pale

114

features. 'But I'll be more explicit. Are you seeking a substitute for your father—in me?'

Shock parted her lips. 'No! No—how could you think such a thing,' she denied vehemently.

'Then what kind of relationship are you seeking?'

Suddenly she felt frightened. She began to stammer and shake her head. 'Isn't it obvious? So—so simple? Can't I have your friendship, without you—without you reading all kinds of—of psychological nonsense into it?'

He shook his head. 'There's nothing psychologically profound about it. And from my knowledge of you I have not come to expect emotional demonstrations of affectionate friendship such as this. In fact, I should say the reverse applies,' he added dryly.

She stiffened. 'How do you know? I happen to be a very affectionate person. And I thought, after——'

'You thought what?'

'I thought you were becoming a friend. Someone I could trust, like Fay, and Paul, and——'

'Don't try naïveté, Tina,' he cut in sharply. 'I'd much prefer honesty.'

'But I am honest!' she cried, and attempted an unsteady laugh. 'As for turning you into a father figure ... it's utterly ridiculous!'

'Is it?'

'Of course!'

'Then perhaps this is what you're seeking!'

Suddenly his hands closed on her shoulders and pulled her hard against him. Her start of shock and tentative beginnings of a struggle were ignored. Max folded first one arm, then the other close round her slender back and held her in an embrace from which there was little chance of escape. He said against the top of her head: 'I've no intention of being a father figure to any girl, even one as young and vulnerable as you, Tina. And there's another thing ...'

His hand slid up to the nape of her neck, cupped its slender stem and forced her head back till her quivering mouth was only an inch from his own. 'Don't you know that the kind of affectionate friendship you appear to need just isn't possible between a man and a woman?'

His mouth hovered, then descended to possess hers

with a fierceness that numbed Tina. She felt only the pressure of his arms like whipcord across her back, holding her immobile within their power, and this hard bruising kiss that was a far cry from the two gentle, sexless tokens which were the sum total of her tender experience with Max Thornton. Deep inside her came the knowledge that without realising it she had given him the impression she sought a romantic response from him, and he had misread her mute appeal as provocation. The numbing of senses abruptly dissolved and flutters of panic took its place. She dragged one hand free and pushed it against his chest, and then as suddenly the frail gesture of repudiation stilled. This was different. This was not the fear which was born when Pierre forced his kisses on her . . .

Of their own volition her fingers moved, to rest as timidly as thistledown on his shoulder and then curl about the open collar of his shirt. Something as basic and as old as time gave way in Tina's heart as her awakening woman's instinct sprang into sudden turbulent life. The long hard pressure of his body seemed to be making her melt against him, making her aware of every nerve and fibre of her being responding to his warm male dominance.

Suddenly she was clinging to him with all the passionate strength of her young arms, her tensed lips relaxing and parting to his demand. His hands moved convulsively over her body, moulding its new fervent pliancy, and she moaned softly with the unfamiliar aching desire they instilled. And then suddenly he thrust her away so violently she almost fell.

The world spun, and only his hand gripping her arm steadied her. A shudder ran through her, and she felt cold, deprived. His features were blurred in the darkness, and she began to tremble with another kind of fear. Why didn't he speak? Why did he just stand there, gripping her arm, after . . .? As though . . .

She took a shaky breath and faltered, 'Don't look at me like that! I'm sorry . . . but it wasn't my fault. You——'

'For God's sake, don't apologise! I might have known . . .' His tone was harsh and jerky. 'Oh, Tina—for a child of the islands you're incredibly naïve,' he groaned.

The sensation of chill and hurt was overwhelming now. One moment the world had stood still and it was as though she had found the end and the beginning of the meaning of her life. Now those brief moments of ecstasy had faded like a mirage, leaving only the need to escape and seek the solitude of a wounded animal. She dragged her arm free. 'I'm cold ... it's late ... I must get back ...'

'No!' The imperative command and his quick barring movement halted her flight. 'Do you want to break your leg, or something?'

'I'll have to risk that, won't I?'

'Tina, listen to me, before you fly off in a rage. Don't you realise——?'

'I'm not in a rage!' she cried. 'Though I should be after that kind of treatment! You——'

'All right!' His tone quietened, but there was a grim note in it. 'But if you're going to get into an emotional lather every time a man kisses you it's time you faced a few facts of life.'

She recoiled. 'How dare you? You started it! You'—emotion almost choked her—'you started it, and then——'

'Yes, I'll admit it.' He sighed heavily. 'And cavalier treatment it must seem. But I had little option.'

'I didn't ask you to start kissing me!'

'No?' His mouth compressed grimly. He put his hands on her shoulders and said more gently: 'Tina, don't you know that a kiss eventually brings a turning point?'

Already the chill warning of inhibition had brought this knowledge. But she stood stubbornly under the warm weight of his hands and shook her head. 'Weren't you taking me a bit too seriously?' she defended.

'I think perhaps I didn't take you seriously enough. The turning point came more quickly than I ever imagined,' he said dryly. 'I'll have to remember that another time.'

'What makes you think there's going to be another time?'

'I'm not going to think anything. And I think it might be better if you didn't. No'—he shook his head as she opened her mouth to retort—'let me finish. There are other things of greater importance. The matter we were discussing.'

The subject of discussion prior to that heartbreaking interlude seemed to have receded far into the distance. Reminded of it, and the offer he had made, she said coldly: 'If you imagine I could accept that now, after ...'

'Why not? Should a kiss make any difference?' Unbe-
lievably his teeth glimmered in a smile. 'It doesn't make
the slightest difference as far as I'm concerned. Nor should
it to you.'

His hands fell from her shoulders and a moment later a
torch beam stabbed the darkness, sending great wavering
black shadows across the uneven ground. He took her arm.
'Come on, I'll take you back. You're coming to have a quick
drink with me, you're not going to say another word until
then, and by then you're going to forget we ever had such
a disastrous kiss. Come on, Tina,' he repeated, and urged
her forward.

Her surge of temper had already ebbed, and it seemed
easier to obey than try to fight, even though the not yet
appeased spirit of pride scorned her weakness. But it was
true; something held her in thrall to this man, had done
so ever since the first moment she met him, she thought
bitterly, and despite everything she could not bear the
thought of being away from him.

In the silence he had ordained she let him guide her
down the long winding path, and the warm firm grasp on
her arm did not once relax its care.

She had never been as close to Max Thornton as tonight,
and never so far ...

CHAPTER SEVEN

ALL during the half hour which followed Tina was unable
to shake off a sense of unreality as she sat in Henri Latour's
shabby living room and sipped the drink Max had fixed for
her. Listening to and looking at him, she thought they
might have been two casual acquaintances of long standing,
who had never had the inclination to encourage acquaintanceship to develop into friendship. He was so polite, cool,
almost detached, as though those fraught moments and
that passionate prelude to love had happened to two other
people up in the eerie darkness of the *marae*.

Max relaxed in a chair, asked after the twins and expressed concern over little Jacques' mishap, and confided
that he was worried about Henri Latour.

'The doctor is of the opinion that Henri should retire, and certainly he must not live alone in future.'

'But his son is coming home. Surely he will care for his father?' said Tina.

'Alex will never stay. This visit is the result of a guilty conscience and one of those sudden impulses better left dormant. This one will do more harm than good.'

Tina stared. It seemed a strange observation. Why should a reunion between father and son bring harm? If rumour were true a bitter family quarrel was to be healed, so why did Max appear to think Alex's visit a mistake? She waited, but Max did not seem disposed to enlarge on his reasons. In fact, he dismissed the subject and asked if her drink was all right.

'Yes, thank you.' Suddenly she felt deathly tired and dispirited. His very politeness was a barrier to keep her at a distance. She said abruptly: 'I'd better go . . .'

He stood up. 'I'll get you something to slip round your shoulders.'

'You always seem to be lending me things . . .'

He did not reply, going from the room and returning a few moments later with a lightweight beige and brown safari jacket over his arm. As he came through the doorway Tina noticed the two cases, one a small overnight bag, the other a grey soft-top, standing just to the left of the door and obviously packed.

She exclaimed, 'Are you going away?'

'For a few days.' He vouchsafed no further information and held out the jacket for her.

She slipped her arms into its over-large contours and turned to face him. The brief touch of his hands fell away, and a whimsical smile touched his mouth. 'You'd better push the sleeves up a bit.'

For a moment she thought he was going to take her hands and roll up the spare length of sleeves in the way a parent dresses a very young child. Her control almost snapped and a great anguish constricted her throat. The longing to go into his arms was unbearable, to feel the hard lean shape of his face warm against hers, to hold him close for ever . . .

Tina fought down the crazy weakness and averted her face. How foolish could she get? To want a man who was merely sorry for her, who in a weak moment, because of that pity, had taken her in his arms, only to make it clear beyond all misunderstanding that he had made a blunder ...

She said curtly: 'You don't need to see me back—I'll go along the beach.'

'I don't need to, but I'm going to.' The brief humour had left his mouth, and his eyes were hard as he waited for her to precede him.

She brushed past, out to where the bike waited and the brief ride along the night-shrouded track to the hotel. She sat stiffly upright, clutching the sides of the pillion seat, determined to fall off rather than subdue pride and take the support of that broad strong waist. This time Max made no comment, neither edict nor invitation, and when they reached the clearing near the hotel he did not dismount.

As she got down he said coolly: 'You can think it over and let me know when I get back.'

She stood huddled in the big jacket. 'I've already thought it over. I can't accept your offer.'

'Why not?'

'Because I may not be able to pay you back.'

He sat there, astraddle the machine, and eyed her impassively. 'I'm aware of that risk.'

'So you see, it isn't practical.' She attempted flippancy. 'I probably wouldn't live long enough to pay it off in easy instalments.'

An unwilling flicker disturbed his mouth. 'At eighteen! According to statistical averages you should have an approximate expectancy of at least another fifty-two years.'

But Tina's heart was too sore to respond to teasing. She said bitterly, 'Maybe, but the joke's gone far enough, Max. You didn't really expect me to take you up on it, did you?'

'Actually, I did,' was the calm reply. 'I'm not in the habit of joking about finance, Tina, still less about the kind of situation in which you seem to be caught. But maybe I'm taking it too seriously. You're a very difficult girl to help.'

'I don't want that kind of help.'

'I'm beginning to realise that.'

The grim note sharpening his voice stabbed into her

mood of self-pity. She cried wildly, 'And it's time you realised I'm no longer a child to be talked down to, and analysed, and advised to do this, or that!'

'Would you take advice?' he asked coldly. 'I doubt it.'

Suddenly she knew an overwhelming desire to lash out at him, to hurt him as much as he had hurt her. 'Not your kind of advice! It's easy to offer money if you have plenty! Do you really believe that it can solve everything?' The words tumbled wildly from her now, and she took a step forward into the brilliant radius of the light. 'Well, it can't! And money is the last kind of help I want from you! Not now! Not after——'

'Tina!'

The shocked voice came not from the man on the machine but from the shadows behind her, and she whirled round, to find Pierre opening the garden gate. He looked alarmed and surprised, his glance going from her to the dark figure astride the bike. He exclaimed, '*Chérie*, what is the matter? Is——'

With a choked little cry Tina ran to him and without hesitation he caught her in his arms. She was crying now, partly with relief at escape from a situation fast becoming intolerable and partly with horror at the things she had been goaded to say, but mostly with the sudden heart-breaking knowledge that tonight something had been destroyed beyond recall. She clung to Pierre while he stroked her hair and murmured soft words of comfort. In the distance she heard the revs of the machine, and glimpsed the swinging rays of light, then silence settled with the curls of dust and there was only the soft golden fall from the lantern above the gate. Max had gone.

Slowly she withdrew from Pierre's arms and shook her head at his puzzled query.

'I'm sorry, Pierre. It was nothing.' She sniffed miserably and began to stumble across the garden towards the hotel while Pierre hurried to her side, his face full of concern. When they reached the terrace he stopped and caught her arm.

'What did Thornton say to you, *chérie*? Why did he offer you money? I do not understand.'

There was deep suspicion in his tone, and Tina said desperately, 'No, it wasn't about money. I—I'd rather not talk about it, Pierre.'

'But I heard you say you would not want that kind of help,' he persisted. 'You cried that money was the last thing you wanted, *Chérie*, what is going on between you and Max Thornton?'

'There is nothing going on between me and Max Thornton,' she said tiredly, and felt the ache of unshed tears still catching at her throat. That was the whole trouble: nothing! she thought miserably, and she had forced a full-scale quarrel to blow up because——

Sick at heart, Tina tried to close her mind to the truth; she had made a fool of herself up at the *marae*, and Max Thornton had tried to forestall her before foolishness became folly. Oh, why couldn't she accept the fact that Max Thornton was not a soft, indulgent type of man, given to the kind of tender gallantry at which Pierre was so adept? The trouble was, that came to Pierre as naturally as donning a favourite garment—and as easily discarded. But Max Thornton was different ...

'And this!' Pierre touched the jacket she was still wearing. Suspicion flooded his handsome olive features again. 'This belongs to him, does it not?'

'Yes, but——'

'I do not like it. I do not like this man Thornton either. And I do not like you wearing his possessions,' Pierre said grimly. 'It betokens an intimacy between man and woman.'

'Oh, Pierre, it doesn't!' *If only it did*, her heart sighed.

'It looks absurd. Take it off!'

'I'm going to!' She seized the excuse to escape and almost ran to the stairs before he could argue further. But she had scarcely entered her room after a shower and change into a cool rose cotton kaftan than Fay tapped at the door.

Plainly Fay had already received a highly embroidered account of the upset from her brother-in-law and now looked for enlightenment. But for once Tina felt unable to confide, even in Fay, and she shook her head. 'It was nothing, Fay,' she said dully. 'I was stupid enough to ask for advice, and disliked what I got. You know what Max is like.'

'Yes, a thorny creature if one got on the wrong side of him, I imagine.' Fay's eyes were sympathetic, none the less, they held a shrewd intentness as they searched Tina's

122

despondent face. 'He's the typical arrogant, know-all male —the chill English variety as well, which makes it worse. But what is this thing about money?'

Tina sighed. She might as well get it over with. Not looking at Fay, she said flatly: 'Max thinks I should go to England for three months, then come back if I don't like it there. He offered to lend me the money for my fare home if I got stranded.'

There was a silence. Then Fay sat down on the end of the bed. 'Well, what was there to get steamed up about in that? It sounds a very practical suggestion. It's also a very kind one. Unless . . .' Fay stopped, and she frowned. 'How were you going to repay the debt? And why did you go to Max? Surely, if money was worrying you, *we* should be the first you think of coming to?'

'Oh, no!' Tina groaned at the sight of hurt dawning in Fay's sweet features. 'It wasn't like that at all! I never even mentioned money! That was what the argument was about.'

Fay was silent again. She bit her lip, then said sharply, 'Are you sure that was all?'

'Of course it was all.'

'Well, it doesn't seem to tie up. At least you could have thanked him . . . even if . . .' Fay paused. 'Even if he suggested it in the autocratic way I imagine he would, you could have avoided an argument over it.'

'I did thank him.' Tina stared at the floor and wanted more than anything in the world to be left alone at that moment.

As though she sensed this Fay stood up, but her expression was troubled. At last she said helplessly, 'Well, for goodness' sake, don't take it to heart.'

'I'm not.'

'No?' Fay looked down at the bowed head, and her mouth compressed. 'You haven't suddenly taken a header for him, have you?'

The sudden homing to target jolted Tina's head up. 'No!' she denied, aghast. Was it so obvious to others, even before she realised it herslf? 'Fay, you know I don't like him!'

'So you've always professed. But maybe it's the kind of dislike which is the most dangerous of all,' Fay said slowly.

'What do you mean?'

'The kind that is really love.'

Tina jumped up and went to the dressing table, to snatch up a brush and begin feverishly tugging at her hair. 'You're imagining things.'

'Am I? I wonder,' said Fay quietly. 'If you dislike him so much then why go to him for advice?'

'Because I—Oh, Fay!' Tina dropped the brush and put her hands to her head, 'I don't want to talk about Max Thornton. And I don't want anything to eat—I've got a splitting headache.'

If Fay suspected an excuse she gave no sign, merely saying softly, 'You'd better take some aspirins and rest for a while.'

Tina, of course, did not have any, and Fay went downstairs in search of them. Tina gulped them down with a drink of water, then managed a tremulous smile of gratitude. 'You spoil me—I don't deserve it.'

'You've done the same for me—on a similar occasion,' Fay observed dryly. 'Remember?'

Tina nodded. Fay's romance with Paul had held its stormy moments, and Tina remembered them very well. But she was still unwilling to venture confidences about the real reason for her present disturbed state of mind.

Fay walked to the door. 'You'll feel better in the morning.'

But Tina didn't. She was too beset by the agonies of indecision and the constant awareness of the letter waiting to be answered, and all the time there was this dark, disturbing heartache each time the thought of Max Thornton came to mind—which was very frequently. He refused to be banished, and in moments of weakness the persistent little inquest would start its mental spiral again. Why had he kissed her the way he had? Why had he made that strange, generous offer? Why, if he was sorry for her, did he behave so brusquely? Didn't he feel any affection for her? Even Tina's limited experience of men told her that a man didn't kiss a girl unless she held some stirrings of attraction for him—or unless he simply wanted a woman in the crudest physical sense. And didn't his subsequent behaviour rule out that dissolute possibility? Didn't he have any feeling for her at all?

It was the question of all questions, and she could find

124

no answer that held even the faintest spark of hope. For Max had never sought her company, except on that one occasion of Corinne's party. And he had made no secret of his motive that time. Perhaps he had stumbled upon the truth, she thought miserably. Perhaps she did subconsciously seek a replacement to fill the dreadful void her father's disappearance had left in her life. But when she remembered her own awakening reaction to Max Thornton's kisses, a rising tide of rapture that even now set every nerve alive at the memory, she knew that Max had found no truth. Had he since guessed the real truth? Had she betrayed her true feeling? And had he chosen that way to divert her ...?

Tina's heart chilled at the thought, and more and more she became convinced that she had hit on the truth. With this perturbing fear came the first serious thought of accepting her grandmother's invitation.

It was Pierre's idea that she should accompany him to Papeete two days later and while seeing to supplies and various business matters concerning the hotel they should inquire at the bank about the draft Mrs Kingman had mentioned. It was a new clerk, who did not recognize Tina, and they had to wait a few minutes while he looked up her account.

Tina did not speak. She hoped that the answer would be in the negative; somehow this would postpone her decision a while longer. Then she saw the clerk returning and read the answer on his smiling face.

Yes, the draft had come through.

'You still do not have to be influenced by that,' Pierre told her, when they were sitting in the pleasant little café frequented by the locals. 'Provided you do not use their money you are under no obligation.'

Tina sipped her aperitif. She had thought of this a myriad times, yet how could she simply ignore the matter? Hadn't she vowed each evening to get out pen and notepaper and write to her grandmother? And hadn't indecision and reluctance won each time?

'You do not have to go!' Pierre said vehemently. 'Why do you not write that letter and finish the matter?'

She looked up at him, desperately wanting to be convinced. Of them all, Pierre was the only one who did not try to persuade her that it would be for the best, as though in some magical way the journey to a new life in England, among strangers, would wipe out the grief of loss and make her forget. As if she could! Even if she were to sail to the far ends of the earth it would not alter the fact that her life had reached the end of happiness, and destiny showed no pointers towards the beginning of a new era of hope. Wouldn't it be foolish to seek it so far away from everything and everyone she knew and loved?

A whimsical smile curved Pierre's mouth as he watched the play of emotion on her wan little face, and suddenly she warmed to him. She managed a smile. 'You always did see things straight without the fog of indecision. I wish it were as easy.'

'Why shouldn't it be? These strangers in England; you have never met them. How can they mean anything to you?'

'I don't know...' She sighed and returned to her lobster bisque. 'Perhaps I'm beginning to see things differently. I know now what it means to be lonely, to lose someone you love dearly. Sometimes I think of my grandparents all those miles away. Perhaps they're lonely. They lost their only daughter, and never saw her again after one brief visit before she came out to the islands with my father. Then they wanted me, after she died. I didn't want to go, and my father refused to go back. Now they must be old, and I wonder if I should try to forget old bitterness.'

'I think you would be foolish. You have said yourself that they are autocratic and stern,' Pierre reminded her. 'My brother and Fay have discussed this with me many times and they are deeply worried. We hate to see you so unhappy and unsettled, *chérie*. It can't go on.'

'I try to think what my father would wish me to do,' she said slowly. She looked up, beyond Pierre's dark head, as though she sought to read the future's answer, and then the unseeing mist in her eyes cleared. Corinne was entering the restaurant.

For a moment Tina thought the French girl had not seen them. She was moving towards the bamboo trellis which screened the bar from the dining area. Then Corinne turned her head and checked. A smile lit her face and she came towards their table.

There was the usual conventional exchange of greetings, and Pierre added: 'Won't you join us?'

Corinne shook her head. 'I am meeting a friend—he may be waiting.' She glanced towards the bar, then bent slightly towards Pierre. 'But ask me again at the weekend, *mon ami.* I will be visiting my father.'

Pierre looked up into her vivacious face, so near his own, and an enigmatic light glowed in his dark eyes. 'I thought you would be otherwise engaged, *chérie*, but *certainement!* As you wish.'

'I will see you, then.' Corinne shot a smile at Tina, in which a hint of triumph lurked. 'On Kaloha one must make one's own amusement, is that not so?'

Tina nodded, and the blonde girl took her hand from Pierre's shoulder. Then, as she seemed about to turn away, she asked casually: 'Is Max back?'

With an effort Tina kept her face expressionless. 'I don't know.'

Pierre said nothing, and Corinne shrugged. 'He is a most infuriating man for keeping secrets. Not a word could I get out of him about his journey. Not even where is his destination! One would almost imagine he had something to hide.'

'Perhaps he has,' Pierre said darkly.

'*Non!* Pierre, you are so suspicious!'

'I see no mystery in that so cold Englishman to excite intrigue in a feminine heart,' Pierre returned with a hint of acerbity, and Corinne laughed.

'Ah, but you do not have a feminine heart, *mon ami.*'

Her amused glance sought Tina's, as though for feminine confirmation of this undoubted fact, but Tina looked away. She could not bear this cross-talk much longer, not while it centred on this particular subject. Fortunately for her, the tall, flaxen-haired man who had just entered proved to be Corinne's date, and after a hurried farewell she moved eagerly in his direction.

'An American,' Pierre observed with scarcely concealed dislike as the unmistakable drawl of greeting to 'Honey' floated across the room. Pierre watched the American smile down at Corinne and then place a possessive arm round her waist as the couple turned to enter the cocktail bar. When Pierre looked back at Tina his mouth had compressed into tight, sulky lines.

Noticing this, Tina sighed and remained silent. She knew that Pierre was not enamoured of Americans, nor, for that matter, of the English, but there seemed to be something more than casual, scarcely formed prejudice eating him at the moment. However, she felt too dispirited herself to probe sympathetically, or take up verbal cudgels in defence of the English and their sister race. In any case, nothing would influence Pierre's opinions once he had formed them, no matter how baseless might be his reasons.

He was unusually quiet during the return trip. To make things worse the weather turned squally and the crossing was rough. Tina clung to the rail, unwilling to retreat to the shelter of the saloon, where it would be hot and oppressive, and tried not to think of the expression in Corinne's eyes as she had spoken of Max. Tina had always suspected that Corinne was attracted to Max; now she was certain. But was Max . . . ?

She stared across the grey, choppy expanse and tried to shut her mind to futile speculation. She was foolish to care whether or not the French girl and Max Thornton were attracted to one another. The only thing that mattered to her was Max's feeling concerning herself. And he had made that perfectly clear already. So summon pride, and forget him, her tired brain urged.

She felt sickly and heavy-headed by the time she was back at the hotel. Her appetite was non-existent and she could scarcely eat any of the superb new prawn mousse which Jules was trying out on the menu that evening. When it was over she excused herself before Fay could start asking well-meant questions and went to her room. She really must write that letter. She couldn't go on putting off the task indefinitely.

But once in her room, confronted by silence and the blank sheet of notepaper, she threw down the pen and got to her feet to pace restlessly across the floor. How was she to make this decision? When every instinct recoiled from taking this step into the unknown? And yet if she refused, what then? Accept Fay's offer? Or return to Papeete and try to draw up the threads of a new life, alone?

Suddenly the room seemed stifling, and a wave of self-pity engulfed her. Why didn't her grandparents give her more time? Didn't they realise she needed time to accept that her life had changed its course? If there had been warm friendship sensed across the sea's distance, remembered throughout childhood and the onset of adulthood, it might have been easier. But there had been only the sense of bitterness passed and indifference in those long silences between the cold, conventional message that marked each Christmas since as long as Tina could remember. And now they had decided to take over her future.

Abruptly she switched off her lamp and let herself out by the veranda door. Shoulders hunched moodily, she wandered along the terrace and down the shallow steps into the garden. There was no one about, and the beach was deserted as she stood by the edge of the velvet dark sea. She listened to the sound of the ceaseless surf against the reef, and the real truth beat as remorselessly against her heart. She couldn't leave the islands. For one reason only. Not because they were her home, but because they held her lodestar. Max Thornton ...

She kicked disconsolately at a small tussock of weed near her feet. Why not admit it? Max Thornton was the one being in her existence who held the power to make her whole world spin right up to heaven. Maybe if she faced it, cried out her heart's longing, tried to analyse why it should be so, she might discover it to be only loneliness masquerading as longing. Perhaps after all her subconscious was seeking a strength and security to fill the great gap left in her life ...

But even after the doubt Max himself had sought to sow was faced and considered she knew it to be baseless. When she looked back, right to that day three years ago, she knew that Max Thornton's attraction had been a potent force seeking to invade her heart. It had taken that night up at the *marae* to tear the veil of ignorance from her eyes.

'*Chérie*, what is the matter?'

Tina cried aloud with shock as Pierre's voice spoke softly at her shoulder and his hands closed on her arms. She gasped: 'Pierre, you startled me—I never heard you.'

'I'm sorry.' His hands feathered lightly up and down the smooth skin of her upper arms. 'Why are you out here alone?'

'I—I just wanted to think.'

'Of what?' He drew her back against his chest. 'Don't tell

me you are still worrying about that same problem.'

'How can I help worrying?' she said a little wildly.

'I thought we had settled it.'

'It isn't settled as easily as that.' She drew a deep sighing breath and broke away from his hold. 'If only it were!'

He was silent for a moment, then he moved forward on quick noiseless steps to narrow the distance she had put between them. 'Tina ...'

She turned wearily, every nerve recoiling from yet another resumption of a now painful discussion. She shook her head. 'I'm tired, Pierre. I don't want to talk about it any more.'

'I do not wish you to talk about it. I wish you to listen.'

'There's nothing else to say. No one can make the decision but me.'

'Not even if I have found a solution?'

She smiled faintly. 'There is no solution. I either go or I stay here. Sounds simple, doesn't it?'

'My idea is the best answer.'

Her eyes narrowed, even as a flicker of hope stirred. What did Pierre mean? 'And what is your idea?'

'That you stay here—and marry me.'

'What!' Tina gasped, wondering if she had heard the words or imagined them. 'What did you say?'

'I said: marry me,' he repeated distinctly.

Tina still could not believe it. A proposal from Pierre was the last thing she had expected. He couldn't be serious!

'Oh, Pierre,' she said wearily, 'please don't joke. This is no time for it.'

He looked hurt and astounded. 'But I assure you; I never joke about marriage!'

'But ...' Incredulous, she saw that he was indeed serious.

He came closer. 'Why shouldn't we marry? After all, I have to marry someone. You have to marry someone. It is expected. So why should we not marry each other?'

This somewhat lopsided logic struck Tina as quite the most cold-blooded reason ever put forward for marriage and for a moment she could only stare at him in amazement. Then she said helplessly, 'But what about Madeleine? I thought you were still in love with her, and still ...' she stopped, shaking her head bewilderedly.

Pierre gave a short laugh. 'That is in the past, *chérie*. I cannot waste my future in vain regrets for a faithless love. Today is today, and one must try to make it a happy yesterday.'

Tina looked away. There was a harsh note in his voice which belied the glib philosophy. Yes, Pierre was glib in so many ways; why had she not realised this before? She said slowly: 'I was beginning to suspect that you were not quite so heartbroken as you would have us believe.'

He shrugged. 'It is expected of a betrayed husband for a little while, is it not?' When she did not immediately respond he put out one hand and cupped her chin. 'Well, my *petite* Luana, what have you to say to me?'

She turned her face from his touch. 'Only that you surprised me. I was under the impression that you had transferred your affection to Corinne.'

'Corinne!' He started, and she saw the dancing lights come into his eyes. 'Ah, yes ... So you have noticed.'

'I could hardly do anything else, after watching you at the party and last weekend,' she returned with some asperity. 'And now you start talking about marriage to me. Do you wonder I don't take you seriously?'

'Are you jealous?'

'Of Corinne? Not in the least. Why don't you try proposing to her instead?'

'Oh, no!' Pierre shook his head, and now the amusement had left his face. 'I do not care to be used by feminine schemers.'

'Is Corinne a schemer?'

'She most certainly is.'

'In what way?'

Pierre gave an incredulous laugh, but there was little mirth in it. 'Have you not guessed, my sweet innocent?'

'Guessed what?' But already a chill had touched Tina, and she thought she knew.

Bitter cynicism curved Pierre's mouth. 'Corinne has her sets—no, how do you say it?—her sights firmly set on another.'

There was a silence. Then Tina whispered, 'Who—what do you mean, Pierre?'

'She wants Thornton.'

The disgust in his voice soured the sweet night fragrance. Tina closed her eyes. 'You mean Max?'

131

'Yes. And I am not prepared to be the lever of his jealousy,' Pierre said grimly.

All her dimly sensed fears crystallised into painful reality. She murmured, 'Oh, no, I don't believe it.'

'It is true enough. Does she think I do not recognise such a very old feminine trick? To pretend affection for one man in the endeavour to make another jealous?'

Tina's shoulders felt as though a weight of sorrow had descended on them. It all seemed so clear now, and difficult to discredit. But didn't Max realise? She thought of him loving Corinne, wanting her, and the thought was like the kiss of gall. Suddenly she turned away from Pierre and said raggedly: 'Isn't that what you are trying to do yourself? Use me in an attempt to provoke Corinne?'

'I would not pretend that it would not give me great satisfaction to let Corinne see that she is not so vitally important to my peace of mind as she imagines. And as for you, *chérie*,' Pierre paused, and his tone deepened with meaning, 'would it not give you an equal satisfaction?'

'Why should it?'

'Oh, come, little one,' Pierre gave a one-sided smile. 'Your own feeling for Thornton is not exactly a secret.'

'What do you mean?' she gasped. 'How do you know that?' Too late she realised she had given herself away. 'Don't be silly! Max Thornton and I are scarcely friends, let alone anything else.'

But her denial was in vain. Pierre's hands closed round her shoulders and his teeth glinted in a smile of disbelief. 'I'm aware of that, *chérie*. I am also aware that it is scarcely your fault.'

'What do you mean?' she faltered.

'That should be obvious. Why prevaricate? It is in your eyes each time you merely hear his name mentioned.'

Tina's hands clenched until the nails bit into the palms. Was she as transparent as all that? She became aware of Pierre awaiting her response, and sensed something almost like triumph emanating from him. She said angrily, 'That's nonsense! You're imagining things.'

'I do not think so.' Her anger seemed only to amuse him. 'Why do you worry?' he asked smoothly. 'You will soon forget him.'

Her anger died as quickly as it had been born. 'There's

132

nothing to forget,' she murmured sadly.

'Good. Then perhaps you are ready to consider my question.' His hands tightened and he made to draw her closer.

She stood stiffly under their pressure and shook her head. 'I'm sorry, Pierre. I believe you do mean it. But it wouldn't work.'

'Why not? You loved me once: I will make you love me again.' He bent his head, until his lips almost touched hers. 'You see, *chérie*, I know how important it is to a woman that she should love—and be loved.'

The wind whispered through the palms and the sea sighed to the dark skies above. Tina felt Pierre's breath come softly against her cheek, and for a moment she stood unresisting. An echo of past enchantment stirred in her heart, and she knew an almost overwhelming temptation to take the balm of Pierre's kiss. She longed for love, and if she could never have Max ...

A soft exclamation of triumph escaped Pierre and his arms tightened about her slender body as his mouth swooped to make its claim. Tina's eyes closed, and against the darkness within them she saw Max Thornton's lean, unsmiling face. A shudder ran through her and she knew the bitterness of delusion, and something like shame. She wrenched free and stared at Pierre with distraught eyes.

'No! I can't! I'm sorry, Pierre, but I can't!'

Before he could speak she turned and fled with anguished steps to the concealing shadows of the garden. She was breathless and near to tears when she reached her room, and thankful that she encountered no one on the way. At that moment she could not have borne curious eyes or explanations.

After a little while she regained a measure of calm, and then the guilt began. Oh, why had she allowed Pierre to believe, even though only for seconds, that she was experiencing a change of heart? Even though Pierre's motives left a great deal to be desired ethically, and at this very moment he was probably indulging the temper of frustration with alcohol, she had betrayed her own code of honour.

Tina sank down on her bed and gave way to the tears of self-disgust. For the folly of temptation to assuage in the arms of one man her futile longing for another ...

The torments of conscience haunted Tina all through that sleepless night, and she arose next morning, wan and dark-eyed, ill-equipped to face the shock that the new day brought.

The arrival of her grandparents from England!

CHAPTER EIGHT

ANY thought of her grandparents was far from Tina's mind when she awakened that morning. There was the recall of Pierre's bitter proposal, with all the subsequent little by-ways of worry to which this thought led, and then the in-evitable hope that Max Thornton might return this day.

It was a forlorn hope for which she despised herself, but one she still could not banish, even as she told herself how vain and foolish it was to imagine that he would seek her out the moment he returned. He had said 'a few days'. How long was a few days? Certainly long enough to realise that when a man was interested in a girl he usually sought her out, made no secret of the fact that he desired her com-pany, desired her ... But what had occurred ever to betray this kind of interest from Max Thornton? Nothing. Only one kiss that she had almost begged for, she told herself scornfully; one kiss of which he had made no secret of its lack of importance as far as she was concerned ...

'Oh, God,' she whispered aloud to the empty morning, 'how does one stop loving a man?'

She was thankful that there was no sign of Pierre at breakfast, and Fay was too preoccupied by a small domestic problem to notice that Tina was more withdrawn than ever that morning. Afterwards, when Tina went to take over her spell on reception, she was deeply involved in the queries of an elderly guest when Pierre entered. He gave her a wry little salute, in which thankfully she read no indication of huffiness, and went on towards Paul's office. Rosa appeared a few minutes later, still wan but assuring everyone that she was feeling much better now that the early stage of pregnancy was past. The problem of petite waistbands which no longer encompassed a once very petite waist now troubled Rosa, and for a few minutes she and Tina stood discussing the matter of clothes that must be chic as well as comfortable for the mother-to-be.

'I hate ze tent kind!' Rosa exclaimed, with an expressive gesture in front of her stomach. '*Mon Dieu!*—when I think of myself in three more months ...'

'And then another three months,' broke in Fay mischievously, coming to join them now that she was free of an inquiring guest. 'By then you will no longer care how you look, *chérie.*'

'Don't depress her,' Tina chided.

'And what do you know about it?' Fay teased. She gave a reminiscent chuckle. 'Oh, that wonderful moment when I looked down at my toes and realised I was flat again!'

Rosa made a face. 'The voice of experience—I do not think I want to hear any more!' She glanced towards the entrance and gave a small exclamation before she darted away abruptly.

She had seen the boy from the village approaching. He sometimes brought messages or helped with supplies, and Fay moved away as well when she saw him handing something to Rosa.

Left alone, Tina tidied the already tidy array of books, pamphlets and sundry articles that lay on the reception desk, no presentiment of anything untoward entering her mind. The casual little exchange with Fay and Rosa had evoked a hitherto unimagined daydream. What would it be like to hold her own baby in her arms? Max's baby ...?

The delicate tinge of colour brightened in her cheeks as Fay re-entered and came towards her. She forced a smile to hide the effect of that foolish, intimate fancy, then saw no answering smile lighting Fay's serious mouth.

Fay said abruptly: 'Prepare yourself for a shock before you read this—they came yesterday.'

'Who? What ...?' Tina stared at her friend, then at the envelope Fay was holding out.

'They tried to get a message to you last night,' Fay was saying, 'but without success, and Mrs Kingman was too tired to face any more travelling. She wanted to go straight to the hotel.'

'*Your grandmother would like to see you as soon as possible.*' The lines of writing in Aunt Wynne's familiar hand blurred and wavered before Tina's eyes. She could scarcely take it in. Her grandparents were here. *Here!* At least they

135

were in Tahiti. A few sea miles away. She could not believe it.

She shook her head, and Fay exclaimed, 'It's true, Tina. For goodness' sake don't stand there like that. You'll have to get over there as quickly as possible. I'll find Paul ...'

Despite her gentle disposition Fay could be both brisk and authoritative, and in a very short time she had urged Tina into a change into more formal dress, requested her husband to organise transport, and assured Tina that this unexpected development was the best thing that could have happened.

'It's going to settle things one way or another,' she asserted firmly as Tina boarded the launch. 'Now don't look so worried! I'm sure they're going to be charming, and within an hour or so you're going to be wondering why you were so scared.'

If only Fay was right! Tina watched the bright water sparkling under the brilliant sun and wished her hands didn't feel so icy. Suddenly memory began to throw up all the bitterness of past dissent, and tremors of fear prickled along Tina's nerve endings. What if her grandparents still harboured all that long era of resentment? How was she going to parry it? A long-past quarrel in which she had no volition, yet it was one in which she had been inextricably involved. For they had wanted her all those years ago. Even before the moment of her birth, when they had wanted their daughter to return home to have her baby in England. Where they could care for her and their first grandchild. But her mother had refused, and Tina had been born in her South Sea Island home. Then they had wanted her to be educated in England, and again Beth Raimond had made the agonising decision to forswear parental influence; her husband had chosen to make his home in Tahiti, and so that was home to his wife and his children ... There the matter had rested, until Beth's second child came, with the sudden complication that brought double tragedy. And then had come the bitter recrimination which John Raimond had had to face. Now there was no gently, tactful Beth to heal the fast widening rift, and John Raimond had been too bereft to care ...

Tina shivered, and looked at the silent figure of Pierre. He had insisted on bringing her over, but how could she go

136

to him for reassurance after last night? As though he sensed her appeal he turned his head and shot her a wry smile.

'So you will probably be leaving us after all, *ma chère*.'

'I—I don't know.' She stared at the outline of Papeete's waterfront, rapidly coming nearer. 'Oh, I wish they hadn't come.'

Pierre shrugged. For a moment he was silent, then he said slowly: 'No, I think it is, as Fay says, for the best.'

'Why?'

'Because it forces you to a decision.'

She said bitterly, 'It's a decision I should not have to make. To me they are strangers. I don't know them, Pierre. Surely you can understand how I feel.'

'I understand too well, *chérie*.' His mouth curved down. 'I think your trouble is that you do not like to hurt people's feelings—except mine, of course.'

Tina bit her lip. Had she made a bad error of judgement? Had her refusal gone more deeply than she imagined? For a moment she was tempted to soften, then in time she restrained the impulse. What good would it do to reopen the subject of his proposal? Far better to leave well alone ...

Again he seemed to perceive her indecision when he had nosed the launch expertly into its mooring place and helped her ashore. 'Well, *chérie*, what now? Do you wish me to accompany you?'

'To the hotel?' Tina looked blank. It had not yet occurred to her that Pierre would land her and then leave her to go alone to meet her grandparents. It was the more obvious course, but suddenly she discovered that she wanted his company very much. 'Would you, Pierre? If you have time ...'

She did not realise how much appeal was in her eyes, and Pierre's sardonic grin softened. 'What does time matter? If you need me to give you—how do you say it?—a moral support.'

Tina's giggle held a tinge of hysteria. 'Did you say immoral support, Pierre! I don't think my grandparents would approve of that.'

Pierre's grin vanished and he assumed a shocked expression. 'You know perfectly well what I mean. But I am prepared to provide both versions if you should so wish.'

'Oh, Pierre, are you ever serious?' she exclaimed as he chuckled and tucked a cool hand under her arm to see her across the bustle of the waterfront.

'I have tried being serious, but where did it get me?' He drew her protectively close as a car shot across their path. 'Remember, I am also prepared to marry the girl.'

She shot a quick glance up into his darkly handsome features and saw his eyes were narrowed intently. With a start of surprise she realised that Pierre had subtly changed during the weeks since his return to the islands. Much of the earlier petulance and egoistic charm had given way to maturity, and she had been too engrossed by her other affairs to notice. Now he smiled whimsically at her regard, and she experienced a sudden warming towards him. The impulse came to say she was sorry for her rejection of his proposal, to reopen the discussion, to ... She bit her lip on the strange compulsion, and as though he divined it he said softly:

'I meant it, you know.'

'I know you did.'

'And even though I know you suspect my motive, I am sure we could help each other to forget.'

Forget! Pierre could not know that his ill-chosen verb was the means of snapping Tina back to reality. Her face shuttered and all the noise and colour of the *quai* rushed back to assail her senses. She forced a light tone. 'Maybe, but it would never work out, Pierre. It's crazy even to pretend it might.'

'And you are not particularly good at pretending, I think,' Pierre chided gently. 'It is one of your charms, *ma petite.* But perhaps I am crazy to pursue this matter at a time like this.' His tone changed and became crisp. 'Let us deal with this business of today first, shall we?'

Tina nodded thankfully, and they boarded a taxi for the short journey to the hotel. Pierre was silent, and not until they were almost there did he murmur, 'I wonder what she will be like ...'

Tina's imagination had already spent a good deal of time trying to conjecture the answer to this. The only clue she possessed was an old faded photograph still tucked away among other small mementoes in the ebony and ivory inlaid box that had belonged to her mother. It showed a tall, upright man of military bearing, and a slender woman in the long, full-skirted fashion of the fifties. A spaniel dog sat at their feet, but the sun had been shining into the woman's eyes and her features were not very distinct. Adding twenty years of time and age made any mental picture pure guess-work. But in a few minutes she would know. Furtively Tina rubbed clammy palms on a clean tissue and entered the hotel foyer.

If Tina had ever thought to sketch her imaginary picture of an English female aristocrat it might well have provided the very image she sought. The woman now walking to-wards her was tall, slender, with graceful hands and narrow feet in immaculate glacé court shoes, and the very simplicity of her powder-blue dress spoke of the classic couturier cut and finish. Her silvering hair held a lilac tint within its softly waved coiffure, and her clear skin had the pink and white smoothness of delicate porcelain, enhanced by eyes the colour of cool, English blue skies. One did not need to glance at the well-manicured pale pink nails to confirm that their owner had spent a life carefully remote from such mundane household tasks as washing dishes or cleaning cookers. But as Mrs Elizabeth Kingman came face to face with her only grandchild, the grandchild she had never seen until this moment, something behind that elegant façade strove to break through the years of habitual control.

The hand outstretched so coolly trembled suddenly, and the graciously modulated phrase of greeting faltered as Elizabeth Kingman took in the slender youthful girl in the pink linen dress who stood there so uncertainly. Tina's own hand wavered as she wondered if she was expected to make a more personal greeting and kiss the smooth, unlined cheek of her grandmother, and it was the tall, soldierly man with the neat clipped moustache who exclaimed in-credulously: 'I can't believe it! After all these years!'

Abruptly he stooped to kiss Tina, then took both her hands in his own while he searched the small drawn features with unbelieving eyes. 'My dear, you're Beth all over again. Isn't she?' He glanced at his wife, and Elizabeth Kingman gave a choked little murmur.

Tina stared back wordlessly and felt a lump come into her throat. Her intention had been to remain polite but cool, uncommitted; now she perceived the emotion struggling for release in her grandmother, and her heart softened painfully as she knew that no matter what past or future held there was only one thing she must do at this moment.

She reached up and put her arms hard round the older woman's shoulders and pressed her cheek against the petal-soft face. 'Oh, Grandmother, you've come all this way to see me ... you must be very tired after——' and then she felt Elizabeth Kingman's arms gather her close and hold her with a kind of hunger that brought a mistiness to the eyes of those who looked on. When at last that tight embrace slackened there were tears in Elizabeth Kingman's eyes. She smiled shakily and blinked hard, and Mr Kingman said gruffly: 'Yes, it's been far too long.'

Pierre, who had been standing by in silence, broke in smoothly: 'I think perhaps a drink ... ?' and almost without volition the little group moved out on to the terrace. Only when they were seated, and Mrs Kingman still seemed too overcome to say very much, did Tina's grandfather glance questioningly at Pierre.

Tina hastily made the introductions, and felt her face go scarlet·when Pierre added lightly: 'Just for the record, I proposed to your granddaughter last evening.'

Mrs Kingman went white. 'Oh, no! Not when we've just found her—Tina's far too young to think of marriage! She——'

'She has not yet done me the honour of accepting,' Pierre said, in the same smooth tones. 'But unless you carry her quickly back to England ...' he added with a hint of suave warning and a lift of dark brows as his glance switched round the three startled faces.

Tina felt a rush of anger. Why did he choose to force the issue like this? When they had scarcely said hello to her grandparents. Conscious of that look of fear in Elizabeth Kingman's eyes, she said sharply: 'Pierre, you promised! Please, there's so much we have to talk about.'

Pierre gave a slight smile and inclined his head. 'I know, petite, but why hide the fact? It is better that your grandparents know now. However,' he quickly drained the last of his drink and stood up, 'I realise that you have much to talk of, so I will make my adieux. What time do you wish me to return for you?'

'She is not returning to this offshore island today, surely?' exclaimed Mr Kingman. 'I thought you lived here.'

'Yes, but I'm staying with Fay just now . . . I thought I'd explained in my letter,' Tina broke in hastily.

'Yes, and we're extremely grateful to your friends for their kindness, but we are here now, and naturally we expect to have you with us after we've come halfway across the world.' The authority of a commanding officer was patent in Mr Kingman's bearing, and Tina bit her lip as she saw the familiar tightening of sulkiness round Pierre's handsome mouth.

Then her grandmother said, 'If there is any difficulty we can arrange accommodation here for Tina. In fact I think that would be by far the best solution.'

'Jolly good notion. I'll fix that straight away.' Without waiting for any assent from Tina, her grandfather got up and went back into the hotel.

'I'm sure your friends will understand, my dear,' Elizabeth Kingman said softly.

Pierre bowed his head. 'If that is what you wish,' he murmured to Tina, but in his expression she read the protest: *I am only trying to rescue you,* chérie!

She said slowly, 'I think I'd better stay—even if I stay at home for a few days. But thank you, Pierre.'

He nodded, then gravely took his departure, passing the tall, erect figure of Mr Kingman as he did so.

'That's fixed, my dear.' Mr Kingman dropped back into his chair, satisfaction in his eyes as he watched Pierre vanish from sight. 'You're not serious about the fellow, surely, Tina?'

She hesitated, the denial almost on her lips. It was too early for confidences and explanations, and these two people were still strangers. She said slowly: 'He's a close friend. But I'm not sure.'

'How wise of you not to commit yourself.' Mrs Kingman leaned forward and touched Tina's hand. 'You have plenty of time before you think of settling down to marriage, my dear. So much to do, and so much to see. And there's so much we want to give you.'

Tina looked at the delicately veined hand still resting on her own and knew she was not misreading the air of possessiveness already present. She took a deep breath. 'I

141

realise that, and I appreciate more than I can say your kindness in coming all this way to see me. But please ... don't try to give me too much, Grandmother.'

'Why ever not, child?' Mrs Kingman smiled indulgently. 'That is why we're here.'

'Yes, I realise that.' Tina drew her hand from under that warm, possessive clasp. 'But I don't want to disappoint you.'

There was a silence. Then Mrs Kingman shot a warning glance at her husband as he cleared his throat and frowned. She said quietly: 'Now don't worry, my dear. We understand that you must still be feeling unsettled—it's natural under the circumstances—and perhaps we were hasty in expecting you to take such a tremendous step, to uproot yourself from the home you've known all your life, and all your friends. But you *are* our only grandchild, you know. It's natural that we should want to take care of you now—that's why we suddenly decided we must come to you.'

'Yes, I know,' Tina said unhappily. It was all proving far more difficult than even her wildest forebodings. She had not bargained for that tremendously strong emotional reaction at the very first moment of meeting.

As though sensing her thoughts, her grandmother smiled and said in a lighter tone: 'I suggest we forget about it for the moment. There's so much to talk about.'

'Eighteen years to encompass,' said Mr Kingman.

'And there is so much we want to discover. Of you, my dear, and your island paradise,' added her grandmother, still smiling. 'You do realise that it's all as alien to us at this moment as we and England must seem to your viewpoint, my dear child!'

The note of indulgent amusement did not entirely mask the subtle reminder of the true purpose behind the visit. Tina smiled back, but her heart was brushed by chill. Already she knew that one of her fears was not unfounded; her grandmother was a woman of strong will: she would never take no for an answer.

But as the hours wore on Tina found it difficult to remain uncommitted. She was by nature warm-hearted and affectionate, and within a very short time it was clear that her grandparents' feeling for and interest in her were completely genuine. If they'd harboured any of the doubts she

142

had suspected these had already vanished, and at first, perhaps with the wisdom of maturity, they did not seek too far into the past. They had brought quite a number of photographs, and suddenly Aldeston Manor took on a fuller dimension instead of being merely a strangely chilling name at the top of a sheet of notepaper. It seemed to be a lovely, warm old house, set in gracious parkland and cool green gardens, and it was obviously a much-loved home. Then there were the dogs, present in almost all the pictures. The spaniel called Floss, the old black labrador called Jax, who was going blind, and Roly, the fat old bull terrier who had been a terror in his young days but now contented himself with an occasional grumble when the postman knocked.

'And this is Binnie with her new foal.' Mr Kingman added another colour print to the little heap on the table. 'We haven't decided on his pet name as yet.'

'Perhaps Tina can think of one,' said Elizabeth Kingman.

'He's not going to be sold? Or going to a racing stable?' asked Tina, studying the beautiful glossy brown mare and her small engaging offspring who seemed all legs.

'Well, we did think he might be perfect for you, later on,' remarked Mr Kingman, and casually brought out another photograph without waiting for any response from his granddaughter.

This was only the first of several similarly oblique indications during the days which followed, each one increasing Tina's feeling of helplessness to parry their determination.

They had reservations for a ten-day stay, and naturally they were eager to see as much of the island as possible. For this Tina was thankful, and she desperately tried to pack as much as possible into a sightseeing itinerary, hoping in this way to avoid the subject of herself and her future. She took them to all the well-known tourist attractions, Point Venus, the waterfalls, the museum, and many less well known places of beauty and interest. She also took them on Le Truck, as the island bus was known, a noisy, happy rambling journey which amused her grandfather but left Mrs Kingman somewhat exhausted. An invitation from Fay and Paul to visit Kaloha was accepted for the weekend, and a day was spent with Aunt Wynne. On the Friday evening they dined late at the hotel, and mischievous discretion kept Tina silent when the 'watered down' version of the Tamure was staged at the late-night cabaret. As danced by the islanders at their own festivities the Tamure was wild and frankly erotic, but here, in the westernised setting of a luxury tourist hotel, it was more in keeping with the new tradition that had spawned concrete swimming pools alongside the sea and plastic leis in the souvenir shops by the waterfront.

'There's certainly something fascinating in Hawaiian rhythm,' Elizabeth Kingman murmured as the dancers swayed and contorted in their grass skirts, 'but it's rather suggestive, isn't it?'

Tina caught her grandfather's eye and saw the twinkle lurking there and could scarcely repress a giggle. He knew! He smiled at her and patted her hand. 'You're looking happier tonight, my dear. I'm glad.'

She smiled back at him, knowing it was true, even though the cause was vain and foolish. A feeling of expectancy had bubbled within her all day at the thought of the return tomorrow to Kaloha. She saw the coloured spotlights dim as the dancers finished, and in her secret mind's eye she saw Max Thornton. He must be back by now ...

No matter how she tried to subdue the inward turmoil she was as taut as a bowstring next morning when Paul, who had come to collect them, brought the launch to the hotel landing stage. She wanted desperately to ask if Max was home, but somehow she controlled the urge. She would wait until she could ask Fay.

Pierre was not there when they arrived. There were children among the guests that week and he had taken them on a fishing trip by outrigger that day. Tina felt guilty at her sense of relief; fond though she would always be of the man who had evoked the anguish and sweetness of first love she dreaded any further involvement. She had problems enough on her hands, and the worst of them rapidly nearing climax as the days rushed by bringing the moment of fate nearer. How was she going to deal with it when it came?

Her grandmother was at her most charming, and Tina saw how favourably impressed were Fay and Paul. They liked the two elderly people who had come so far with such purpose-ful intent, as Aunt Wynne had been won over during the day

144

they spent with her. For the first time Tina began to wonder seriously if she should take the long step into the new life they offered. And yet every instinct rebelled. How could she leave everything that meant home? But wouldn't it be for the best? A new life that would help to fill the void of sorrow, and help her forget the hopeless longing for a man who saw her only as a bereft child?

Engrossed in her thoughts, Tina failed to see the anxious glances Fay gave her during lunch, and she felt no warning twinge of foreboding when Fay suddenly drew her aside for a moment while the others were distracted by the antics of the twins.

'Have you seen Max?' Fay said in a low voice.

Tina's heart gave a great lurch. 'No—I've been wanting to ask you—is he back?'

'Yes, but I didn't want to mention it in front of the others in case you ...' Fay bit her lip and glanced across the terrace. 'Haven't you heard?'

'Heard what?' The lurch came again, this time painful with fear. 'What's happened? Is Max——?'

'No, nothing like that.' Fay's eyes filled with concern as she stared into Tina's frightened face. 'He's all right, but ... Honestly, I don't know what to make of it. It's all over the island, and it must be all over Tahiti by now, but probably you've been too busy to have heard any rumours.'

'What rumours?' Tina's cheeks whitened under their tan. 'For heaven's sake, tell me, Fay!'

'Max came back on Tuesday. He brought a girl with him.'

'A girl!'

Fay nodded.

Tina's hands felt like ice. 'Who?'

'An island girl. Her name is Tiare.'

'Tiare!' Tina realised she was echoing every word and pressed her trembling lips together. Her eyes pleaded mutely for something to ease the growing nightmare of fear into which she had plunged, and Fay shook her head.

'No one knows where she is from, except that she's very young, fifteen, sixteen, maybe, and very beautiful. The best of all worlds,' Fay added with a sigh.

Those few words told Tina all she needed to know to visualise the unknown Tiare. They told her that Tiare would be of Chinese-French-Polynesian extraction, the mingled heritage that produced what many claimed to be the most beautiful form of womanhood in the world. Tiare would have the exquisite fine-boned daintiness of the Oriental, the lustrous hair, satin skin and vivacity of the Polynesian without the unfortunate tendency to an obesity and ageing that was premature by Western standards, and in addition she would be gifted with the superb feminine élan of her French blood. She would be irresistible to men, and few men would resist for long.

And Max had brought her to Kaloha!

Tina sank weakly into a chair, still unable to believe it, and Fay shook her head again.

'I'm afraid it's true. She's definitely living there.'

Tina sat as though stunned. 'But why?' she whispered stupidly.

'No one knows.' Fay sighed deeply. 'Of course there may be an explanation, but so far it isn't circulating. Corinne was completely shattered.'

Tina's fingers twisted feverishly on the chair arm. She had almost forgotten Corinne. But she could feel no satisfaction at hearing of the French girl's reaction.

'The island's been agog ever since they came.' Fay's eyes were troubled. 'It's difficult to believe. Max Thornton, of all men! I know you've developed quite a thing about him'— she smiled sadly as Tina made a numb little gesture of denial—'oh yes, darling, I could tell, we all could. But to me he seems such a chilly personality.'

There was a silence, then the chuckles of the twins and the laughter of her grandparents came as though from a long way distant. Tina said almost desperately: 'But what about Monsieur Latour?'

Fay shrugged. 'He's still convalescing—but you probably haven't heard the latest about him. He's staying with Cécile!'

'Cécile?' For a moment Tina looked blank. Then slowly, as though emerging from a thick fog, the name registered and a picture of the little French lady amid her embroidery silks broke through. 'Oh, yes, I remember,' she said dully. 'I believe Cécile used to know Monsieur Latour many years ago.'

'The rumours are flying thick and fast,' Fay smiled. 'I never knew they were old flames. But it seems that poor

Henri won't be running his plantation again for a long time, if ever. He's still on anti-coagulants, mustn't smoke those endless cheroots of his, and is on a strict diet. I should imagine that Cécile is finding him quite a handful to look after.'

Tina nodded, but it was an automatic response. Fay sighed, looking at her, then murmured softly: 'I'm sorry.'

Suddenly Tina sprang up. 'Can you cover for me? Just for half an hour? Please, Fay.'

'Oh, darling ...' Fay's mouth twisted with pity as she instinctively divined Tina's purpose. 'You're not ... ?'

'I must. I have to see her. Just see her.'

Fay tried to hide the pity in her eyes. She nodded. 'I'll say you've slipped up to do your hair, or something. Go out the side door.'

Without stopping to think twice on the wisdom of her impulse Tina sped from the hotel and took the path through the plantation instead of the quicker way along the beach, which was visible from the hotel terrace. As she hurried through the shadowed groves her mind had gone numb to everything except the one appalling thought of Max. She still couldn't believe it. Max bringing a girl back to Kaloha. Not Max. He couldn't have taken a mistress, a *vahine*. Not *Max!* her anguished heart screamed in her breast.

When Tina rounded the curve of the track and saw the house her heart was pounding so fiercely she could scarcely get her breath. Abruptly she halted, staring at the white picket fence, the familiar doorway, the tumbling mass of blossoms in the untidy garden. Nothing had changed. Inside it would look the same, beyond would be the veranda, the white cushions on the lounger, the steps down to the beach, the steps up which Max Thornton had carried her high in his arms ... *'You're too young to wear the flower of love ...'*

With a trembling hand Tina thrust the gate open and walked to the door. It was ajar, would swing inward to her touch, and there was only silence within. Instead, she moved slowly around the side of the house until she reached the veranda. Still no one appeared, and she paused on the top step.

The lagoon lay below, calm, green, translucent, fringed by its palms and smooth sand. An ageless scene, older than man. How many human loves and tragedies had it witnessed? A great sigh escaped Tina as she searched its beauty for a sign of life. Then she saw the movement, the tiny dark spot bobbing on the shimmering emerald water. A girl was swimming down there.

Caught by some power she could not resist, Tina descended the steps and became aware of music playing. A huge luxury beach towel made a vivid orange splash on the sand near the foot of the steps, and on the towel were sundry articles: a smaller, yellow towel, a pair of white-framed sunglasses, a scarlet flask of sun oil, and a cassette player from which came the music.

Tina halted. The dark head in the ripples had turned shoreward; the girl had seen the newcomer. With languid, effortless strokes she came into her depth and stood up in the water, shaking moisture from her hair. For a moment the two girls stared at one another, and Tina felt a chill creep down her spine. This was Tiare. And she was exquisite. Lustrous black hair to her waist, smooth satin skin and curving voluptuous body, dark glowing eyes filled with challenge at this moment—but it took little imagination to picture their slumbrous invitation should their owner desire to attract.

There was no smiling 'Iorana,' the Polynesian greeting, only that sultry, challenging stare. Tiare stepped on the sand and eyed this newcomer in the plain white linen dress. 'Who are you?' she demanded.

Tina's head came up. She returned the stare. 'I came to see Max, not you.'

Too late, she realised how unguardedly the more intimate first name of reference had slipped out. She saw suspicion enter Tiare's already unfriendly eyes.

'Why do you wish to see Max?'

'Because he happens to be a friend of mine.'

'*Aue!* He never mention you!'

Something in her inward despair gave Tina strength. She said coldly: 'As you asked my name and I haven't yet told you who I am you can scarcely claim to know whether Mr Thornton has mentioned me or not. Not that it really concerns you,' she added icily.

Tiare's red mouth turned down sulkily at the corners. Abruptly she flounced past, tossing that glorious mane of raven hair back from her face. She stooped to pick up her towel, casually unhooking the top of her scarlet-flowered bikini as she did so. Her small perfect breasts were the same sun-kissed honey colour as her limbs, and Tina could not help a start of shock at the sudden flaunting smile Tiare directed at her. Still smiling, yet as though Tina had ceased to exist, Tiare mopped the glistening droplets of sea water from her arms and body, then turned to move with a lovely wanton grace towards the foot of the steps. There she paused, reached out to pluck a pink blossom and tuck it behind her ear, and then glanced up at the house.

The vivid blue of the sky silhouetted that beautiful naked outline, and then another movement caught Tina's attention. She looked up and gave a choked gasp.

Max was standing on the veranda, staring down at Tiare.

There was a rush of movement before Tina's eyes and a fierce exclamation almost spat at her, then Tiare was tearing up the curve of rough steps as though on winged toes. The towel slipped unheeded from her shoulders and again the firm sculptured lines of her body were silhouetted like naked bronze against the sky.

In a numb trance of shock Tina saw the flying figure reach the top and fling itself against the man who stood there. His hands came round the bare shoulders and slim arms fastened possessively about his neck before the two intermingled forms misted in a swimming blur before Tina's eyes.

She could not bear to look.

With a choked cry she turned to flee blindly along the beach, shock, anguish and heartbreak pursuing her like venom-tipped arrows. And now Tiare's violent, triumphant exclamation caught up with her, its message branding like fire on her brain.

'To'u!' the intimate possessive.

'My Max! Max is mine!'

CHAPTER NINE

DURING the weeks of disillusion that followed Tina never knew how she got through the rest of that weekend. Somehow she arrived back at the hotel and managed to don the cloak of conventional response necessary for day-to-day existence. But that was all it was, a frail defence that scarcely hid the turmoil that wrung her tormented spirit. She avoided Fay's questioning eyes, avoided being left alone with anyone lest they ask the question she dreaded, imagining the pity of knowledge in every glance. For once she was thankful to leave Kaloha, and grateful that her grandmother decided not to extend their stay there beyond the Sunday. Again to Tina's relief it was Paul who took them back on the Sunday evening, and once back at the hotel in Papeete she pleaded a headache and went to bed without bothering about the evening meal.

In the solitude of her room she could give way to the anguish and the bitter memory of those two intermingled forms. The cloud of black hair flying as Tiare's piquant little face closed against Max's lean brown profile, her slim pliant body moulding its warm nakedness against his white shirt ...

-'Oh, Max ... why? Why?' Tina whispered aloud, over and over again to the dark night. If only she hadn't gone, hadn't seen with her own eyes. Perhaps then she might not have believed, would have been spared the pain and humiliation of disillusion.

But she had gone, and she had seen, and there was nothing left, nothing except to believe—and weep for her own foolish vain love.

She was wan and listless on the Monday morning, picking at her breakfast fruit and roll, scarcely caring whether she ate and drank ever again. Elizabeth Kingman watched with increasingly anxious eyes, and asked at last: 'Are you feeling off colour, darling? You look so peaky.'

'I'm all right,' Tina said listlessly.

'You don't look it,' Mrs Kingman returned flatly. 'Maybe we should have the doctor.'

Tina gave a shuddering sigh. No doctor could cure what ailed her now. She shook her head and made a valiant attempt to smile. 'Where would you like to go today?'

Mrs Kingman still looked doubtful, then her husband said eagerly: 'I thought we might browse around the town—you still haven't taken us to see your father's studio. We'd like to see some of his work before we go home.'

'If it wouldn't be too painful for you, darling,' Mrs Kingman put in gently, her expression still holding a trace of worry.

Tina shook her head. She had known this must come sooner or later, and exhaustion was bringing a strange sense of fatalism to numb the anguish.

They went that morning, to the lonely, shut-up studio where John Raimond's brushes and paints still lay in the neat order in which Tina had placed them that day just after his departure. Silently she turned over for their inspection the few canvasses that remained, and said in a flat little voice: 'I took the rest home—his favourites—I couldn't bear to sell them.'

'Of course you couldn't.' Her grandfather paused, studying a vivid beachscape in oils. 'This is excellent. By the way, did he own this property?'

'Yes.'

'And the house?'

'Yes.'

He nodded, but did not press the subject farther. It was not until they were out in the sunshine again that he said casually: 'What were you planning to do about it all?'

'I wasn't planning anything,' Tina said dully. She looked away, knowing that they meant well and that they were unwittingly reminding her of the painful task she would have to face sooner or later. But how could she part with the last links of her old life? The things dear to her father, his pictures, his paints, the studio? Especially the studio.

Her mouth quivered. It was hopeless. Why couldn't she realise that she was trying to build a fool's paradise on hope? She took an unsteady step forward, and felt an arm come firmly round her shoulders.

'Take no notice of him, my dear,' Elizabeth Kingman said softly. 'Men don't think ... they see things in black and white more than we do, always trying to tie up the ends neatly. What he is really trying to say is: we want to help you over this difficult time. Isn't there anything we can do?' she added pleadingly.

'I—I——' Tina began, and then her grandfather interrupted:

'Aren't you going to lock up, Tina?'

She realised she was walking away with the studio key still in her hand. She turned back, and then suddenly everything blurred and the stupid tears flooded into her eyes. She groped with the key, but it wouldn't go into the lock, then her hand was gently thrust aside.

Mr Kingman turned the key, tried the lock, then handed the key to her. 'Beth's right, you know, darling. Why not just let us take care of everything?'

The two pairs of eyes watched her steadily, intent on her pale, distraught little face, and then her grandmother made a curiously appealing little gesture. 'Please, darling . . .'

Why not? Suddenly Tina was too weary to resist any longer. She bowed her head and gave a choked little murmur of assent, and Elizabeth Kingman opened her arms and said simply: 'Yes, my dear, I think it's time to go home.'

It was all arranged with bewildering speed.

When the Kingmans took off three days later at the close of their stay Tina was on the plane with them, ostensibly for a hastily arranged holiday, but she knew that as far as they were concerned it was to be no brief package tour.

There had been a flurry of unease over her passport, fortunately ironed out, and an anxious discussion between her grandparents regarding this, for although Tina's parents were both British she had been born on French territory. 'We don't want to get you home and discover that our own immigration officials class you as an alien,' Mr Kingman said grimly as he took charge of Tina's birth certificate and those of her parents, along with the rest of the family papers which Tina hunted out from her father's bureau.

But by the time the plane rose above the moonlit beauty of Faa Lagoon Tina was too weary to care. There had been a hectic shopping trip, at her grandmother's insistence, to buy a new travelling outfit and a luxurious set of matched luggage in the same deep blue as her dress and jacket. There had been a farewell dinner for which Fay and Paul and Pierre had made the crossing, but no farewell journey to Kaloha for Tina, which she did not regret. The island she loved now held too bitter a memory for her . . .

She looked down for a last glimpse of the lights of Tahiti, and a sudden wave of panic wrenched her from the grip of weary apathy. Stark cold realization flooded back and she almost snatched at her seat belt, as though to escape. It was really happening. She was on her way into the unknown. But what if she hated England? What if she never came back? How had she ever imagined that in new surroundings, amid strangers, she might find forgetfulness ... ?

The lights dimmed in the long body of the aircraft, and most of the passengers settled down to sleep away the night lap to Acapulco. But despite her weariness there was no sleep for Tina, only the long dark hours that began that seemingly endless journey. The sense of unreality returned, persisting with each touchdown and take-off at the subsequent stages of the flight. Acapulco, Mexico City, Nassau, Bermuda, places hitherto only names on a map, until Tina began to feel that the great Boeing was the only tangible security in her life. And when at last the moment came of her grandfather saying thankfully, 'It won't be long now, my dear, we'll be home within an hour,' she felt a resurgence of fear at the prospect of stepping down at last from the plane. The vastness of London Airport surrounded her, and the plane she was leaving seemed to be her last link with Tahiti—her real home.

But there was no turning back. She had to go on, following the tall, authoritative figure of her grandfather through the crowds and the noise, and out to the gleaming limousine with the uniformed chauffeur who waited. And then the speeding journey by road, south into the beautiful leafy avenues of Hampshire, a countryside alien, yet somehow known, as though some strange quirk of inheritance had passed its recognition from her mother; this was her mother's home.

The house was exactly the same in reality as in the photographs Tina had seen. The long curling driveway, beneath oak and beech, giving way to open green and gardens with the scent of late roses, and then the great house, its Tudor brick pink-mellowed in the sun and its mullioned windows throwing a myriad diamond reflections. The dogs came rushing, snuffling and barking and leaping, almost crying their delight at the return of their owners and darting ecstatically between Mr and Mrs Kingman. The housekeeper, a plump woman in her fifties with greying hair, greeted them and said lunch would be ready within half an hour, and Tina scarcely had time to take in the wide, panelled hall with its smooth parquet floor, heavy-framed paintings and huge stone fireplace at one side before she was guided up the broad staircase and along the gallery above to the airy, spacious bedroom which was to be her room.

Her room. Her home. For always?

It was a new way of life entirely, so many things to see and discover, and with a kindness that made Tina feel almost ashamed of the stubborn core of reserve that would not let her relax and accept it all completely. No matter how hard she tried to obey the voice of logic that told her to forget the past and look to the future, letting time work its particular alchemy, she could not escape the memories that returned with inexorable force each night when dark and silence dropped their folds over the countryside and only the great old clock down in the hall chimed its sonorous markings of the passing hours.

In her lonely bed, warm under the rose silk quilt, Tina lost all defence against the pictures that still haunted her; a tall, sunburnt man with black-lashed grey eyes that turned blue in bright sunlight, a mouth that could be grim, compelling, and quizzical in turn—and unforgettable in its sweet strength against her own ... taking her heart from her that night in the dark eerie shadows of the *marae* ...

And then Tiare ...

Where was Max now? Was Tiare still there, still running from the beach, to throw herself in wild abandon into his waiting arms? Tina shivered violently and thrust her face deep into the lavender-scented pillow. This was crazy; torturing herself, longing for yet dreading the first letter from Fay, wondering what news it might contain.

Yet when the longed-for airmail finally came it was disappointingly brief.

'There hasn't been time for much news to gather up,' Fay wrote, 'and I'm not like my mother, who can make reams out of nothing yet still be interesting. But we are all thinking of you and I thought a few lines might help. You're bound to be a bit homesick until you've had time to settle in ...'

Homesick! That was the understatement of the year. And not a word about Max ...

Tina gulped and looked up, to find her grandmother

watching her with somewhat worried eyes.

'That intense young Frenchman?' queried Mrs Kingman, and seemed relieved when Tina shook her head. Almost instantly Mrs Kingman launched into the plans for the day. Tina was to have her first riding lesson that morning, then they were going to lunch at the Grange. 'You'll meet their daughter—she's about your age—and she'll introduce you to the young people round here. You'll soon make lots of friends.'

Tina nodded tremulously. It sounded so easy. If only she could forget the past and accept and return the affection they wanted to lavish on her. Perhaps it was true, that she would forget. Perhaps in three months' time she wouldn't want to go back...

In her heart Tina was not convinced. She lived for the post each day, for the warm-hearted letters from Aunt Wynne, and the hurried but affectionate notes from Fay. She longed to ask about Max, but forced herself to deny the longing, and it was three letters on before Fay said casually, 'I hope you've got over your yen for Max Thornton—you must have, as you don't mention him. I'm afraid she is still there and I wish she wasn't—she's always looking for lifts to Papeete and trying to flirt with Pierre, who is so susceptible, and this caused him a real uproar with Corinne last week. I wish he would make his mind up about her ... I expect Mother told you the main news—that Henri Latour and Cécile are to marry. It's to be when Alex arrives. I believe he's due next week ...'

Tina looked up with shadowed eyes. So Tiare was still in possession ... *Oh, Max* ... she moaned softly, fighting the misery that rose again. She mustn't comment when she answered the letter; let Fay go on assuming that she no longer cared or was interested. It was crazy to let herself grieve. Max Thornton would long since have forgotten her existence.

And so the days slipped by, and imperceptibly the little homely incidents that made up the daily routine at Aldeston Manor began to weave into a frail acceptance of her new life. The antics of the dogs, and the daily argument between Floss, the spaniel, and Mrs Greenway, the housekeeper, when Floss sneaked past her each morning to race upstairs into the bedrooms she was supposed to be forbidden. She would land into Tina's room, all floppy ears and huge paws and ecstatic pantings of joy as Tina fondled the silky head and Mr Kingman's voice demanded to know who had let that animal up here! Then there was the skirmishing between Mrs Jackson, the widowed daily help, and Matt Meadows, the grizzle-haired gardener, who was courting Mrs Jackson. She swore that his blandishments were only cupboard love—because she made the best steak-and-kidney pie for miles around—while Matt would slyly affirm that a good steak pie would certainly warm the stomach—but not a cold bed! To which his reluctant inamorata would retort: 'And why should I be worrying about that when I've a perfectly good electric blanket?'

In more serious moments Mrs Jackson would recall Tina's mother, and the anecdotes she recounted did more than anything else to remind Tina that Aldeston Manor was indeed as much part of her heritage as the life she had always known.

Her grandfather arranged a course of driving lessons for her, there were shopping trips to London, concerts, and an evening at the ballet, and Tina discovered that the only way to push down the memories of heartbreak was to force herself into activity whenever a leisure moment became a vacuum that threatened to fill itself with reflections best left in limbo.

Until the morning that brought an unexpected letter from Pierre.

It began with somewhat warm and fulsome greetings and an anxious inquiry as to her health. Everyone sent their love, everyone missed her, and then: 'Kaloha is disgustingly dull at the moment. Everyone has gone now—even our suzerain has departed for shores unknown, which is not surprising after the excitement and the scandal. Papeete talks of nothing else! But I'm sure Fay will be telling you the whole story, embroidered as only the feminine hand knows how! And now, *chérie*, I must go and console the fair Corinne. After all, we have only each other now. I await your response! *Jusqu'alors* ... Pierre.'

Tina felt her hands beginning to shake. What scandal? Was it ...? What had happened? Why had Max left? For it could only be Max. Only Pierre had called him the Suzerain of Kaloha. And Corinne needed consoling ...

Tina swallowed hard on the sick feeling that threatened to choke her and shook her head at the succulent rashers of bacon her grandmother wanted to put on her plate.

'You don't eat enough, Tina,' Mrs Kingman protested. 'Your appetite——' She stopped as the housekeeper appeared at the door to say that Mr Kingman was wanted on the telephone.

'At this time of morning?' He wiped his mouth hastily with his napkin and hurried out, while his wife, with a despairing look at Tina's empty plate, returned to her own breakfast.

Tina scarcely noticed him return and gesture to his wife, who immediately got up and followed him from the room. The letter from Pierre, with its disturbing content that told so little and hinted at so much, filled her mind to the exclusion of everything else. It was not until later in the day that Tina noticed her grandmother's preoccupation and that Mr Kingman had not yet returned from his hurried departure to London. Tina felt a pang of guilt as she looked at Elizabeth Kingman's strained face at dinner that evening.

She said slowly, 'Grandfather isn't usually as late as this. Is something wrong?'

The older woman hesitated, then shook her head uncertainly. 'No—don't worry, dear. It's just ... I've a bit of a headache.'

Tina felt sure that this was not the cause, and she bit her lip. She was becoming more fond of her grandmother than she had realised and she did not like to see her so pale and worried. But she did not dare press confidence further.

The meal over, they watched a film on television, and then Tina went to make the bedtime drinks, deeply worried herself by now at the failure of her grandfather to arrive home. Had there been an accident?

She wanted to wait up, but Mrs Kingman would not hear of this, and Tina went reluctantly to bed, leaving her grandmother alone downstairs in the now silent house.

It was almost midnight when Tina heard the car.

She sat up uneasily, wondering if she should go downstairs, but some instinct kept her where she was, listening for sounds of reassurance, while the long minutes ticked by. A full hour elapsed before she heard the muted voices, and a shaft of light under her bedroom door told her that

157

her grandparents were coming up to bed at last.

What had happened?

The air of tension was like a charge of electricity in the atmosphere when Tina went down to breakfast after an uneasy night's half sleep. But after their normal affectionate greeting neither of her grandparents made any reference to the previous day and whatever had occurred. The mask of control was back on Mrs Kingman's patrician features, and her husband seemed immersed in his paper. Yet Tina's unease persisted. Something was wrong. But what?

Mr Kingman rose. 'No riding lesson today, I'm afraid, Tina.' He folded his newspaper and instead of handing it to his wife as he usually did he tucked it under his arm and went from the room.

There was a moment of silence, then Mrs Kingman stood up. 'Can you amuse yourself until lunch-time, darling?' she asked. 'I have the Red Cross ladies coming this morning.'

The local branch of the Red Cross was only one of the many organisations with which Mrs Kingman was involved. She was president of the Senior Citizens' Welfare Association and the Child Care Action Group, and was chairwoman of the Hospital Friends League, besides her church work. The ladies' cars began rolling up the drive shortly after ten, and their occupants made their way to the big drawing room. Tina wandered down to the stables to talk to Jemma, the placid mare who was so indulgent of Tina's first wary efforts at horsemanship, and Hassan, the spirited colt who was to be her own, but on whom she could not imagine herself astride and being borne swiftly towards the horizon.

But the wind was cold—Tina thought she would never get used to the sudden onslaughts of English chill—and she returned indoors to the warmth of the kitchen, where Mrs Jackson was just starting to wash the trolley load of coffee cups from the committee meeting. Tina got a tea towel and started to dry, and she was almost finished as the housekeeper hurried in, looking rather flustered.

'There you are—I've been looking all over for you, Tina,' Mrs Greenway exclaimed. 'There's someone to see you— your grandmother is still busy with her meeting, so I put him in the library.'

Him! Tina clutched the tea towel. 'Someone to see me? But——'

'I didn't catch his name—that dratted poodle of Mrs Lane's is yapping its head off. You'd better go—it's nearly lunch time.'

Tina hung the tea towel over the rack and made perfunctory smoothing motions over her hair as she hurried along the corridor. Mrs Greenway must have made a mistake; she didn't know anyone who would call on her specifically. The poodle was still indulging in heartbroken whines split by bursts of yapping because his mistress was not yet out of her silly old meeting, and Tina whispered a few words of consolation before she crossed the hall to the mahogany-panelled door leading to the library. It felt heavy as she swung it inward on soundless hinges, and she paused, her gaze entering the book-lined room in search of its occupant.

A man was standing by the high marble fireplace, his arm resting on the mantelpiece as he studied a photograph he had taken in his hand. A man whose back was suddenly achingly familiar.

Tina froze, incredulous, and gasped, and the man swung round abruptly.

It was Max.

'Hello, Tina,' he said quietly.

She still stood like a girl stunned, unable to believe her eyes. The room wavered, and the tick of the clock was like a drum beating in her ears. She blinked hard and whispered: 'Max—is it really you? Or is it a dream?'

'It's no dream.'

His voice was crisp and down-to-earth. He stood there, unmoving, watching her, and she had a wild impulse to fly to him, to touch him, to assure herself that he was indeed the real, flesh and blood Max. But something kept her immobile. If she moved he might waver and vanish before her eyes.

She whispered, 'When did you arrive? I—I never expected . . . No one told me . . .' Her lips felt stiff and she bit back the incoherent murmurs, aware that the shock was already causing weakness to pervade her limbs.

'I arrived yesterday, to tie up a few business matters before I return to the islands.'

'I see.' She didn't, but he looked so strange in the dark formal suit and green shirt and dark green tie, standing there like a polite stranger. At any moment he will mention the weather, she thought on a rising note of hysteria. Then he moved, and the sunlight cut a burnished swathe across his dark head, and she saw the grey eyes, the lean curve of his tanned cheek, and the chiselled shape of his mouth, all the heart-aching features that were imprinted on her memory for ever. And then all the other memories rushed back, inescapably real. She said stiffly, 'Why did you come?'

'To keep a promise.'

'What promise?'

'To see if you were all right. If you were happy. If you needed money,' he itemised in the same crisp tones, and waited.

'Why—why shouldn't I be all right?'

'You tell me,' he returned equably.

'I'm all right.' She looked away miserably, wishing the cotton-woolly sensation would go out of her legs. 'It was kind of you to remember—I never expected you—that you——'

'Yes,' he prompted, after an appreciable pause, 'you never expected what?'

She twisted icy hands together. 'I never expected that you would take it so seriously, the stupidness of a child afraid of its own grandparents.'

He glanced coolly round the room with its unobtrusive signs of wealth, and then at the spacious garden stretching away outside. 'No,' he said dryly, 'you don't look particularly deprived in the material sense, but I've always gained the impression that the material facts of life mattered far less to you than——'

'Tina . . .!'

The interruption came from the doorway. Tina spun round to see her grandmother standing there, staring inquiringly at Max.

'I didn't know we had a visitor.' Elizabeth Kingman waited, her eyes holding a chilly blue light, then added smoothly, 'Well, my dear, am I not to be introduced to your—your friend?'

Stammering, and suddenly cold at this renewed manifestation of her grandmother's autocracy, Tina did so and Mrs Kingman smiled coolly. 'My granddaughter never mentioned you, Mr Thornton, or that she was expecting a visitor.'

'As she was unaware of my intention to call, she could scarcely inform you of the fact.' Max's voice held as much chill as that of the older woman.

'I see. Would you care to stay for lunch?' Mrs Kingman asked graciously.

'No, thank you, Mrs Kingman, I have business in town. This was only a brief call.' With a formal inclination of his head towards her he crossed to the door. Only when he reached it did he look at Tina. 'I'm glad to see you looking so well, Tina. Are there any messages to take back?'

She shook her head dumbly, conscious of the deep sick emptiness back in the pit of her stomach. In a moment he would be gone, and the ache would start all over again, worse than ever after this one glimpse of him.

He put his hand on the door. 'I'll see myself out, Mrs Kingman. If you should wish to get in touch with me, Tina, I'm staying at White's until Friday.' He paused. 'By the way, haven't they told you yet?'

'Told me what?' Tina stared.

'That your father has been found.'

CHAPTER TEN

'My father!'

Tina caught at the desk corner to steady herself. Her father! She stared imploringly at Max, wondering if she was dreaming it all. Then the sick horror of fear struck. Did he mean . . .?

Max read the desperate little play of expression and shook his head. 'No, Tina, I would have told you another way if it had been bad news. Your father is alive, and safe.'

'Where? When? Is he . . .?' She couldn't go on as the room began to swim and she thought she was going to faint.

Max came to her side in two rapid strides. His hands caught her shoulders, easing her down into the chair by the desk. 'We still have a lot of gaps to fill in, Tina. The news only came through three days ago, just as I was about to fly out. As far as we know your father was adrift for about two weeks in the yacht's dinghy, with only the emergency rations that were in it, until he was picked up by a fishing outrigger and taken to a tiny island at the remotest end of the Roa Taurea Group. From a communications point of view he couldn't have landed in a worse place. No Europeans live there and the islanders are practically self-sufficient—they have a boat call only once in six months. We don't know exactly how long he was there, before the islanders decided to take him to Roatu, the main island of the group, where there's a small settlement, and a tiny mission run by two nuns. They nursed him, but he had lost his memory, probably due in part to the deprivations and exposure he had suffered, and he had no identifying papers or anything on him. They, good souls, decided he must be either a fleeing criminal or a political escapee and considered he should be nursed back to health before any possible shocks might be administered to him. And then they remembered of the loss of the yacht and wondered if he were one of the survivors.'

Max paused. 'There'll be a great deal more, which your father will tell of himself when you're reunited.'

Tina was crying now, the tears of relief and wonderment and joy. She looked up tremulously. 'It's really true? Daddy's alive and—and—he will get better, won't he?'

'It's true. And he will get better,' Max said quietly.

She swallowed convulsively, then dashed the tears away and sprang up. 'But I have to go to him. I have to go back! He'll not know where——'

'He's on his way home now.' Max put a restraining on her arm. 'He——'

'Yes, but I'm not there! I must——'

'Your father is on his way to England,' said Mrs Kingman.

Only now did Tina remember the presence of her grandmother, and a sudden flood of anger surged through her. She whirled to face the tall, dignified woman who stood there so coolly.

'You knew!'

'Yes, Tina, since yesterday.'

'And you didn't tell me! You kept it from me! Why? How dare you not tell me?' Tina raged. 'You——'

'Tina! Calm yourself. Of course we were not trying to keep it from you—why should we? I should imagine that a cable to you, from your father, is already on its way.' Elizabeth Kingman betrayed impatience, then her tone softened. 'My dear, we did it for the best. We wanted to make sure that the first report was not unfounded—that was where your grandfather was yesterday, with his friend at the Foreign Office and making innumerable phone calls. He was also trying to make arrangements to have your father's arrival kept quiet, to save him being delayed and exhausted by a full scale reception—the media are certain to follow up the story, and we don't know if your father is well enough to cope with a lot of excitement.'

'Yes . . .' Tina did not look entirely convinced, however, and the sparkles of anger still glinted in her eyes.

'I think your grandmother is right about the excitement,' Max said flatly. 'Your father's homecoming should be as quiet as possible.'

Tina had no quarrel with this, but she could not forgive what she saw as a cruel, high-handed action on the part of her grandparents. To think that they had known for more than twenty-four hours and held silent. But for the advent of Max she might still be in ignorance of the miraculous tidings.

Watching her, Elizabeth Kingman sighed. In what was for her an unusually placatory tone, she said: 'We were going to tell you today, as soon as your grandfather gets home, and he should be back any moment now.' She gave a small, tremulous smile. 'We only wanted to be sure, darling, and to be able tell you definite, confirmed facts.'

Tina nodded. Suddenly she began to comprehend their viewpoint. Supposing it had been a mistake? Supposing it hadn't been her father . . . How would she have felt to have new hopes dashed so violently? She gave a shuddering sigh. She wanted to laugh and cry and shout and go deliriously mad. Her father was safe. He was coming back. They would be going home; together. Oh, they would have the most wonderful reunion of all time, and Aunt Wynne, and Fay, and Paul, and the babies, would all be waiting, and all their friends . . .

Reaction had set in now, and for once Max receded in a kind of unreality. She made automatic responses as he took his leave, her mind afire with excitement and impatience. How long before the wonderful moment came, when at last she would see her father? Oh, she would look after him and care for him—he would be thin and weak after his dreadful ordeal. He would need lots to eat, and new clothes—he would have lost everything he had—and she would certainly insist on him having lots of rest until he was completely recovered ...

Tina spent the most of the next few hours at the front sitting room window, in a fever of impatience for the sight of the postman or telegraph boy, or the summons of the phone. Her grandfather returned just after twelve-thirty, bringing the news that as far as it was known John Raimond was 'somewhere en route for Apia', from where arrangements were being made to fly him home.

'He must be on one of the inter-island schooners,' Tina fretted. 'It could be ages before he gets here—you don't know those little island boats—they take *weeks* to get anywhere, calling at every island in a group.'

'I suggest you set to work preparing your father's room,' Mrs Kingman said with a smile. 'It'll help to occupy your mind.'

Tina seized on this idea and it was decided to prepare the big guest room that faced south and had an adjoining bathroom and smaller room which Tina could move into if she wished. She was sorting blankets from the linen room when the first cable came.

It was from Aunt Wynne. *'We have just heard the wonderful news. Fondest love to you both.'* It was followed a short while later by one from Fay and Paul, and then, just as Mrs Kingman was trying to persuade a reluctant Tina to go to bed late that evening, the phone rang.

Tina stood at the foot of the stairs, dark-eyed with tiredness but knowing she would never sleep, while Mr Kingman went to take the call in his study.

She watched him through the open doorway, and then ran as he turned and beckoned. He smiled but did not speak as he put the receiver into her hand. Suddenly trembling, she whispered, 'Yes ...? Tina here ... Who is it?'

'Is that you, darling?'

The world seemed to tilt crazily as Tina received her

164

third shock that day. The voice she had thought she would never hear again.

'Daddy! Oh, Daddy!' she whispered incredulously. 'Is it really you?'

'Yes, darling girl—have I surprised you?'

'You certainly have! I only heard today—but where are you? When——?'

'I'm in Samoa—just having the best breakfast I've had in months. But what on earth are you doing in England? How did this come about?' John Raimond's voice was alternating ebbing and sharpening owing to the atmospheric effects of the long distance involved, and Tina had to strain her ears to catch every word. 'I didn't know what had become of you until last night.'

Of course he wouldn't! Tina gave a gasp of concern, and then bit back the instinctive launch into explanations as her father cried, 'Hello—are you still there, Tina?'

'Yes—when are you coming home—or shall I go home— I mean are you coming here?' she gabbled.

'We're flying out on tonight's plane—we should be with you very late tomorrow night—or will it be the next morning? What time is it there?' He sounded almost as confused as Tina. He went on, 'I must say things are moving at this end—somebody's got every line in the Pacific buzzing for me!'

'It's Grandfather—he knows somebody in the Foreign Office who knows all the ropes!'

'Or the strings to pull!' There was a brief muffled exclamation, as though someone else spoke at the other end, then her father's voice came again. 'Time's up—au 'voir, my darling, for a little while.'

Tina did not know how long she stood there, the now purring receiver still clutched in her hand, until Elizabeth Kingman came and gently took it from her. Firmly she shepherded Tina upstairs and did not speak until she turned down Tina's bed and began to unbutton her granddaughter's blouse.

Tina came out of her bemusement and stepped out of her shoes, and Mrs Kingman smiled. 'It's a long time since I undressed a child for bed—yet if I close my eyes I can see Beth standing there, protesting that she *had* washed her neck thoroughly and brushed her teeth properly.'

Tina reached for her nightgown and giggled feverishly. 'I'm not even going to bother tonight—it doesn't matter for once.'

The older woman's eyes had misted. She shook her head. 'No, it doesn't matter for once.' She waited until Tina had climbed into bed, then drew up the clothes and tucked her in as though she were that much-loved child of long ago. For a moment she stood looking down at the flushed young face and bright eyes so like those of Beth, before she stooped and kissed Tina's brow. 'I'm so happy for you, my dearest. Even though I fear we're going to lose you again, just as we've found you.'

Tina's eyes sobered and something in her grandmother's expression brought a tightness to her throat. Impulsively she reached up and put her arms close round Elizabeth Kingman's neck, pulling her into a tight embrace. 'No,' she whispered unsteadily, 'you won't lose me, not ever. Even when I go back—because we will be going back—I don't think Daddy would ever leave the Islands now—it will be different. I'll write to you every week, and you'll know I'm thinking about you. And perhaps you'll come for another holiday, a long one. So don't be unhappy, please, Gran.'

It was the first time Tina had ever used the affectionate diminutive, and with a little cry Elizabeth Kingman hugged her and then straightened. 'I won't. That's a promise. Bless you, darling—goodnight.'

For a long while Tina lay in the darkness after her grandmother had put out the lamp and quietly gone from the room. So much had happened on this momentous day it made the thought of sleep impossible. First Max ... The thought of him cast its shadow, she almost wished he had not come, reviving all the painful memories, the bitterness of loving a man who didn't want her, who had turned instead to the sultry pagan intoxication of Tiare ... With a muffled little groan Tina burrowed deeply down under the clothes. Max was part of the past; soon her father would be home, miraculously restored to her. They would begin life exactly as it was before. He would paint, she would look after him, they would be happy again ...

Tina fell asleep at last. She had forgotten a tiny blank spot in her memory of that wonderful telephone conversation with her father. When he had said: 'We're flying out tomorrow ...'

We ...

Twenty-four hours had never seemed so long. But somehow they got over, and once again Tina was trying to sleep, this time, however, in the knowledge that when she woke up it would be to set out at last on the journey to the airport. Aldeston Manor had been a hive of activity all day, with polishing and preparing, planning a welcome menu, getting out the best china and the silver, raiding the garden for the pick of the blooms. If only the sun shone brightly ...

It seemed that the fates were all relenting now. The sun blazed down, granting Tina's small wish, as the car sped towards the airport on a perfect autumn morning. There wasn't a hint of fog or storm, no delays, no hitches, and the great jet slid down from the stacks and roared to a halt on the runway at the precise moment it was due. Someone unseen in high places had kept his promise; there wasn't a trace of a camera eager to catch a man given up by the relentless sea, nor were there any delays in rushing John Raimond as smoothly as possibly through Customs and clearance formalities.

Tina strained her eyes over the stream of disembarking passengers, almost frantic for her first glimpse of her father, and actually failed to recognise him. She was seeking a man alone, prepared for she was not sure what in signs of emaciation from the ordeal he had undergone. Her glance noted, then passed over a slightly built man in dark glasses and light-weight tropical suit accompanied by a tall girl with auburn hair who was wearing a cream and blue dress. Then suddenly Mr Kingman was motioning Tina forward, the man in the dark glasses was waving and starting to run, and the girl was looking puzzled, then smiling and following. And then John Raimond was whipping off the disguising glasses and Tina was in his arms.

There was confusion for a few minutes, everyone exclaiming at once, Tina in a delirium of excitement, laughing first then distraught at the lines of illness and strain in her father's features. He had gone so thin, and his hair betrayed tinges of grey certainly never present before. Then she started to introduce him to her grandparents, only to break into confusion as the two parties indicated that they had met already, albeit rather a long time ago.

'Far too long ago,' Mr Kingman said quietly, and Tina knew a moment of peace; the old rift had been healed at last.

Then John Raimond turned to the girl who had drawn a little aside from the poignant family reunion. He said, 'Tina, I want you to meet Marion. Marion, this is my daughter, Tina.'

Tina looked sharply at her father, then at the girl who was several inches taller than herself and very attractive in a cool capable kind of way. Marion smiled first. 'You look exactly as your father described you.'

Tina proffered her hand, puzzled and a little wary, then relaxed, instantly ashamed of her own lack of warmth as Marion drew back.

'Now that Mr Raimond is safely in your hands I'll leave you,' she said with a smile at them all. 'I'm travelling on to Edinburgh straight away.'

Marion must have looked after him during the long flight, Tina thought, and said impulsively, 'You've been looking after him, haven't you? Thank you so much.'

'I haven't done anything special.' Marion shook her head and put out a contradictory hand as John Raimond started to protest. 'No, I'm going to leave you to your family reunion now. Goodbye.'

Before anyone could respond she turned and moved briskly away.

Within a few moments Tina had forgotten her. There was so much to talk about, not least John Raimond's account of the dreadful storm during which the yacht had foundered, and how his companion had been there one moment and then gone the next, vanished for ever in seas as dark and mountainous as only the Pacific can be.

'I remember thinking I'd never see daylight again,' John recalled, 'and yet that sun came up over as benign and blue an ocean as anyone could wish.'

He was to curse that sun as the days dragged by without a sign of another vessel anywhere on the boundless horizon that surrounded him and his tiny craft. 'I didn't believe that I'd be adrift more than a few hours before being spotted and picked up,' he went on, 'and then I began to lose count of the days—what point in trying to notch them up when my precious water was almost gone? I think I just went slightly mad.'

They could only try to imagine but would never fully comprehend what he had gone through, Tina thought when they were gathered round the big gleaming mahogany table that evening. A superb meal was over, the candles were burning low in their silver sconces and reflecting a myriad glittering facets in the crystal wine goblets, and the rich peace of the beautiful room must seem a far cry from that nightmare of blazing sun, empty reaches of sea, and thirst ...

'I can't remember those last days before I was picked up, except that I suffered hallucinations and was getting salt sores,' John went on, his eyes shadowing reflectively as they stared unseeingly at the glass within his curved fingers. 'I know I slipped and fell across the thwart, cracking my head on something, and that was the last thing I knew until several weeks later when I found myself in the little mission on Roatu, and Marion filled me in on the missing gaps.'

'Marion?' exclaimed Tina. 'She was there?'

John nodded. 'She's a nurse. She had been working in the Gilbert group for two years. She also has a sister who joined a religious nursing order—her family have always been very closely connected with the Church—and Marion went to visit her before returning home. This of course was the mission of Roatu—Sister Blanche being Marion's own sister—and Marion decided to stay on until the next trading schooner called and help to nurse me. Then she sailed with me, and came home on the same flight.'

He fell silent, and Tina saw the same expression in the eyes of her grandparents as must be in her own. There was much yet to be told about Marion. The flicker of disquiet she experienced at the airport returned as John stood up abruptly and asked Mrs Kingman if he might make a call to Edinburgh.

'Marion should be home by now—I just want to make sure she got home safely.'

Consent readily given for this, John went from the room. There was silence for quite a while, then Mr Kingman murmured, 'What an extraordinary story!'

His wife nodded, reserving her comments, but Tina tried

to banish her own feeling of unease. She ought to be feeling wholeheartedly thankful that someone had looked after her father as devotedly as apparently had Marion. The questions she wanted to ask were lining up by the dozen, but when her father returned he said firmly: 'I think I've talked enough today—I want to hear all your news, Tina.'

There wasn't so much to tell, she thought ruefully, except the sorry state of her love life—and this was not the moment for those confidences. She was not sure that she wanted to tell anyone, not even her father, much as she loved him.

Soon afterwards John pleaded weariness and Tina, instantly protective, fussed over him until he was settled comfortably in the room she had prepared so lovingly. She hovered by the bed, to say goodnight, yet reluctant to leave less some cruel fate should snatch him away again. At last she stooped to kiss him, but as she reached out to the bedside lamp he sat up abruptly and caught her wrist.

'It's no use, Tina pet—I wanted to wait until we were more settled, but I can't. I must tell you.'

'Tell me what?' She sat on the edge of the bed and stared at him with frightened eyes. 'Are you ill? I mean, has it all had some awful effect, that——?'

'No, nothing like that—the American doctor on Samoa gave me a thorough overhaul and there's nothing that time won't put right. No, it's Marion.'

'Marion?' Tina whispered. 'What about her?'

'I've fallen in love with her. I want to marry her.'

Tina recoiled, wondering if she had heard aright. Her father remarrying! After all these years! It was something she'd scarcely given thought to—he'd never given the remotest sign of being interested in another woman since Tina's mother died.

He was watching her, with something like fear in his eyes. He said sharply: 'Does the idea shock you so much, Tina? I realise I must seem like Methuselah to you, but I'm only forty-three—still young enough to seek new happiness without ever detracting from the love with which I remember your mother.'

'Yes, I realise that.' Tina shook her head. 'It's just that ...' She stopped, not knowing how to express the

170

shock of his announcement in a way that would not hurt him.

John sank back on the pillows. 'I was afraid of this. That's why I intended to wait a while—I wanted us to spend some time with Marion so you could get to know her and, I hope, come to love her in time. But I'm not much good at keeping secrets, and I saw your expression the moment we all met this morning. You sensed it, didn't you?'

Tina nodded. 'Have you—does Marion——?'

'No, I haven't asked her yet. But I think she loves me. Oh, Tina, she's an angel, a wonderful woman. I think she saved my sanity.'

'Did she?' Tina whispered, still trying to adjust to this fresh shock.

His mouth curved with tender memory. 'She spent countless hours, patiently trying to jog my stupid amnesia. You see, I had no identification on me and no one knew who I was. She was so certain that I was married, perhaps with children, and so worried that somewhere they were grieving their hearts out for me. And then one day I was doodling on the back of an old envelope, making a rough sketch of the view from the mission veranda without realising what I was doing, and she cried, "You can draw! You're quite an artist." I was despondent that day—you've no idea what it's like to lose one's past until it happens to you. But Marion was overjoyed because she'd made a breakthrough. She said it was a start. By then I think the loss of the yacht had been forgotten, so many new tragedies are jostling for headline space each day,' he interjected bitterly, 'but it must have struck a chord in her memory, and that night she remembered. From then on it began to come back—it was the trigger she needed. But for her patience and determination it might have been months.'

Suddenly he smiled and touched Tina's cheek. 'I think we ought to call it a day—tomorrow you may be more used to the idea.'

But Tina knew it would take her a long time to get used to the idea of her father getting married. She was honest enough to own to a certain amount of selfish possessiveness with regard to her father—they had made their own routine of living in the years since the loss of her mother and a strange woman, no matter how sweet and good, would change everything. But there was also the uncertainty. Could Marion make him happy? Would she be able to cope with his moods and his appalling untidiness when he was in the throes of creation? Tina had many doubts.

Her grandparents, however, made no secret of their disapproval. They were convinced that it was simply an infatuation born of the particular circumstances; that in the return to reality in both his own and Marion's lives they would discover the attraction shortlived. But Tina had to give them credit for being fair; they invited Marion to spend an extended visit at Aldeston Manor and within a very short time of her arrival they were won over. So was Tina.

Marion could be placid without being dull. She had a sense of humour, she was sunny-natured without being gushing, and she didn't intrude on family conversations. She was also cool and practical in an emergency, as she demonstrated the afternoon when Mrs Greenway gashed her hand rather badly while trying to prise open a wooden chest of special tea ordered by Mrs Kingman. Marion coped and soothed, took poor Mrs Greenway to have it stitched, and then helped with many of the countless household tasks the housekeeper was unable to fulfil during the following days.

'She really is a sweet girl,' said Mrs Kingman.

The wedding was fixed for the third of October, less than a month ahead.

Tina and her father went to Scotland, to have a brief holiday and meet Marion's family, and the days flew like wildfire. John and Marion were to spend a short honeymoon in the highlands, and stay a few days afterwards in Edinburgh for the sake of Marion's family. For, as John Raimond said, they had lost her for two years and only got her back prior to losing her again. Tina was bridesmaid, along with Marion's youngest sister, and suddenly the excitement was all over and she was travelling back to Aldeston with her grandparents for the two weeks before her return to Tahiti with her father and new stepmother.

It was a strangely sad interlude.

The house seemed so quiet, yet the underlying tensions were building and Tina sensed that her grandmother was deeply troubled. Tina was well aware of what must come, and dreaded the moment when she would have to make the decision. It came when she least expected it, as she looked up from the tartan and thistle picture postcard to find her grandmother watching her.

'Are you sure you're doing the right thing, my dear?' Elizabeth Kingman said in a low voice.

'In what way?' Tina tried to meet those intent blue eyes casually.

'You know what I mean, darling. Haven't you considered that it might be better to let your father and his new young wife make a new life together, alone? Wouldn't it be fairer to them?'

'You mean ...?'

'They're young enough to start a new young family. Are you prepared to fit in with that probability? The very fact of your being so close to your father all these years makes me wonder how it's all going to work out.' Elizabeth Kingman gestured as she saw the dismay and shock on the distraught young face. 'Oh, I don't mean it wouldn't work out, or that you should never see them again. I'm merely trying to see ahead, what is best for you all. Heavens, you can visit them—we're not exactly penurious and you're our only grandchild. We've no one else to spend it on. Or leave it to,' she added quietly.

'Don't talk like that! As though ...'

'Why not? We have to face it,' the older woman said calmly. Then her calm broke and her mouth worked painfully in the travesty of an attempted smile. 'It's losing you again so soon that worries me.'

Tina did not know what to say to bring comfort to the sad-faced woman who suddenly looked so old. How could she make the decision demanded of her? Was her life always to be torn apart by conflicting loves and loyalties? Part of her was now living for the moment when she would step down once more on her native soil, to savour the scents and hear the surf on the reef, to feast her eyes on the familiar blaze of colour and walk again in the pagan motley of the waterfront. And yet, imperceptibly, England's cool green land had begun to creep into her blood, as though it bid to claim her, and the parting from these two elderly people would not be without its tears ...

173

'Don't try to decide this moment. I know how difficult a decision it will be,' her grandmother said gently. 'I ask only that you think it over.'

Tina knew the subject would not be mentioned again—her grandmother's pride was still an indomitable thing—but the seed of doubt had been sown. Was the older woman, with her wisdom of maturity right? Tina wondered miserably. For there was that other secret she had to live with; could she ever face the island paradise of Kaloha as long as it held such poignant memories?

By the eve of the return of her father and his bride Tina was no nearer a decision. She could only wait until she had discussed the matter with them. Only then would she decide.

And then the letter came.

Tina read it three times, to make sure that Fay's hurried, tumbling scrawl conveyed exactly what it seemed, then she folded it like a precious thing. She was not sure how she would tell her grandmother, or what ultimately would be the outcome of the sudden wild, unbiddable instinct that seized her reason. She knew only that she was going back. There was something she had to do before she committed herself to the point of no return.

She had to go back.

She had to see Max—just once more ...

CHAPTER ELEVEN

'I think I'll go over to Kaloha.'

'Yes, we must take Marion.' John Raimond put his hands to his head and grimaced. 'God! I can still hear those blasted jets.'

'I mean now—today.' Tina tried desperately to make her voice casual. 'I must see Fay.'

'But you'll see her tomorrow!' exclaimed Aunt Wynne. 'She's coming for the celebration, with Paul and the children, and Pierre. *Everybody's* coming tomorrow.'

'Tina, you haven't even unpacked!' Marion betrayed astonishment. 'We've just *got* here. How will you get there —I thought the ferry, or whatever you call it in this part of the world, went in the morning?'

174

'I'll find somebody to take me over—I'll probably stay the night and come back with Fay in the morning. Look after each other while I'm gone,' Tina added flippantly, and grabbed her bag as she made her escape before they had time for further protest.

But once outside the assumed flippancy fell from her like a cloak, to be replaced by the feverish haste of compulsion as she hauled her old bike out of the outhouse where it had been stored for so long. If she was lucky she would make Kaloha by sunset, after that it didn't matter. But what if Max wasn't there?

She pushed the thought away, the warm sweet wind flying through her hair as she pedalled furiously down the long winding road to town. At the first *tinito* she stopped and thrust the bead curtain aside. The elderly owner of the store, who had known Tina since her childhood, turned from the bales of brightly patterned materials he was stacking and his grave lined face lit with recognition.

'You back, Miss Tina?'

'An hour ago—can I leave my bike, please?'

The solemn permission readily granted, Tina stowed it away in the little warehouse behind the store, paused long enough to thank Mr Chang, inquire after his health and that of his family, then continue her way on foot along the quayside.

She was looking for Jake Logan, one of Papeete's many characters, who owned a small, deceptively ramshackle-looking cruiser, the appearance of which masked a briskly reliable turn of speed. It would depend on Jake himself, who had a habit of disappearing every so often on one of his sprees. But she was in luck; there was the boat, and the thin, weatherbeaten figure of Jake himself.

A little breathless from hurrying, she made her request and waited. Jake always took a few moments to weigh up whether he would or whether he wouldn't. Then he tugged at his small straggling beard.

'She needs fuelling.'

'I'll pay, Jake.'

'Now we're talking business!' Jake grinned. 'Give me twenty minutes—go and have yourself a Coke or something.'

'I'll give you a hand,' Tina said grimly. She knew Jake

175

of old. If he met one of his cronies . . .

Jake shrugged, as though at the distrustful dispositions of females, and Tina went on board. When at last they were heading out for the pass she gave a sigh of relief; all she had to hold on to now was her courage.

She was thankful that Jake, once afloat, was not a garrulous man, and she could retreat into silence, rehearsing the things she would say . . . It was not until the small green hump of Kaloha was showing its familiar individual landmarks that a possibility occurred to Tina. What if Max were not there?

She thrust the notion away; he had to be; it would be too great an anti-climax if she had come all this way in vain. Just in time she noticed Jake bearing through the small pass in the reef towards the hotel end of the beach. She said hastily: 'Not there—the plantation jetty, please.'

Jake turned in the cockpit, his grizzled brows aloft with curiosity. 'If it's old Henri you're looking for he's gone—hadn't you heard?'

'Yes.' Tina's mouth compressed. 'Just land me there, please.'

Jake shrugged, and a sly glimmer came into his eyes. 'But of course, ma'am. After all, what would a pretty little thing like you be wanting with a poor old crock like that? I must be going soft in the top storey.' With a grin he returned his attention to navigation, and Tina sat silent, looking up at the old plantation house on the rise.

Jake nosed the craft in and remarked casually, 'Don't see no sign of life up there—though they say Mister Thornton got back a coupla weeks ago.'

'Mind your own business, Jake,' she said with grim humour, 'I'll be going along to the hotel tonight, so I won't need you to wait. Thanks.'

He touched the peak of his grubby cap, and she was conscious of his gaze following her as she walked along the beach to the foot of the path. It would be all round the bars of Papeete tonight that Jake had taken young Tina Raimond over to Henri Latour's place, and she scarcely off the plane from Europe, but Tina no longer cared. She was thinking of the letter in her handbag and wishing Fay had been more explicit. Half the letter taken up with the news about Pierre and Corinne getting engaged, most of the rest with Fay's

176

own joy about Tina's father, and then, almost as an after-thought, the postscript. 'All is quiet now at the plantation, but Pierre told you about the Latour skeleton-in-the-cupboard, didn't he? I suspect we misjudged Max Thornton—though the men won't believe it, naturally!—thinking of Tiare!'

But Pierre hadn't told her. He'd left it to Fay.

Tina's heart was thumping painfully in her breast as she climbed the rough steps, but it was not caused by the physical exertion of the ascent. The torment of mental suspense that had held her in its grip all through the long journey home was taking its painful toll, and now the climax of trepidation was near. Strangely, the thought of Tiare and all the agony of humiliation she had invoked now receded and Tina could think only of Max. Could she face him and say those things she wanted to say? And if she did, what if his reaction was the same old arrogant impatience, or worse, amusement? But whatever he thought or said she had to take this course. For despite Tiare, nothing was changed as far as her own feelings for him were concerned. She could despise herself for all her foolish weakness, but the sight of him during his visit to Aldeston had told her that her heart had not changed. The journey to England had proved merely a futile attempt at escape, and now Fay's statement had awakened the turmoil to agonising life again.

I suspect we've misjudged Max Thornton . . .

Did it mean . . .? Tina reached the top of the steps and paused, staring at the house. The breeze had lulled, and the waxen blossoms were closing their petals, petals tinged with the reflected glow of the setting sun. Tina reached up to touch one, then withdrew her hand before the impulse could effect the action. The wearing of a flower was a stupid, pointless custom. Silly and sentimental—and heart-breakingly wonderful. Tina bit on her lower lip until it hurt and walked blindly up the slope to the veranda step. She must be insane. There was no one here, the place looked deserted. If she had any sense she'd turn and run away, along to the hotel, to Fay, and to people who cared about her. Instead of pursuing a man who had made it perfectly plain he found her a troublesome child who made his con-science a penance.

The door was closed and fastened. There was no light within, no smell of cooking, nothing ... She turned the corner, to the dark side of the house, felt the cooling breeze meet her bare arms, and recoiled suddenly from a ghostly white movement that almost flapped in her face. She gave a choked little cry and touched the white shirt that hung there. It was nearly dry, except where the moisture had dripped into the hem, so it had been laundered only a short while ago—things didn't take long to dry here.

She completed her circuit of the house and returned to the veranda overlooking the sea. She looked at the glory of the sunset, the first she had seen for many weeks, and decided that she would wait for twenty minutes, no more. If no one came by then she would give up her foolish quest.

The long shadows darkened and the light patches began to merge into them. The distant black peaks of Moorea were outlined in a fan of gold rays, and Tahiti itself lay in a haze against a sky streaked with green and indigo as the deepening night encroached from the east. The last of the flowers bowed its heavy head, and a late-homing bird circled overhead before it dropped down towards the trees. Then it was dark, and everything was still. Tina sank on to the lounger, curling her toes up under the fullness of her skirt. The darkness and the stillness had a hypnotic quality ...

Tina did not know that she had lapsed into a curious languor halfway between sleeping and waking. When the crack of sound snapped her back to awareness she began to tremble with a sudden, overwhelming fear. She sprang up, and her bag fell with a hollow thud, and as she bent to snatch it up the veranda door swung open. The man within stepped through, and light streamed forth over the startled invader.

Instinctively she cowered back, but too late. His voice came like a whiplash: 'What the——! Who's there?'

Then his arm shot out and her shoulder was seized in a grip of iron. He yanked her into the light and exclaimed incredulously: 'Tina!'

Tension snapped in her and she sagged, suddenly very tiny against his tall, looming strength. She whispered, 'Did you think—I——? I didn't hear you come back. I——'

He stared down into her white face. 'But why? How did you——?'

'We just got back. We——' She stopped, trying to summon back her voice to its normal tone instead of the shaky whisper it wanted to be, and abruptly Max released his grip, as though he too became aware of force overriding logical control.

He said more casually, 'You'd better come in and have a drink, or something. There isn't much—I wasn't expecting visitors.'

'No!' Instantly she sheered away from the prospect of facing him in the revealing clarity of full light. 'I—I feel stifled still—after being cooped up so long on the plane—I need air.'

The excuse must have sounded inane if not feeble, she thought wildly, but if he noticed this he made no comment, merely turning back to her and resting one hand on the veranda rail. 'You didn't waste any time, did you?' he observed coolly. 'But then you were always a somewhat unpredictable child.'

She closed her eyes despairingly; it was going to be far more difficult than she had envisaged. 'Just how old do I have to be before you stop considering me a child?' she sighed. 'Eighty?'

But he made no response to this, except for a slight movement of his shoulders. He looked across the dark sighing sea to where the lights of a fisherman's canoe glimmered like golden fireflies. 'I was more glad than I can say to know of your father's safe return,' he said quietly. 'It must have been a wonderful occasion for you—more like a miracle.'

'It was.'

'And how does it feel to have a new parent?'

'Oh, Marion . . .'

'Yes.'

'Oh, fine. We get on very well—she's a sweet person.'

'Not a bossy stepmother?'

'Heavens, no! More like a newly discovered long-lost sister—at least so far.'

There was a silence, and Tina knew that the moment could not be postponed any longer. Already Max was shifting his stance, half turning his head, then looking back to the night. He must be wondering why she was lingering, why she had come in the first place, within hours of her return from England. Tina took a deep breath and put her hands tightly on the rail.

'Max, you must be wondering ... but there's something I want to say. You see, I've reached a turning point in my life, and there's something I have to straighten out. Something I——'

She sensed him stir, and she said quickly: 'No, please don't interrupt—not until I've finished.'

'Very well. Go on, Tina.'

'This isn't very easy for me, but I can't go away again until I know for certain ...' She hesitated, keeping her face averted and praying her courage would not run out. 'I think you are the kind of man who—who wouldn't think ill of a woman who spoke her mind, or would denigrate her for making a confession on which convention still frowns if she makes it without a certain preliminary convention still demands. I don't know why it should still be so these days, why there should be any loss of pride involved. The events of the past few months have made me see things in a different perspective.'

'What are you trying to say, Tina?'

She bit her lip, suddenly wishing with all her heart that she had never embarked on this perilous course. But she made herself remain there, unmoving, and whispered: 'Try to be patient, please.'

'Go on ...' There was a peculiar intensity in his tone that was far from encouraging.

'First, I have to thank you for coming to see me in England. It was kind of you, but I was too confused at the time to—to——'

'You didn't make a special journey here just for that?'

'Not entirely. I wanted to explain why I left Tahiti without seeing you—I meant to, but I——'

'Tina!'

The exclamation was so sharp she jumped.

'No, save your explanations—I'll say it for you,' he said scornfully. 'This thing you are finding so difficult to put into words. You thought I'd taken a mistress, didn't you, Tina? Moreover, you believed I'd followed the well trod path of the *popaa* who takes a *vahine* into his bed. I thought better of you, Tina.'

She gasped, and before she could start to stammer a response he swung to face her. 'Oh yes,' he said savagely, 'I'm well aware of the gossipmongers' little heyday at my expense. Did you really believe I'd taken Tiare for my mistress?'

The directness of his challenge brought the scarlet of guilt into her cheeks. 'I didn't know what to believe,' she choked. 'I saw Tiare that day and—and——'

'Yes. I saw *you* that day, as well. And you immediately assumed the worst. You should have known better—you're a child of the islands yourself. You know the possessive streak in the island girls, that they're frank, single-minded and determined in all their desires, and that the fulfilment of a sexual relationship is as natural as eating and breathing.' Max turned away and planted heavy hands on the rail. 'It wouldn't occur to you to try to imagine things from Tiare's angle. A stranger arrives out of the blue, to tell her he's taking her to another island to some people who wish to meet her. He holds out the promise of clothes, possessions, money, a possible trip to the mainland, but no more, because his instructions are to keep the real truth from her until her real family have inspected her. But how was I to know that Alex would be delayed, and that Henri's heart condition would prove so serious, and that he would insist on the whole business of Tiare being kept quiet until he was home and his son had actually arrived? Imagine trying to keep a secret like Tiare! In Tahiti of all places,' Max added explosively.

'I was caught in an impossible situation,' he went on bitterly. 'The only thing I could do was to hustle her over to Kaloha as quickly as possible and try to amuse her until Henri could deal with his own family problems. Why they couldn't leave well alone, instead of suddenly taking this quixotic notion of assuaging old guilt, is beyond me. But it's over now.' His voice changed abruptly, regaining a flat control that was almost weary. 'If you've come to make apologies for assuming what everyone else did you can spare me them—nobody else bothered.'

His words echoed into silence, a silence in which Tina still groped to fit everything together. She gave it up, for the moment it was enough to know that she had been guilty of

181

a grave error of judgment. The knowledge at once both elated and saddened, for it changed nothing as far as she herself was concerned.

She whispered, 'But I *am* sorry, Max.'

'Are you? For what?'

For what? She looked down, dreading what must come next, knowing that his mood was as arrogant and unhelpful as ever, and sharpened by bitterness. Yet a dogged determination kept her there. She had come so far, she had to finish what she had set out to do—and pray that the result might help to expel the fever from her blood once and for all. At least she would know.

'I've not quite finished, Max—I won't keep you much longer,' she said in a low voice. 'I didn't know Tiare had anything to do with Henri Latour, and now ... it doesn't matter. You've always been pretty honest with me, Max, ever since a day I believe you remember as well as I do, and I think you know in your heart why I've come and what I'm trying to say.'

'Tina—I think——'

'No, Max, for my peace of mind and for the sake of my future I have to say it aloud. I love you, Max. I think I've always loved you, but——'

'Tina—please!'

She heard his step and felt the darkness of his shadow fall across her, but she ignored the pleading note in his voice and put out her hand with a mute plea for his silence.

'I'm sorry if this is embarrassing you, but please let me finish, then I'll go away and you'll never hear from me again.' Her head lifted defiantly, and strangely, her courage had returned. 'I feel no shame in confessing the way I feel about you, and I see no reason why I should. You see, Max, so often my instinct—that woman's instinct that's so often derided—has told me that you were never quite so indifferent to me as you'd have me believe, I made up my mind to find out how true—or false—it has played me. Probably I *am* mistaken. Maybe you were just sorry for me! It doesn't matter now. But I have to know. Because I want to draw a line after this part of my life.'

'What do you mean? You're going to draw a line in your life?'

She knew she had not mistaken the sudden note of shock

in his words, and her heartbeat quickened to painful intensity.

'I'm going back to England.'

'To England? But why? When?'

She made a small movement of her shoulders. 'I don't know, but soon. My grandmother wants me to make my home with her—I think she's desperately lonely—and now my father has Marion, they'll have children, I think it would be for the best if I did. But I can't until I know—until I know for sure that I was mistaken and I'd cleared up misunderstanding, and wouldn't go on always wondering if—if——'

Her voice broke and her mouth began to tremble so much she couldn't go on. The tight-drawn thread of control was fraying to its last frail strand. She took a shuddering breath. 'You were very kind to me in so many ways. You offered the most practical form of help each time I most needed it, and asked nothing in return. That to me is a kind of love, and I just couldn't help responding to it. And so . . .'

She turned blindly, hardly able to distinguish the tall broad outline of him through a sudden swirling mist of tears, and thrust out her hand.

'I've come to say goodbye, Max, and—and——'

The brave, choked little utterances were stifled at last. Hard arms enveloped her and pressed her face into his shoulder. 'No, Tina, it's not time for goodbye. Not yet. Not until—Tina, don't weep, my little darling, please!'

'I can't help it.' She tried to drag herself from this longed-for haven. 'It's no use. I—I should never have come here. You're just sorry for me, and——'

'I am *not* sorry for you!' He seized her arm and pulled her back to him. 'Tina, look at me! And listen—for a change!'

Almost afraid now, she looked up slowly, and met a stare of burning intensity that quelled her into frozen obedience.

'Of course I love you, you wayward, generous, gallant child! And had you been just a little less impatient for a little while longer, you would have spared yourself this—this emotional havoc tonight.'

'But—why? If——' She faltered into silence again, hardly daring to believe she'd actually heard the wondrous declaration from his lips. 'Max . . . ?'

'Because my instinct is no all-knowing oracle—and you certainly had me fooled,' he said wryly.

'You mean . . . you *were* attracted to me? And never guessed how I felt about you?' she breathed wonderingly.

He searched her upturned face with eyes in which an equal sense of wonder glowed.

'But why, Max?' She gave a deep sigh and wound her arms round his neck, ruffling the thick dark hair at the nape. 'I longed for you so much—I can never tell you how much.'

He pressed her slender body within the circle of his hands and a tremor passed through him as she responded.

'Because I had to be rational and wise for your sake more than my own. Right back to that very first day when you treated me to a choice sample of teenage tantrums— oh yes, you did, my treasure—and yet I was drawn to you then despite myself. But after deploring Pierre's rakish approaches to a fifteen-year-old as innocent as you undoubtedly were, how could I behave the same way myself? A man must be true to his own ideals, Tina.'

'But I wanted you to.'

'To what?' His mouth quivered, then sobered. 'You didn't —not then. You wanted Pierre. And three years later, when I came back to the islands, it seemed you were still caught in an unresolved situation with him. Even so,' Max paused reflectively, 'things might have taken a different course if your father had not disappeared so tragically. After that, any declaration from me would have been unwise.'

'But why?' She put her hands on each side of his face and studied him with puzzled eyes. 'I did everything I could to encourage you, but I thought you fancied Corinne.'

'Corinne never even came into it as far as I was concerned.' Max shook his head. 'Look back, Tina. You were distraught over your father, then you were torn by the claims of your grandparents. Supposing I had asked you to marry me at that time. Without being aware of it, you might have accepted me, simply because I offered an escape from all your problems. But I'd never have been sure if this was so, and in time you might have wondered if I'd simply been sorry for you. Then when I came to England there was still no chance of getting you to myself, not until you'd got over the excitement of your father's homecoming. But when I heard of your father's marriage . . .'

'Yes, I'm happy about that,' she said slowly. 'He needs someone to look after him.'

'Yes, and that was just another cause for concern.' Max rested his chin on her hair. 'You've obviously always had a very close bond with your father—I'd no wish to become a substitute for him.'

Tina jerked from under the pressure of his chin. 'Oh, Max!' she cried despairingly, 'you *were* trying to be wise and sensible. I wonder how long it would have taken you to find the right moment!'

'I was planning to gatecrash your party tomorrow—although I hadn't been invited—now that the future looked free of obstacles.' Abruptly he gave an exclamation and pulled her fiercely to him. 'I think I've earned this!'

He began to kiss her, long passionate kisses that set Tina's senses on fire and dispelled any lingering doubts of his feelings for her. She quivered under his hands, and when at last he broke off to whisper, 'Love me? Sure?' she nodded and trembled against the hard strength of his warm body. She had no doubts now.

Long moments later he put her away from him, albeit very reluctantly. 'I think we'd better have that drink!'

She followed him into the room, unable to bear being parted from him now, even by such a short distance. When he had mixed the long cool drinks they returned to the veranda and sat down on the lounger, Tina drawn close into the hollow of his arm and shoulder. The heavens were ablaze with stars and tiny ridges of phosphorescence danced and glimmered on the sea.

Tina said softly, 'Tell me about Henri—and Tiare. Was she his child?'

'No,' Max set down his glass and drew Tina closer. 'She was his grandchild, Alex's daughter. You would be only a baby when Henri and his son were estranged, and Henri finally disowned him. Alex was always wild, refusing to settle down and help Henri to manage the plantation. He drifted around the islands, getting into scrapes, and coming back to his father when he was broke. Then he went to Raviva and lived with a *vahine* called Luna, a most beautiful girl by all accounts, and Tiare was born. Unfortunately

185

Luna met another man, a wealthy painter, and persuaded him to take her back to the States with him. She left the baby with her family and Alex came home, broke again. There was a hell of a row, and Henri then disowned his son, and the last anyone heard of Alex was that he took a deckhand's job to work his passage to the States to try to find Luna. He wrote once, but Henri refused to let his wife answer, and it wasn't until this year that Alex tried again to contact his father. He'd married and had a son, but his marriage had crashed. He'd been ill, and near a breakdown, and suddenly decided he wanted to make his peace with his father. He also developed a guilty conscience over the baby he'd scarcely known. That was when he asked his father to make inquiries about what had become of Tiare.'

Max paused and sighed. 'It was this letter that brought on Henri's heart attack. He was furious. But the heart attack gave him such a fright he discovered he had a conscience too, and he'd better heal the family rift in case the worst happened. And that was where I came in,' Max went on grimly. 'Henri begged me to find Tiare, see what kind of a grandchild she was, and what kind of circumstances she was living in. But his pride was still fierce. He wasn't going to recognise her as a Latour until he'd seen her, and until Alex came. So I had to bring her to Kaloha and try to hush things up until Henri was recovered. And of course Cécile was another complication. Having rediscovered the home comforts a woman can provide, Henri didn't want to spoil his chances in that direction until he'd got everything well settled and sealed. I never want to go through anything like these past weeks again,' Max added feelingly. 'And as for Tiare ... heaven help the college that has to admit *her* through its portals!'

Tina gave a derisive little sniff, and Max asked sharply: 'Just what happened between you two that day?'

'You mean, what happened between *you* two that day?' Tina retorted. ' "My Max" indeed!'

'Is that what she told you? Before she landed at me like a tornado!' Max chuckled. 'I'll admit it must have looked slightly compromising.'

'It did!'

'Yes, and you'd better believe me, but I took to sleeping out down by the drying sheds—safe from temptation!'

'Really?'

Max rose to the teasing bait, as Tina knew he would, but her protest was not very convincing as he turned suddenly and locked hard arms round her, the amusement in his eyes rapidly darkening to passion. Long moments later he said against her mouth, 'Where are you supposed to be sleeping tonight, anyway?'

'At Fay's.'

'So I suppose I'll have to escort you there, sooner or later.'

'Well,' Tina nestled her face into his shoulder and savoured the delight of his warm muscular hardness under her cheek, 'she doesn't know I'm on Kaloha.'

'And what is that supposed to convey?'

'I don't know ... oh, Max, I wish I'd known ...'

'Known what, my darling?'

'That you love me. I—I still can't quite believe it.'

He sighed softly. 'God willing, I've the rest of my life to convince you, but you know, Tina, while I maybe haven't matched up to your dream of a man who would storm down all defences, that doesn't mean my love was any less deep.'

He tipped her face up towards his. 'A man doesn't usually try to do what is best for a girl, subduing his own personal desires and asking no return—as you yourself recognised—unless he does love her very dearly.' He sighed again. 'Perhaps I was wrong. Perhaps I should have tried to rush you into marriage months ago. But too many people were trying to influence you. I wanted to be sure you knew your own heart first, and how could you know that during all those weeks of stress?'

'That was the only thing I did know,' Tina whispered. 'That night at the *marae* ... I wanted you so much.'

Max tightened his arms about her. 'I know. You felt the first stirring of physical need for a man, but despite this you weren't really seeking physical fulfilment, my darling. Your body was seeking one thing, but your heart another.'

She gave a tiny inclination of her head, knowing he had perceived a truth she'd scarcely realised herself. Then he went on softly: 'Tina, if I hadn't stopped when I did it would have been too late. And taking you that night, at the *marae*, of all places, wouldn't have provided the answer to

187

your problems, but might well have destroyed such peace of mind as remained to you.'

She sighed as she recognised yet another facet of Max's unselfish wisdom. For she would have experienced guilt, and almost certainly the fear that his inevitable proposal of marriage afterwards was born of duty instead of love. Yes, he had been wise where she would have been foolish.

In a sudden surge of sheer love she clung fiercely to him, every part of her straining to meet the warm urgency of his instant response. His searching mouth explored the slender line of her throat, touched her closed eyes, and homed to the softness of her breast. Until at last he groaned and turned away.

'That wasn't very wise—little temptress!'

He took her hand and drew her to her feet, to hold her within his arm and look at the star-decked night. After a moment he sighed and reached out to the cluster of sleeping blossoms. As he had done that day so long ago he plucked a flower and turned to her, to tuck it into tresses now sadly tumbled from his lovemaking.

'Remember?' he said quietly.

She nodded and stood on tiptoe to print a small, intimate kiss on his lips. 'You won't ever make me weep, Max?'

'I'll try not to—as long as you stay— *ta'u vahine?*'

'Oh, yes, please, for ever and ever . . .'

He kissed her again. *Ta'u vahine.* His woman. All she had ever wanted to be . . .

Complete and mail this coupon today!

YOU'LL L♥VE
Harlequin Magazine

for women who enjoy reading fascinating stories of exciting romance in exotic places

SUBSCRIBE NOW!

This is a colorful magazine especially designed and published for the readers of Harlequin novels.

Now you can receive your very own copy delivered right to your home every month throughout the year for only 75¢ an issue.

This colorful magazine is available only through Harlequin Reader Service, so enter your subscription now!

Now available!

COLLECTION EDITIONS

of Harlequin Romances

Harlequin proudly presents a nostalgic collection of the best-selling romance novels of former years. It's a rare series of 100 books, each one lovingly reissued in a beautifully designed new cover. And the cost is only 75¢ each.

Not sold in stores

Send for free catalog

Most of these old favorites have not
been reissued since first publication.
So if you read them then, you'll enjoy
them again; if they're new to you,
you'll have the pleasure of discovering
a new series of compelling romances
from past years.

Collection Editions are available only
from Harlequin Reader Service. They
are not sold in stores.

Clip and mail this special coupon. We
will send you a catalog listing all the
Collection Editions titles and authors.